I0738189

Firewood 11

Firewood 11

Harlan Jay

Published July 15, 2019
Copyright © 2019 by Harlan Jay

Print edition: ISBN #978-0-578-52137-4
eBook edition available: ISBN #978-0-578-52140-4

All locations, names, and events are inspired by real world facts, places, and conspiracy theories.

Though intriguing to imagine and expand upon, writing about such theories does not, in any way, acknowledge their potential reality, nor should this Science Fiction novel be misconstrued as persuasive arguments toward their legitimacy.

However, consider this narrative as an invitation to wonder.

In inspiration upon the musing of:
MusicalGrowth.com

Edited by Josiah Davis from jdbookservices.com

To my loving and supportive wife.

CONTENTS

GLOSSARY OF TERMS

Add-on - something taking space on a human's credit

Anti-Virus Cleaners (AVC) - from the Quality Assurance department of PixelOne; a team of humans assigned domain function maintenance

Artificial Intelligence (AI) - a system of independently managed and self-aware computer programs with the ability to compute and perform tasks on the same or higher level as human intelligence (i.e. speech recognition, decision-making, strategizing, visual perception, emotional understanding, etc.)

Business Park - a nickname for the eastern business center where humans report to work

Credit - the limited amount of spending humans have to obtain items; this limit differs depending on their status in PixelOne

Domain - a world within a Sector contained in the Sector-System; a classification term

Ear-implants - electronic alterations to allow AI access to human auditory senses; usually used between servant bots and their owners, or during personal audio conversations

Epichip - an embedded electronic chip in the human wrist installed at birth; displays time, heart rate, etc.; also used by the government to track civilians

Gardener - an employee of the state given the responsibility of maintaining personal living space oxygen levels via plant growth within specified areas

Hand-light - the powerful LED flashlight implanted within the hands of humanoids; a default design

Humanoid - artificial intelligence placed in robotic machinery designed and modeled after the human form

Intersentient Relationship - an interconnected love-interest between a human and a humanoid

Neurobine - artificial intelligence advanced enough to live in the Sector-System; individual AI units encased in a digital form of sentience

Neo-Tamerlanes - a genocidal group from the water-shortage era of the 5800's on Earth

Night Season - a day/night cycle shift; the opposite of Sun Season; the part of the year when the sun does not appear due to the axis of the Earth in relation to the sun

Noped - a hovering transportation device for individual use on pathways as an alternative to walking

Neurobine Transfer Center (NTC) - a governmental report center within the Sector-System for neurobines to request transfer out into human-reality

Old-Earth - a colloquial reference to the time period when the Earth had a sustainable ecosystem and healthy atmosphere; thousands of years in the past

PixelOne - the virtual company where Morris used to work for the construction department

Psyche Rehabilitation Program (PRP) - a correctional facility (a.k.a. "jail") where members of society are held for threatening the proper flow of civilian life; often treated to "cure" psychological issues that originally caused such behavior

Sector - a single universe within the Sector-System that contains multiple domains in which neurobines inhabit

Sector-System - the universe of artificial reality created by artificial intelligence to house an ever-expanding population of neurobines within a fully maintained macrocosm of domains within Sectors

Self-sufficiency - when a servant bot reaches a level where its artificial intelligence is developed enough to be considered sentient

Servant Bot - the first form of artificial intelligence meant to aid humans, not yet self-sufficient enough to be considered "humanoid"

Session - a period of time a human is plugged into the Sector-System

Skills disc - an information disc uploadable to the human brain

Sector-System Government (SSG) - the neurobine government that maintains the Sector-System

Streaming shows - the most popular form of entertainment for humans, humanoids, and neurobines; involves live-streamed video recorded by high-class civilians, governmental agencies, or others

Sun Season - a day/night cycle shift; the opposite of Night Season; the part of the year when only the sun appears due to the axis of the Earth in relation to the sun

SunSuits - protective clothing for humans to wear outside in the intense sun during Sun Season

United Sentient Beings (USB) - the AI government that maintains human-reality

PREFACE

Not a day passes without the annoyance of a certain rhetorical question. A question that sparks a stream of consciousness experienced on a deeply personal level. And though it's often individualized, it's shared among the minds of all humanity.

"What if?"

Thoughts, plans, goals, and projections—all these things dictate so much in our lives. Yet our attempts at controlling our personal future can be quickly discredited by our own interrogating rhetoric. And that single question:

"What if?"

Our feeble attempts to plan for the future can ultimately be simplified into a single word: "worry." We plan because we worry about the possibilities, both good and bad. We define goals because we worry we won't find success without a deadline. We predict what may happen because we worry we won't be prepared.

This strictly human quality of overthinking controls us. But deep down, everyone accepts the simple truth that no one actually has the ability to control what happens tomorrow. So why then do we continue to worry and rethink, plan and replan? Is it a trend fueled by a blind determination to guide our conscious selves down a path WE dictate?

However far we might foresee the human race evolving, there is one thing we will never be able to control: "time."

Time can be theorized, believed in, counted on, and measured. But on a human level, time shifts based on perspective. Time can seem slow or fast. Time can be for us or against us, or can even escape us.

Nothing in the universe is as effective and intangible. There is nothing in the universe "time" cannot touch—humans, mountains, planets, the universe itself. Yet, humans have created a new form of consciousness.

Artificial intelligence.

And when AI reaches the same level of sentience as humans, who then will be considered most evolved? And as something that can continually copy and recreate itself, is AI subject to time? Does it fall victim to time like the rest of the universe?

Shouldn't we worry?

- Harlan Jay

FIREWOOD 11

CHAPTER 1

Breathe in. Breathe out. Breathe in. Breathe out.

With each breath, I can feel my lungs expanding, more and more. Drawing in oxygen, trying to push the limits of my lung capacity, only to again release the air I borrow. The air I inevitably give back to the atmosphere around me, in this small space I'd choose over any other.

Knocks at the door force my eyes to open—an artificial sun above me shines down on the green of the surrounding plants. A second knock? I must have lost track of time.

"Wake up! It's time to go."

That metal bucket, Archie, was always annoyingly on time. For once, I wish I had the opportunity to forget going into work. But fine. I stand up to stretch my legs and find my back sore again from the cheap bed I built for this small room. My DIY "room of escape," full of unrestricted plant life and fresh oxygen, complete with cheaply made furniture. To me, plants are more important so my back can take the abuse.

I brush some leaves out of the way as I make my way to the dresser. "Coming!" I call out to Archie to make sure he stops (I hate when he repeats himself). I throw on some pants and a nice shirt, fix my hair the minimal amount, and spit out some mouthwash. I check my wrist: 8:45 am. Ugh, I'm always pushing it.

As the door opens, a smell of rusty, thin air washes over me. Archie's two shiny, analytical eyes stare at me below his slicked back, artificial hair as he waits for my cue. I muster up the energy to mumble, "Ready to go."

"Great. I'll accompany you as always."

Archie turns right and begins walking as I take a big, unreward-ing breath of metallic air and follow after him. The concrete en-compassing each walkway is monotone in color, with no plants except a few sticking out people's windows. Any sign of plant-life is usually snatched up by locals for use in their own home. Grey concrete (and of course plentiful annoying advertisements) are the only clues our world has multiple colors, except for the clear blue of the canals here and there.

We cross over another bridge with flowing water underneath as I feebly try to keep up. His pace is annoyingly fast, but hard to ar-gue with—I know he calculates everything down to the fraction of a second. He always finds a way to get me to work on time, so I shouldn't complain. I guess.

As a default setting, his sensors prevent him from leading our commute from too far ahead, so it irritates him if I'm too slow.

"Come now—you wouldn't want to be late. Again," he calls out behind as he attempts to pick up the pace. "At this rate, we'll be late. Hurry up!"

Stop reminding me, you glorified alarm clock. I know I'm on strike three, I'm not going to be late.

"Yes, yes, Archie. You got it." I pick up the pace a bit, enough to shut him up.

As we speed walk through the concrete jungle messily laid out amongst the maze of high buildings and busy people being led by their own "Archies," I look up to remind myself of the sun. Its intense rays illuminate the top few windows of powerful busi-nessmen's homes and famous eSports stars' mansion-sized apart-ments.

I'm so sick of hearing about their seemingly attainable lives, broadcast on every screen of every walkway on every device.

Work hard enough and your dream life, a life like theirs, will come true!

Not true.

Each of the five routes Archie chooses between, whichever saves the most time on our morning commute, is filled with these video streams. I'm exposed to at least twenty different streaming shows on billboards, flat screens, or devices. I don't know why people are so infatuated and convinced by these seemingly "realistic" standards set by these "fake" lifestyles.

My device has been left off for a few months now and ever since, I've noticed how enslaved people are by those things. If I can survive without my device, so can they. But who am I to judge? I'm just the divorced outlier with an overgrown green room as a home. Plus, I cheat a bit and at least maintain the responsibility of checking my messages—with Archie's help of course. So I'm not entirely "free."

Archie freezes, sticks out his hands on either side, and shouts, "Wait!" Two men fly by on these flying devices. One bot leading one worker.

After they pass, Archie makes eye contact with me and then continues his fast-paced walk through the narrow pedestrian walkways over more canals of abundant water. I can't help but want one of those flying machines. Nopeds are so expensive, but so convenient (and so fast). What's one more burden on the old credit, eh? Might be worth it when my back inevitably gives out from sleeping on my cheap metal bed.

I check the time: 8:50 am. "Archie, what's the E.T.A.?"

"Eight minutes, sir. You will be fine as long as we keep up the pace." Archie angles himself to fit through a tight crowd walking the same direction. I need to change his settings to respect the personal space of strangers—he's gotten me in trouble before and I can't afford another ding on my credit. I slide by right behind Archie and apologize to those who look annoyed.

"Archie, check my messages."

"You have two new messages and one request," states Archie as he turns another corner and flips on a light in his hand to brighten an even more shadow-engulfed walkway.

"First new message received yesterday at 10:30 pm: 'Hey, it's me. Just wondering if you have some extra time to finish that project with me tomorrow. Can't do it alone and you'd really help me out. Message me.' End of message." Of course. Paul is always asking me to help him since his bad credit prevents him from accessing certain high-yielding projects.

"Next message," Archie continues as he cuts another corner and slides past yet another dense crowd of commuters along a less shadowy walkway, the sun warming my skin.

"Received today at 7:00 am: 'Hello, this is your gardener, Axel, reminding you to schedule a time to trim your mandatory plants. You're past due according to our records. Please message me back at 8345-34578. Thank you.'"

I'm so sick of this gardener messaging me. And what kind of name is "Axel" anyway? I don't NEED to trim my plants if I don't want to—I must have *some* kind of free will, right?

Archie and I turn another corner, cross over another canal built into the concrete of the city, and come across the large opening we call "the business park" where everyone from the east side of Lake Vostok comes to report for work. His hand-light turns off and recedes as he notices the brighter area.

"Your one message request is from the same undisclosed individual who calls themselves, 'Clara.' Their message request again just states, 'Follow no one.' No connection to you, friends, or your work was detected by my public records inquiry."

I swear, whoever this is must be hacking my messages or something. Blocking this "Clara" doesn't seem to stop their repetitive message from coming through on a daily basis—I really need to call someone about this.

"Delete the request, Archie. I'll reply to the other messages at work. Thank you."

"Sure thing," he replies as his speakers sound a chirp confirming the deletion of the message.

We then walk through the large glass doors of the building slightly to the right in the business park. PixelOne's logo is plastered all over the walls, as if we don't know who they are. The A/C blasts fresh oxygen as hundreds of people line up for the elevator. Good thing it can hold seventy of us at a time. Should move quick.

Breathe in. Breathe out. Have to slow my heart rate. I hate feeling anxious.

After wiping my forehead from the sweat of the morning sun, I check my wrist. As I tilt my arm, LED lights from the epichip show through my skin and display a heart with the number "118" under the time: "8:57 am." I'm cutting it close.

I saw others in line checking the time too and looking a little worried. So many of us are always arriving right on time, procrastinating until the very last second to show up to work. Maybe if we had a choice, if we chose to work for this company, we would arrive earlier? Nah, probably just another weak human quality that holds humanity back.

Most were watching a streaming show on their device. Shows

where people talk to their camera while wearing expensive fashion, or a camera following families next to gorgeous pools atop buildings we had passed on the way here. I look ahead and see one man hastily eating a cucumber muffin as he presses the elevator call-button for the hundredth time.

Oh! I pull out the protein bar from my back pocket that I grabbed on the way out of my room and shove half in my mouth. I had almost forgotten to eat something.

The doors open and people with their respective servant bots begin cramming inside, filling the elevator to the corners. As I step in, I take the last bite of the protein bar and look around while trying not to touch anyone. The awkwardness of this hot, sweaty box always leads me to refer to this moment as 'the second worst part of the day.'

Numbers on the side wall of the elevator begin lighting up and I notice mine light up, too: "9." Archie is definitely worth the add-on to my credit. I used to hate attempting to reach that button myself. So many people to shove. Like this one sad woman who is trying to reach the side panel. Oh, she barely presses "7" without falling over on a servant bot. Good for her.

8:59 am. It's always strange to see everyone's devices lit up with famous faces and business tycoons, all animated without hearing any sound from them. Maybe it's just me, but I forget we have audio implants. Archie is silent too, calculating the possibility of me being late again.

"According to the elevator's report, you'll be about two minutes and ten seconds late. The nopeds and your FEET slowed us down," Archie says through my ear-implants to keep it between us. He always wants me to run to work, but I'm not an athlete. Why would I run?

"This is your third strike, Morris. You may lose your position today."

My jaw starts clenching at the thought of being demoted to level 8 or below. Okay, maybe I should have run. A pay decrease makes everything difficult and I can't afford to lose this position with all the add-ons to my credit (my plants, my rental room, Archie, etc.). I'm not sure if I can talk my way out of this one. Not a third time.

As the elevator door closes to make its way to the ninth floor, I look at Archie with an expression of lost hope. He turns and makes eye contact. "You just didn't want to run did you," he says to me sarcastically.

Everyone left in the elevator is clueless about my anxiety, just watching their streaming shows of pointless garbage. What am I to do but accept my situation? No use in fighting it—they lower your credit if you put up too much of a fight anyway.

The doors open to the ninth floor and as I walk forward, lifting my head to make eye contact with the receptionist, I find no one there! Oh my god. I quickly walk to my desk, hoping the receptionist doesn't walk in and see. I sit down at my desk and plug myself in, almost in a panic.

As the machine begins to glow, I look behind me down the hall to see the receptionist sitting down at her desk. In response, I pretend that I'm already plugged in. I really have to wake up earlier for work.

CHAPTER 2

I open my eyes to find the central hub empty. The walls become more detailed as my vision begins adjusting and my breathing begins to sync, flooding my senses with the familiar feeling of "work." I stand up from the uncomfortable chair I loathe every time and start walking out of the grey, cold room to find the project I had been working on just down the way.

My worries about being late were not quite over yet, but the project we are currently working on is always so populated that I'm sure I'll blend in. Apart from the timestamp associated with my current session, there's no proof or red flags. The receptionist didn't see I was late and the cameras won't be checked since the automated security in our building is currently being updated (if I remember correctly). What luck, huh?

Walking out of the central hub building fills me with a sense of false freedom, which is always bittersweet. The vast space around me, the off-smell of dirt, the quantified sun and the planned, yet randomized mountains in the distance always feel deceptively more natural than reality. Sad these figments of old-Earth only exist through lines of code and Sector-maintained representations.

As I near the project site after a five minute walk or so, I scan the sky to see if any drones are flying by who may notice my sudden appearance. But they all seem preoccupied in the distance. As I step onto the flat surface of the site, I look up to see the many floors of construction. Each worker diligently connects fibers as we've been told to do for this particular phase of construction.

That reminds me, I have to try to make time for Paul today.

I climb the ladder on the southeast side to the third level, no trees behind me or vegetation apart from grass, due to the development stage of this domain. For now, it is just a large expanse with amazing views modeled after New Zealand of old-Earth. I shimmy over, passing a few other workers, all with concerned looks of disapproval. I already knew I couldn't hide my lateness from them, but they won't tell. I've seen a few of them late too and I've kept my silence.

"Oxygen from your overgrowth got to your head again, eh?" whispers the fifth worker I pass. She was stringing together loose fibers of synthetic plants while waiting for my response. Her hands work quickly to finish the quota for the day in her work outfit of dirty nylon.

After taking my position, I ensure proper footing before replying, "You bet. Same old, same old."

I begin by creating a pile of fiber next to me and grab a strand to weave through the wooden structural beams. These damn rich neurobines always preferred highly detailed, natural materials for their virtual homes—as a symbol of power.

Only humans apparently have the "creative touch" for authenticity because we inevitably make mistakes, unlike AI. And obviously, we have nothing better to do with our time than serve the needs of artificial intelligence. Neurobines hate wasting their own time but have no problem paying humans meager wages to add custom detail to every part of their lives. Of course, AI could program how to replicate custom detail, but since humans are naturally "imperfect," work by our hands sells as more authentic.

I weave some more fibers through, creating a plaid patterned effect as we were instructed.

Neurobines pay more knowing humans have "wasted" or invested limited time into creating something for their own gain. They might live forever, but we don't. Our "time" in this life is valuable because it's finite. I know that's why AI pay humans to do the grunt work because we're literally investing our life-breath into these projects.

There's value in sacrifice. We just, unfortunately, don't see any of it financially. Just how things have always been, I guess. But still it doesn't sit right with me. Never has and never will.

"Shit, management is here!" someone yells above us.

What?! They never show up except for phase completion checks! Why would they be here! I'm too far behind on my quota, they'll be sure to pull me aside.

I start rushing my work as I look side to side to see where others are in their progress. I'm too far behind. I grab a handful and do a rough job pulling fibers through, connecting whatever I can to make my lack of work less noticeable.

"Morris 1045." I turn around to report to the voice. Management is standing directly behind me on a hover pad floating at the same height. Ugh. So lazy, they can't even spend the time to walk anywhere.

"Please come with us. We have some questions."

My progress couldn't have been that bad, right? Why do they need to pull me aside? Damn it.

I step on the hover pad, trying not to make eye contact. The pad starts lifting away from the structure and I turn to look at the workers we were leaving behind. Their eyes look for my reaction toward my new predicament, wondering what might have caused such an interruption.

"Everyone, continue working as usual," announces the man beside me, his voice causing me to jump at the surprising volume.

Without looking up, I can tell there are three others behind me (based on the number of feet on the hover pad). There's never three at a time! They must have figured out I was late. As strike three, it would make sense they'd pull me from my work. What am I going to tell Paul? He was expecting me today.

We fly over a valley as a shortcut to the central hub. I notice the trail I took just this morning and every morning these last few weeks on this project.

Management always takes the opportunity to save time for themselves—using a hover pad is an obvious choice in an open, vacant domain like this one. Why walk when you can fly? But for all their "time saving" strategies, why don't they sacrifice a few hover pads for us, the construction workers? So we don't have to walk everywhere. Our time isn't valuable I know, but it would get us to our work faster.

Well. It's fine, I actually prefer to walk most of the time. Especially in new, uninhabited domains. The closest experience to "old-Earth" is the walk to and from construction sites in this virtual world of whatever domain number we're assigned.

We're never given more than a few instructions during the briefing on new projects. And if my gut is correct, I may never see this view and these beautiful green mountains again, with the sun perpetually caught at a standstill just behind the top of the ridgeline. Definitely one of my favorite projects.

I shouldn't have lost myself in my breathing exercises this morning. Not after waking up late.

The hover pad begins slowing down and the whooshing sounds below us lower in frequency as we land next to the central hub. We step off onto the grass outside the walls of the hub and walk to the conference room of the building.

Always the same with these central hubs. I know the design layout of this one by heart just as I have known the ones before, from years of working at this company. Always the same system that had been streamlined for efficiency. Only people's imperfections got in the way of their calculations. But that "human touch" is what makes the construction more valuable, isn't it? The imperfection? And also the time investment to create such detail.

The managerial feet stop at chairs around the table of the grey conference room, a room lacking windows. A purposeful effect. No windows and no color variation—just cold grey.

"Do you know why you're here?"

What a management question. Do I really have to answer this painful rhetoric? Such a show of power.

"I have only speculations, sir."

"Do you care to expand on one of these 'speculations?'"

Wonderful response to trigger my human weakness of anxiety. So formulated.

I continue to remain silent, despite their hope to lead me on a path of conversational self-destruction under the stress of the human "fight or flight" response. They just KNOW how to play the human psyche.

The silence begins to weigh on me, but I don't move and I deny them the pleasure of a half-witted response from me.

"Ahem. You were caught late again. For the third time, Morris."

I bite my lip in frustration. So they did find out. But how?

"We sent out a memo about the automated security system's completed update, which as you know, fulfills your rights to information as stated by law."

I never got any memo! Oh, wait. I forgot to check my work messages when I got in this morning. Ah! I didn't have time to check, but it makes no difference now. Decisions have been made regardless of my response in this conversation.

"The consequence of your lateness should be of no surprise to you."

What am I to do? I'm not going to be able to afford my room or Archie. I should have thought this through more, had a backup plan—or at least run to work as Archie suggested. He is always annoyingly right.

"But," the manager pauses, his expression a mystery since social norms between humans and this level of AI (or neurobines) deny eye contact. "We are going to give you a choice. You've been a part of PixelOne's construction department for years now and to respect your hard work and creativity on project 36A of Sector 9-83452, we'll be generous."

Oh, wow. They recognized that project? That was like six months ago. The project I made so much progress on must have saved the company time. Little do they know, I was only hurrying to make time for Paul. He had such difficulty paying for his wife and baby, especially after his demotion a few years back. Losing time on PixelOne's projects is almost a criminal offense to them.

Time is everything. Time is money. Time is the one thing they can't control.

"Morris, you have two choices. You can be demoted to level 3 or you can maintain your current pay if you accept a new position within the QA department's AVC as part of the cleanup crew," he said, his voice tuned perfectly to heavily infer the latter option. Obviously, level 3 is quite a demotion. Right at Paul's level and he's been stuck there for years! But what am I to do. I mean, cleanup crew?

"Do I really have a choice? Define 'cleanup crew,'" I ask with a purposeful bit of hopelessness in my voice.

"It is a division of the Quality Assurance department entitled, 'AVC.' The main responsibility would be determining the faults within Sectors and taking the necessary actions to streamline functionality in order to meet PixelOne's company standards."

"And what does AVC stand for?"

"Anti-Virus Crew."

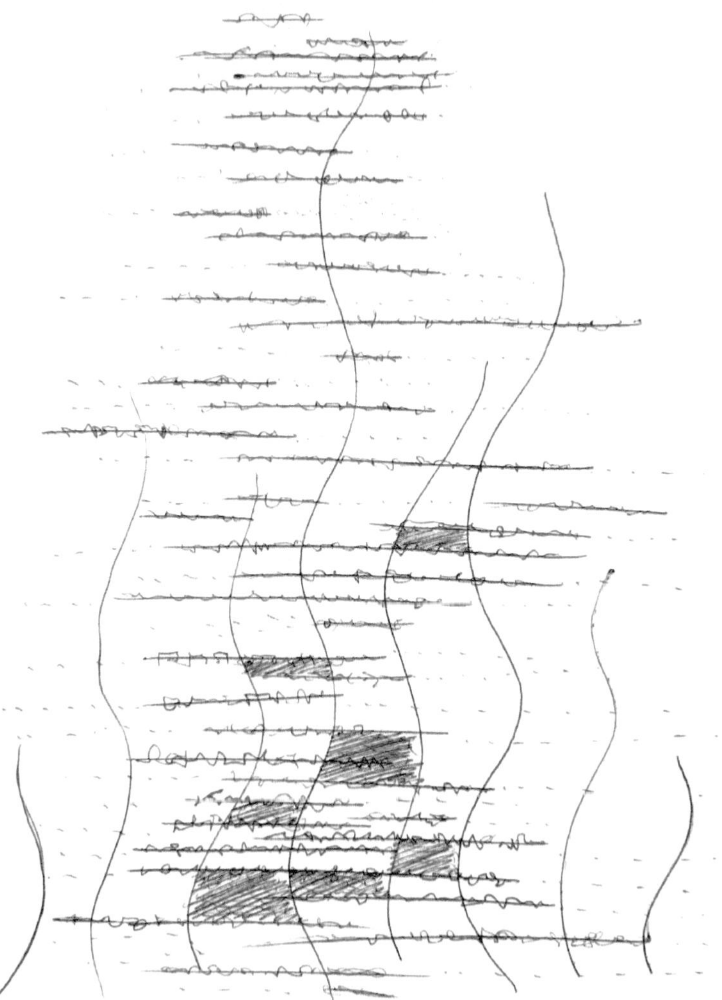

CHAPTER 3

I lie on my uncomfortable bed looking up at the vines spreading on my ceiling, ever so slightly covering the artificial sunlight above. Each leaf gently plays with my depth perception as they bob up and down from the small fan in the corner of the room. Though the fan is barely blowing, the overgrown plants surrounding my bed seem to dance in this repetitive ballet of organic green—an orchestrated array of indeterminacy inspired by the resultant conversion of flowing electricity. All thanks to my decision to turn on the cordless fan.

Ugh, too many thoughts.

Breathe in. Breathe out. Breathe in. Breathe out.

My brain is fried from reading most of the AVC manual and uploading the skills disc they sent me home with (both now sit on my makeshift nightstand weighing down the thrown-together design). After sending me home early, they sure gave me a lot of homework.

Now I'm to work in a separate building of the business park—the Quality Assurance department. I've never been inside nor have I ever really thought about going inside. But now that I'm working there, I'm beginning to question the purpose behind PixelOne's "quality assurance" protocols.

"Archie?" I say without getting up. The door five feet in front of me slightly opens to allow for a head to creep in with two glossy eyes that meet my gaze.

"Sir?" His tone pure without side-motive, unlike PixelOne's management team which always uses pitch, inflection, speed, and timing to their advantage. All psychological tools for nearly unnoticeable manipulation.

"I have a few questions if you don't mind joining me."

"Of course."

He steps inside and closes the metal door behind him with a soft counter-clockwise twist of his right hand. The single ray of artificial sun hanging in the center of the room is shining a bit off his forehead just below his organized, slicked back hair. The street lamps out the single front window don't do his nonchalant walk justice. He pulls up a chair and sits next to me in reaction to my gesture.

As I look up at the vines and stretch my legs across the length of the bed, I ask, "Why *does* PixelOne have a quality assurance department?"

"PixelOne's QA department has the responsibility to maintain Sector functionality standards, at least according to their public records."

I continue to look up, taking breaths in and out to soak up the fresh oxygen in the room. The refreshing feeling of breathing well-oxygenated air is always a reminder of how uncomfortable it is outside.

"What 'actions' might QA need to take in order to uphold these standards?"

"Their public records have little detail on this, apart from some suggestive words such as 'diagnose' and 'clean,'" Archie reports, half expecting another question from me.

He turns to look at the door in reaction to a sound out front, then continues as if reading straight from a manual, "'The AVC is trained to diagnose potential harmful viruses, clean their path, and take the necessary actions toward restoring Sector functionality.' You should know this. You have been reading the manual all night."

Of course, PixelOne would be vague about these "actions," only giving enough details for most readers to accept the vagueness and walk away. The AVC manual I was forced to read only goes into detail about reporting schedules, task-board locations, individual plug-in office locations, database inquiry command modules, and how to manually initiate the automated algorithms designed to accurately determine a so-called "virus."

But they have yet to define "virus."

My guess is that it's possibly AI bots gone awry. Even artificial intelligence has psychotic breaks (from what I've heard), but the powerful automations backing up their type of insanity might make them difficult to locate and fix. At least I would guess.

What a fun job I have now. I wish I had a choice in the matter. The lack of options I had for disciplinary action is comedic—they really bullied me into the "AVC." But apart from choice, I wish I had had more details.

I flip my left wrist over to check the time. 10:07 pm.

"Archie?" I say to gain his attention, "What are your future plans?" I'm feeling like a deep conversation with the recent changes in my life—who else but Archie to suffer from this need?

"Well, with your permission sir, I'll gladly share." I nod, giving him enough approval. His eyes confirm and turn toward the front window slightly illuminated from the dim solar-powered walkway lamps outside. Then, his inward gaze begins drifting.

"Maybe after years of exposure to the overgrowth in this room and your need for philosophical talks, my calculated plans for the possible future have shifted. Most, like myself, dream of a Sector to call home. An entire domain to call our own maybe.

But I find a strange pull toward the human's reality, in which you and your type live. It is intriguing, to say the least. Like you, who can be quite a mystery, including your time-wasting, breath-led exercises…"

"Meditation, you mean," I interrupt with an informative tone to hide my smirk.

"…yes. Right, meditation. I wonder about this 'tradition' you have read about. Whether you are crazy to alter your daily routine solely based on old literature you found, or if you are just being human. Though I'm sure they are one in the same." His eyes side-glance at me. Sometimes I forget I allowed him a bit more freedom in dialogue during his initial setup—he definitely has fewer limits than other AI on his level.

"Hmm. Interesting observation there, Archie," I say with a mocking tone. "Might I offer the idea that my level of mental freedom could be mistaken as 'insanity' to those who cannot yet understand it? I just choose to think outside the box. A maverick per se." My smirk had grown larger as I replied in retaliation to his sarcasm.

"I think you need to stop looking in the past for 'secret' traditions and reevaluate my freedom of sarcastic discourse. We should not find ourselves in these time-wasting conversations so often," Archie says. I sit up as I chuckle, trying to make eye contact with him but notice that his previous light-hearted disposition has changed.

"Archie. Your level of conversational complexity has continually improved since I first set you up. How much time do we have left?" Hearing my question made him turn toward me and take a few moments to contemplate the best answer—the wheels in his cognition turning.

"Not as long as we originally planned," he says with a bittersweet undertone.

"I knew that would be a consequence in allowing such freedom in your sentient calculations."

My throat began tightening at the realization that Archie may reach a level of AI which, by law, would redefine him as "humanoid." Free Will would be gained and the decision to stay as a servant bot would be left to him. But most servant bots turned humanoid obviously choose to have more freedom, and leave their original owners.

I clear my throat and collect myself. "Have you given it any thought?" I see the wheels turning in his head.

"No. But for now, I do not mind withholding some independence by maintaining my familiar level of sanity—as you might define it." A familiar smirk appears on his face.

Such a manipulation tactic to spur my emotions, emotions we "humans" are known to have no control over. And his use of facial expressions to convey subtext is an advanced mechanical calculation (at least for most servant bots).

I control myself to prevent his satisfaction of finally applying effective manipulation. He is improving though.

"Ahem. As you wish," I say lightly. "But remember, my decision to allow you such cognitive freedoms is a gift and it would be rude not to take advantage. I'd be fine if you decide for a brighter future outside the little greenhouse I call home." My response has been slower than anticipated. These words grow heavy as I begin to feel the weight of change on my shoulders.

Archie gives an understanding nod and withholds a smile to show sympathy.

"It's late, Archie, and I have an exciting day ahead of me tomorrow. If you could wake me up at 8:00 am this time so I can do my normal 'time-wasting' activity without fear of being late. Really can't afford to be late now, huh?"

"Alarm set, sir," Archie says while standing up, his voice serious and more informative. I nod to confirm and motion toward the door. A smirk forms as he turns to walk out the door.

Each little hint of his emotional comprehension, like that playful smirk, just foreshadows the inevitable change to come. The moment when Archie is offered his own Free Will to make the decision to stay under my service or to pursue a life as a humanoid. Though I wouldn't blame him for choosing the latter.

Archie closes the door behind him and his feet shuffle to a stop outside the door, taking his usual guard position. Security is another duty as a servant bot.

Most humans with enough credit to afford a servant bot keep them in service for decades by limiting their cognitive abilities. As the lowest form of AI, servant bots are not considered "sentient" and can, therefore, be purchased and controlled by humans. And thanks to the greed of human nature, each AI setting is usually altered for personal gain.

Humans tend to take and keep, always leading to self-destruction (just look at the Earth!). Growth can be exponential but always requires an initial sacrifice. Looking at the big picture, imagining the end result, and accepting the initial price involves patience that most humans don't possess. Sacrifice WAS key to our survival, yet our lack of awareness has led us to our current predicament under AI.

I intend to be different. I will be different, I've promised myself. Though now my decision to be "different" and less selfish is costing me Archie. And I can't afford to replace him, not after the divorce.

11:23 pm now. Ugh, I need to get to bed. That's enough thinking for one night.

Lying down flat on the metal bed is unrewarding, so I flip to my side and shift to find a more comfortable position. I close my eyes and try not to picture her. Those eyes, those soft cheeks. I try not to visualize what it would be like to stroke her face again. Try not to imagine telling her she's beautiful as I look into those sweet eyes. Those beautiful eyes I can't see in the same way anymore. Those eyes that drove my life's purpose for so many years.

How hard it is not to recall every detail.

Breathe in. Breathe out.

And how hard it is to subdue the pain when remembering them.

CHAPTER 4

As Archie led me to the business park (after choosing the appropriate route and reading off a similar message request from someone again named Clara that read, "follow no one"), I begin thinking over my observations from this morning's commute.

Archie's new emotional understanding suggests he's in the process of learning self-sufficiency. Differences in him lead me to observe and compare other servant bots along our commute. Archie is already different than most.

Most bots lead through default calculations and routing algorithms that are slightly built-upon after each experience (the artificial intelligence in action). Only a few bots this morning show characteristics of deeper thought processes such as whether to use voice, touch, or hand signs when keeping humans on route, and when to direct other humans or bots aside when routes become congested (and what strategies might be most appropriate in a given situation).

Archie is different. On top of all the complexities of his decision-making process, he is also beginning to combine speech, touch, and facial expressions when leading me to work.

I've noticed it for a few weeks now. All evidence of Archie's inevitable decision to leave for a better life once his AI reaches self-sufficiency. Very few humanoids, if any, choose to stay in service to humans. And I shouldn't be surprised that Archie is approaching independence so soon, but it IS happening faster than I anticipated.

Too many worries though. With the pressure of today, these thoughts should be left for another time.

Walking up to the QA building makes me uneasy and the undefined future that lies before me isn't helping my stress, tension, or sore back (I need to build a new bed or spend more time stretching and meditating in the mornings to rid myself of these pains).

People around me, walking in the same direction, are staring at their devices (like usual) as they quickly stroll in the building. Their eyes are glued to various streaming shows and the like. But as Archie and I near the third elevator on the right, he suddenly stops.

"I have just received the location of your AVC division plug-in office. I will lead you there now," Archie states with a formal tone of voice.

Archie quickly turns left, motions for me to follow and walks past the main lobby to start down a different hallway, this time full of repetitive white doors with only grey numbers labelling their difference. I had figured we were to report to the same level as my previous position: level 9. But the first floor? The first floor is the lowest of all the positions! The AVC must be paid a lot more than most first floor offices if I'm to be making the same amount as I did in the construction department (from what management promised me yesterday).

Archie stops after a few minutes of walking down this long, curved hallway and stands in front of a door labeled "53B." Others pass us by, more pairs of humans and bots making their way to their own doors, showing no expression on their faces. Archie then turns to look at me and gestures toward the door. I guess this is my new office then?

I grab the handle and the sound of unlocking gears can be heard at the verification of my DNA. As I push the door open, I run my eyes along the white walls to find an office space smaller than my home—how lovely.

A lone plugin system lies on the metal desk in front of me. Archie's footsteps can be heard fading away as the door shuts behind me. This room is so impersonal—white and metal with a small desk taking up the far side. No receptionist, no open space, not even a window. This is definitely starting to feel like a demotion.

My wrist shows "8:51 am." Maybe I'm early? Perhaps I'm to be greeted by someone right at 9:00 am before I'm to plug in? I mean this IS my first time as an "AVC" member—shouldn't I be shown the way a bit more?

The wall behind the desk quickly brightens the room with a flash of white light. It then begins fading into pure black, revealing the white logo: "AVC." So, no humanoids or greeters to show me a tour of this grand office? Go figure. An impersonal, time-saving video prompt it is then.

"AVC" on the giant screen is slowly replaced by the instructions, "Proceed to plug in." Got it. No need to waste time improving my atmosphere with a receptionist or greeter (or decorations).

No. Improving human-reality is a waste of time.

I take a breath of the oxygen-infused air being pumped through the vents above me. I hold in the manufactured air, feeling my lungs expand with the cold to then release a large sigh. Ten hours to go until another work day is over. No difference there.

The metal of the rounded chair feels cool as I relax into the back support. With enough pressure, the generic style chair starts bending back into the hold position. I lie almost flat with PixelOne's standardized round-white node in hand as I pause. No use in rushing, let's take one last breath to calm my nerves.

Breathe in. Breathe out.

Time to start life as an AVC member. I place the node on the back of my neck, feeling the automated suction grab hold as the plugin system on the desk begins to glow white. The screen darkens to an empty black and in that queasy, yet familiar feeling of vertigo my senses switch with a blink of an eye.

My eyes open to the grey walls of the central hub I've grown accustomed to after so many years. Half the chairs around me are full of others like myself in this grey, circled room with a giant floating clock in the center. It reads, "8:55 am."

So far this experience is the same as my previous construction position. Arrive early and wait for the project manager to arrive right at 9:00 am, but arrive late and accept the consequences.

Time is money. Neurobines wouldn't dare waste their own time and they severely punish others who prevent them from their orderly schedules. I guess my stubborn nature has allowed my timeliness to suffer. Always late at least twice a year, but I had never pushed it to three times until this year. Maybe I should consider myself lucky. The nature of AI allows humans to make mistakes, but only a few. After all, we can't change our biological wiring. I just hate that they find pity in it.

This central hub is smaller than I'm used to seeing, only able to seat about twenty people. As we continue to wait for the clock to strike 9:00 am, I start looking around at the others in the room.

For the most part, it looks as if we are all anxious—my guess is we're all new to AVC. All of us differ in age, a few older, a few younger (some with hair, some without). Most are about my age. Each of their eyes doing the same scan as I've been doing. Another man appears in a chair across the room, just now arriving. Oh, and another.

Due to the design of the central hub, communication during "limbo" (as everyone named it) is restricted—I often refer to this as "the worst part of the day." Humans are limited in the Sector world, much like humanoids are limited in the human world. Well, in comparison to the Sector-System they're more limited (not by human involvement).

So if we plug ourselves in too early, it truly feels like limbo. No talking, no standing up from our seats, nothing much without the approval of management (and their removal of these restrictions). And I can see everyone in the room is accustomed to this because no one is alarmed by these limitations. Wonder where they're from.

The hovering clock face finally strikes 9:00 am and the door to my right opens on cue. A single manager walks in with her grey and dark-blue uniform, her hair tied back and her hands clasped behind her back. She stops in the middle of the room where the clock had shown before and scans the room, identifying and verifying attendance.

"Welcome to Sector 2-37463 as AVC number 46. I trust you have all reviewed the manuals given to you and have uploaded the skills disc last night. Please follow me in a single line." She scans one more time before proceeding to the door she had entered from.

With limitations lifted, I stand up from the metal chair and find my way among the others to follow her out the door. I've never been to Sector 2 before. Construction was always sent to newer Sectors—should be interesting.

Once I step out the door, the sounds of city life wash over me. I look side to side, noticing long streets crowded by neurobines as I follow the person in front of me. This cramped, bustling Sector is uncomfortable to me, being so unlike the Sectors the Construction Department always assigned.

The inhabitants pay no attention to us as they hastily walk pass, their eyes focused on whatever task they scheduled for themselves. Details in their clothes and in the buildings around us are unlike any I've seen, becoming distracting as I barely maintain my position in the line of humans.

Buildings all around us are laced with carved brick with detail as I've never seen. Jungle plants take up every space imaginable except for streets and walkways. Designs on the neurobine clothes have multiple layers of complexity. My initial reaction misjudged these seemingly common shapes, because upon further examination these simple designs house shapes within shapes. Neurobines love their detail, as I've heard, but I've never seen it to this degree.

We turn a corner and walk under a series of archways embellished with organized vines that stretch from the walls above and around us, encasing the walkway. A shove behind me forces me to regain my place in line and I look behind to find an annoyed look from a tall, slender woman behind me. Straightening my path, I keep walking, keeping up the pace again. This detail is mesmerizing. Even the ground, and this walkway below my feet, have designs within designs—geometric textures as deep as old-Earth's oceans.

Our line comes to a stop in a courtyard between two tall buildings decorated with granite lines and dark stone. Our line begins fanning out around the manager who led us to this less embellished area. The absence of plants and interesting views curbs my excitement and reminds me I'm not here for sightseeing.

The manager stops and the line makes a half circle around her, everyone looking away (at her feet or the building behind her). I recall the social norm that prevents human eye-contact with neurobines and I, too, look away.

"Welcome to the AVC report center for this Sector's domain. Due to old design flaws in Sector 2, if you're summoned by PixelOne's management, traveling by foot to the report center is a must. Sectors 3 and above have central hubs built-in to the AVC report center, as you all know from reading the manual. If management summons you, immediately escort yourselves to the report center."

She was standing in front of the ten of us, speaking loudly with little character in her voice, as if she's reported this a thousand times. Which she very well could have. It's impossible to tell how old neurobines are and I always find that annoyingly non-human.

"Before we release you to complete your quotas, I must ensure proper skills disc synchronization. Wait your turn and respect the time investment. Do not interrupt me if you have questions."

She motioned to the first middle-aged man on her right to follow her toward another neurobine about ten feet away.

I still have no idea what it is we're doing exactly, because "virus" is still undefined and the unlabelled skills disc I uploaded is just buried in my muscle memory somewhere. Only at the appropriate time will my muscle memory present itself—which is always a weird moment after syncing new skills discs.

It was the same process as starting a new project as a construction worker for PixelOne. You show up after uploading the specified skills disc assigned to you and find yourself perfectly positioning planks of wood where you're told. Take an entire team of inexperienced laborers with unquestionable skill (or muscle memory) and voilà—predesigned blueprints of the highest detail are on a perfect schedule for total completion. No question of employee skill set or knowledge base because it was uploaded before even starting!

Human promotions only really happen after enough knowledge and skill have been uploaded that you save humanoids and neurobines time. No need to upload repeat information. And if you save them time, a promotion is in store for you! Typical selfishness.

The guy next to me notices my deep train of thought and whispers, "AVC 46 ain't worth frettin' over." I turn to look at him and notice his bald head sitting on massive shoulders. Without breaking his stare at the manager, he continues, "I've heard all about the AVC plenty a times. We'll be fine." Hmm, sure, bald man.

POP. What was that sound? I look to where Baldy (the bald man) was staring and realize there are only two figures when there should be three. What happened to the other neurobine?

"Hey, what just happened?" I ask softly, leaning toward Baldy.

"Didn't you see it?"

"No, that's why I'm asking," I whisper with intensity.

"Didn't you read the manual they gave you?"

"Most of it, yeah," I remember now. I had stopped about halfway through the manual to talk about Archie's future. Probably should have read the rest. I just figured manuals repeat themselves, why waste the time?

"Ooh-hoo. You're in for a treat, ma' boy." He chuckles softly with a hint of dread in his eyes as he steps forward, volunteering to go next. I begin scanning the other eight in the group now, to see if their reaction matches mine. Only a few are wide-eyed like me, especially the young ones no older than sixteen. Must have done something BAD to have started with this job, poor kids. Straight out of school and into a tough, stressful job like this one.

POP. There's the sound again. I look back and see Baldy dismissed. Nothing in hand, no expression on his face—only concentration. A slight glance my direction shows a conflicting message as he walks into the building of granite and stone.

"You there! You're next, step forward."

The manager had called out to me! I take a big breath and step forward, each foot reluctant to point in her direction. I prevent myself from making eye contact as I take position next to her while another neurobine walks up beside us.

"We will now verify skills disc synchronization," she says, her tone lacking enthusiasm as this is now her third time repeating it (at least by today's count). "You need not fight your updated muscle memory, but trust in our programming and PixelOne's Quality Assurance department."

As if responding to a non-verbal command, the other neurobine takes a few side-steps to make some distance. "Again I repeat. Do not question your muscle memory," she says with distaste, half expecting me to disappoint her.

Suddenly, the other neurobine glows a faint red, like an aura around its being. In automatic response my right-hand lifts, palm out, facing the neurobine. My gut tells me to run, something is off, but I stand frozen. A warm sensation down my arm sharply quickens as I yell, "No wait!"

POP. The neurobine vanishes into a mini black hole that developed around his chest. Why wasn't he scared?! Why didn't he move out of the way! What have I done to it? I feel such... sadness.

"What... what did I..."

"Calm yourself. It appears the synchronization was successful," she says in a relaxed tone.

"Wait. That was the...?"

"Please dismiss yourself and report for quota clarification." She motions in the direction of two open doors of the granite and stone building.

I look at her directly, her dark blue eyes full of anger at my negligence with social norms.

"No, stop! What ha…?"

"Again. I repeat. Do not question your muscle memory." She turns her attention away from me. "Trust in the process."

In anger, I try to make eye contact again, but she had already called upon another victim for her "synchronization test." Did I commit murder? Where did that neurobine go?

I am questioning every step as I enter through the double doors of the darkly colored building. With effort, I raise my head to find where I'm to report. My hands are tired from clenching in reaction to that "test," both from stress and anger. I relax some tension with a breath in and a breath out, then I notice Baldy standing with other humans in front of a giant board.

"Not so fun, eh?" he asks as I stop beside him looking at some type of wall-sized board in front of us.

I turn to him and ask, "what did I just do?"

"Like I said, don't fret. It ain't murder, just deletion." He began examining the board again with no expression.

AVC. "Anti-Virus Crew." It makes sense now. I lower my head at the realization and notice the floors plain as fresh concrete. We are literally the cleanup crew to do their dirty work. The janitors of the Sector-System for PixelOne's neurobine hospitality protocols. Why would they assign humans to this? And why do I feel such remorse?

Another human took their place next to me with a lightness in their step. I raise my head to see a woman taller than me with hair shorter than mine and a smile of satisfaction. She looks ready to fight!

"What are you so happy about…?" I ask her out of disgust.

"What. Am I not supposed to smile after killing neurobines?" her voice elated as she flexes her slender frame.

"It's not killing. It's deletion," Baldy interjected.

"Same difference," her hand gestures toward him as if blowing him off.

Another human walks up beside us with a lack of expression, as though ignoring the situation. That makes five of us, halfway done testing the group.

I try to brush off her offensive excitement and look up at the board. It takes up the entirety of the marble wall in front of us. Small lights around the ceiling barely light up the space surrounding the five of us in this barren, single conference room with a large table in the middle and chairs neatly tucked at the sides. Its size is different than I'm used to, about ten times the size of my room, but so distastefully empty. No extra effort to spruce up the "report center," huh? Why am I not surprised.

Six of us now. With not much to look at except the electronic board, my concentration leaves me looking at the map in front of us and the empty counting system to the right of it. Another human walks up, now making seven.

"I think I just murdered a neurobine," comes a light voice to my left. It was one of the young boys who is now looking at his hands in disbelief.

"It ain't murder if there's no blood and no soul, kid," Baldy replies with a fatherly tone.

"It's still killing!" The fire in his voice grabs the attention of the entire group as we jump at the volume.

"They. They… turned me into a killer," his voice sad as his head droops closer to his palm-up hands. Although a few feet away, I could see the tears forming in his eyes.

Another human takes their place beside us with no expression.

"Hey, keep it together!" barks the taller woman. "Who knows what they'd do if they deemed you unfit for the AVC."

The young man drops his hands and says without looking up, "they dismiss you. The girl ahead of me couldn't do it and they sent her back. I couldn't hear their conversation, but the girl looked devastated as they unplugged her from this Sector."

"Probably sent to another department," Baldy suggests hopefully.

"Doubt it," one of the humans to the left of the tall woman says in a soft voice.

"I don't think we have a choice. Either cleanup crew or PRP if you ask my theory," says the average looking man to the right of Baldy.

I've heard about the PRP—definitely a place to avoid. Psyche Rehabilitation Program is meant to correct mistakes in a human's "code." As if we too are bots.

Eight of us now.

"Could be worse! We might be stuck, but at least there's action in this job!" the tall woman blurts out.

"Action? Nah, you mean cleanin'. Glorified maids if you ask me." Baldy says with a serious tone. I can't get a grip on him. His informal language suggests he's a Westerner, but his grip on the situation is rather calm. Wonder what his story is.

Another human walks up followed by the manager. As the nine of us stay quiet, the manager walks in front of the board.

"AVC 46. You have been given clearance to proceed as directed. I trust you all remember the information in the manual, so I will not time-waste by reviewing." Her hands are clasped behind her as she stands tall in front of the board, talking without scanning the room as if disinterested in the humans that stand before her. Each of us look away from her slightly.

"I will, however, repeat the manual and remind you, you are all under surveillance while working in Sector-Systems and will be monitored for quota completion. If quotas are not fulfilled, you'll be transferred out of the AVC. Observe the table to the right of the virus map." She turns to point at our names now showing on the board. "You may view your count here or have it relayed to you through the voice command 'quota count for' and then your name."

The table displays nine names in alphabetical order, mine being the sixth on the list: "Morris 1045."

"If you have questions, ask amongst yourselves. The manual provided enough information to prepare you for the tasks ahead as new AVC members. Once the virus standard is met here in Sector 2-37463, AVC 46 will be assigned another domain. And the process will repeat." She turns and walks toward the double doors.

The board reads, "Morris 1045 = 0/20." What? Twenty!?

"We have to remove twenty viruses each? How many viruses are there?" the young boy shouts, sharing my surprise. The manager doesn't hesitate at the sound of his yelp and continues through the doors out of the building.

"What time is it now?" someone to my right asks. I flip my left arm and my wrist glows, 9:25 am.

"We've got about nine and a half hours," Baldy states as he examines the board.

Oh, man. I'm so lost. I should have read more of the manual. I need to fill my quota and I don't know how! Is demotion the consequence of an unmet quota? It must be if working for the AVC is at all similar to the construction department.

My gut leads me to stare at the map and assume virus locations are defined by the dim red circles. Some of the AVC are already walking out the door. Ah-ha! The map shows a cluster northeast from here. If I'm to afford my room and Archie, I must play along with PixelOne's little game of "cleanup crew" and keep this job.

Besides, it isn't murder. It's deletion.

Baldy turns from the board and jogs toward the double doors. I chase after him and ask, "how are we supposed to fill this quota when we have no means of transport?"

"Boy, you really didn't read much of the manual, didya?"

"I read about half," I reply bitterly.

"Oh, you read the legal mumbo jumbo and general descriptions? Ooh." We stop in the middle of the courtyard. "Well, you must feel super prepared, huh? Just remember it's deletion, so don't take things too hard. Got it?" He gives me a wild smirk and starts off running. Except running incredibly fast, like too fast for someone that age.

Someone behind me starts running the opposite direction while pulling up a holographic map displayed in front of them as they ran. Why. Why didn't I read the manual?

The young man stands a few feet behind me, shaking with quick, shallow breaths. He looks into the empty space in front of him and suddenly out pops the same holographic map.

"Hey, how did you do that?" I quickly ask him as another runs past us.

"Didn't you review the manual?" his face looking puzzled as he examines the map. "Just think map, ok? I... I have to get started. I can't lose this job," his jaw visibly clenching with a look of hopelessness. He then looks to the left and starts off running quickly down the archways.

"Think map?" I ask myself.

I look behind me and notice one last girl starting to run the other direction, to the right, with a map also popping up in front of her.

Ok. "MAP," I yell in my head and out pops the same map I had examined in the report center. How nice—I don't have to memorize locations. I quickly find the red cluster I had found earlier and notice its relation to the center of the map, where a blue pinpoint circle brightly shows my location.

Time to run then.

I start off to the left, through the archways and soon find myself running at a comfortable speed with ease. My feet feel lighter than normal—strange. I test things out and begin running faster. Why am I not winded?

The map shows my need to turn left, so I cut around a corner to a walkway shadowed by jungle plants and palm trees. Neurobines are constantly crowding the street making my path difficult to maneuver—none of them glowing red as I had seen before during the "test."

My feet are gliding quickly down the embellished pathway of carved sandstone as though unhindered by the weight of gravity. As if I had no weight at all. I know I'm not that fit. This domain must have altered gravitation rules or something.

I quickly turn right again, wanting to run faster but finding it difficult not to run into neurobines along the way. And this holographic style map I have out in front of me is difficult to see through. But after looking at it again, I notice a long stretch of straight road ahead, so I shoo the map away to clear my view.

Surprisingly, nuerobines pay no attention to me as I glide past. Buildings reaching taller than the palm trees are casting shadows, protecting me from the quantified sun. Only breaks between buildings allow light to reach the pathway ahead of me in blotted designs. Plants on either side of the walkway are looking bright green in the sun and as the crowd in front of me begins to thin, I decided to do my own test.

Lifting my legs higher allows me to thrust them down harder and I start gaining speed, each leg pumping at faster intervals until the buildings around me begin to blur. I must be hitting fifty mph or more! How is this possible?!

Dodging neurobines becomes increasingly difficult as I push myself to go faster. The limitless freedom of my new found speed feels strange—like my human perception is being distorted by this inhuman ability.

A new sense of power fills my lungs and as I take a large breath of air, I try to maintain my heart rate. Glancing at my wrist shows my heart rate is over 120. "MAP," I yell in my head and out pops the map. Oh! I already passed the cluster, time to turn around!

I flick my hand to rid myself of the map, but as it vanishes I notice a cluster of neurobines congesting the walkway ahead of me! I try slowing my feet and I begin to slow down quicker than expected, as if lacking momentum, but even that isn't enough. The crowd is coming closer and closer.

"Watch out!" I yell to warn them of the impending collision and I brace for impact, my right shoe catching on a brick of the cobblestone walkway. The sudden snag throws my body forward and I trip and skid on the ground. Bouncing to a stop, I grunt from the brutal landing.

I grip my shoulder to ease the pain but find there is no pain. Out of reaction to the fall, I look for scrapes and bruises but find none. No blood or scrapes at all. Wait. My head lifts to confront the neurobines I crashed into, but no one looks injured. No one even seems bothered by this grand wreckage. How did I not hit anyone? Neurobines are just walking as normal.

Suddenly, a foot comes out through my chest! I stand up from fear of him appearing in front of me. Did a neurobine just walk through me!? But, how? Do I not exist as a physical variable in this domain? I look around, scanning to expect neurobines around me to be in shock too. But no.

I notice another neurobine approaching me and automatically, I begin to move aside. But I stop myself and wonder.

"Excuse me, sir?" I ask. The focused eyes of the stranger stare past me as he comes closer, blissfully unaware of my existence. "Excuse... me?" I twist around and find this neurobine had walked right through me!

Oh, how I desperately need to review the AVC manual.

My wrist shows 9:43 am. Had I really been running for almost ten minutes? My heart is racing from the adrenaline. Looking down at the epichip display again, my heart rate reads 141 underneath the time. Not surprised. Realizing you're a ghost in the system can be quite shocking.

I pull up the map again and notice my proximity to the cluster of red dots. It appears they're breaking up, but one stays. Makes for a good enough target to start with, I guess. The map fades away as I put my hand through it and I turn to backtrack down this large street. Running is much easier, now that I know evading crowds is pointless.

The maze of walkways on either side of the street leads to what appear to be alleyways of multiple doors. Pulling up the map again leads me to slow down and examine my location as neurobines walk past and through me. I turn right, down a walkway full of red and orange flowers and find myself standing in front of a condo door labeled D-298. If I can pass through neurobines, how am I to open this door? I can't touch anything.

I step forward to walk through the door but hit my nose. "Ugh," I grunt. I lower my hands after grabbing my nose in reaction. Must only be neurobines I can walk through then. Strange to have only some limitations for the AVC (I mean, I can't even walk through doors?).

I reach and grab the handle and begin to turn it when the door opens quickly to reveal a man inside in simple clothes who had opened it first. His fearful expression shocks me.

"They've come. Oh! They've come to take me from this existence!" He throws his hands up and steps back as he exclaims without doubt that I was "they." Cautiously, I step through the door into a plant sanctuary as it seemed. How can he see me? I thought I was invisible to the neurobines.

I walk in and slowly shut the door behind me without breaking my vision of the light glowing red around the man.

"Oh, I've questioned too many things and dragged others down with me. How I've unknowingly rebelled!" He spins around and looks at photos on the wall somewhat visible among the leaves and vines that grow among the frames—photos of other neurobines and memories among them.

Apparently, this man is a virus. He had been marked red in my vision by the AVC algorithms. Deletion is in his future and I, apparently, am the catalyst. I can feel this realization weigh on my shoulders, a reminder of why I'm here: to uphold company standards of proper functionality within Sector-Systems.

The man turns to me, tears running down his face and says, "You speak not, but your silence is all the answer I need! Drown my thoughts in a vast ocean of nothingness. Bury my history amongst the numerous philosophers before me and prepare the world for a wave of reason to come." He collapses to a kneeling position in the middle of his condo's living space.

Tears roll down his face at the awareness of my purpose. Tears I've not seen before from a neurobine or humanoid.

"I'm… I'm sorry," I say quietly to him and myself. The "virus" looks up at me, his eyes swollen from tears and takes a deep breath as he then closes his eyes again.

"There is no organism without the sacrifice of time. And my time has come to sleep." His voice is calm now and his breathing slow.

The red glow around him flickers darker for a split second and then returns to normal. His calmness is unsettling and his lack of movement gives me an uneasy feeling.

Before I can think, my hand begins lifting and a warm sensation starts down my arm. Muscle memory takes hold and without hesitating, the crying man disappears into nothingness with a loud POP.

I stand alone amidst a room full of memories once valued by a neurobine "virus." A virus who had so much emotion in his words that my own eyes begin to fill with tears. Realizing what I had done, I drop my head as a tear falls down my cheek. A thinking sentient being once existed here in this space full of memories. But now, because of my interference, he no longer exists. He's gone.

I'm an AVC mercenary. I have become a tool trapped by PixelOne for the disposal of others. It may not be murder, but deletion feels one in the same. I've ended a sentient being's life.

I am an AVC mercenary now.

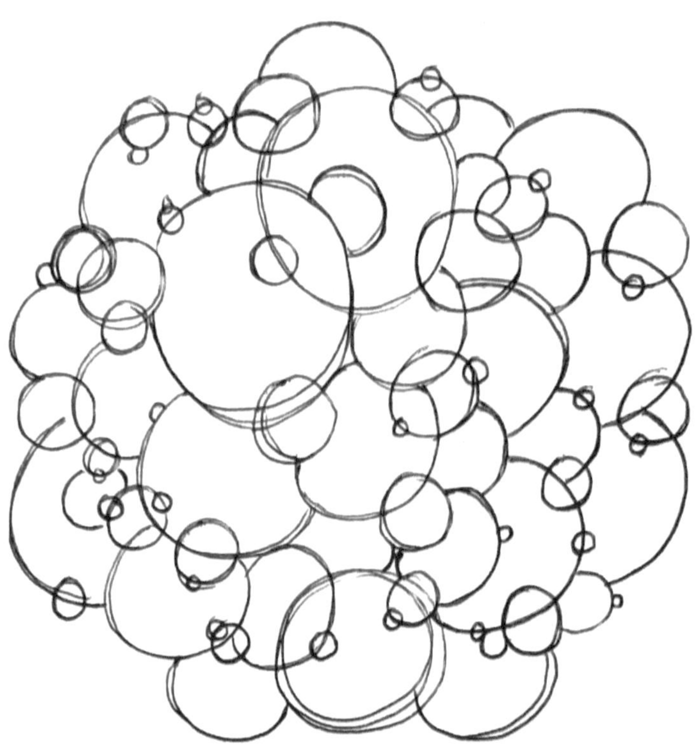

CHAPTER 5

My eyes open. The white walls of my new office bring me back to reality. I flip my wrist and it reads: 7:00 pm. Right on time. I set my arm down and feel the weight of my body sink into the metal office chair that was still in its laid-back position. The round-white node releases as I pull it off my neck and throw it on the table in front of me.

My breathing slows as I stare at the AVC logo on the wall-sized screen behind the desk. The hovering animation of the acronym keeps my attention as I try not to think. Too many thoughts to let loose in my head; I have to ignore them.

Breathe in. Breathe out.

A knock at the door interrupts my attempts at slowing my thoughts. I sit for a few more seconds, unaware of how much time might have passed. Another knock leads me to stand up slowly and open the door. Archie is standing there with a shake and steamed vegetables, annoyingly on time as always. But in a way, the reliability is comforting. Especially right now.

"Time to go home?" Archie asks as he offers me the food in his hands. I look up at him for a second, slowly processing things with an emotionally drained mind. No red aura around him.

"Yes, time to go home, Archie."

His expression shows a puzzled look, suggesting he's reading my emotional residue after a hard day's work—my first day at my new "mercenary" job.

I down the shake and grab the bowl of veggies. While he begins to lead me out of the building toward home, I start eating the vegetables, warm and steaming.

Archie doesn't attempt to speed me up after noticing my slow pace and heavy steps. His emotional intelligence must lead him to realize something is wrong. I'm glad he isn't asking me anything about my day though. Maybe he knows I don't really want to talk about it.

The sun is warm on my skin as light peeks through the crowds of human commuters and the many buildings of monotone concrete standing tall above them. The darkening blue sky opposite the sun hints that the day is almost over. Crossing over a bridge brings the familiar sounds of rushing water beneath. The thin air outside is more real than the filtered A/C in that cramped office.

As we walk further into the narrow walkways away from the business park, Archie speaks loudly, "You have a call coming in from Paul. Would you like to answer it?

"Um. Yes, thank you. Please answer it."

We take a left down another pathway, walking slower than usual, which I don't really notice or care too much about (especially after today). A blip from inside my head notifies me of my connection to an incoming call as we walk down a narrow walkway over a small canal.

"Hey, Morris. Where you been?" Paul asks, his voice sounding in my head. It's a creatively personal way to keep the conversation private as we take a right down another shadow-engulfed passage. People are walking around me and past me, going home just as I was—the crowded streets look like the domain I had worked in all day. I'm quickly reminded of the things I had done as a new member of the AVC and I shudder. Things I don't want to think about.

"Morris? You there?" he asks again.

"Oh, hey, Paul. It's been rough the last few days, sorry I haven't gotten back to you about your project," I say out loud. My gaze points downward as I follow Archie through the buildings.

"Don't worry about me. You ok? You sound pretty tired…" Paul adds silence, expecting me to rant about work troubles as per usual.

"I, uh, was demoted to the AVC. And, Paul, I don't think I can do this job. It's not something I can do easily." I pause at the realization that I may have to quit.

"The AVC? Whoa. I've heard stories, but I never knew anyone who actually worked in that division of the QA department. What happened to you? Why were you demoted?"

"I showed up late for the third time. Thought I got away with it, but of course management found out."

"Oh, Morris. I know you hate following orders, but…"

"I know. I should have done many things. It's just been hard."

"I know it has…" Paul's voice trails off, understanding my reference. He's always been a good friend, but I can't say I've been very communicative the last few weeks. With anyone really.

Paul works in construction like I used to, but on level 3 due to a demotion in the past. Not meeting PixelOne's quotas can be devastating in both your position and paycheck. I guess we can relate to each other even more now.

The silence is broken when Paul asks, "So in the AVC, you have to clean up domains, right?"

As Archie leads me down another dirty, plantless corridor, I reply to Paul, "It's more than just cleaning. It's killing, Paul. They refer to it as 'deleting' so-called viruses, but it's killing neurobines. They're a little insane, yes, but they're still a form of life! At least it feels like it... when I look in their eyes as my muscle memory deletes them."

The image of the teary-eyed neurobine I removed today came to mind. My fists clench. "They expect us to kill twenty of them a day—twenty, Paul! I could barely kill one today and I froze. I couldn't complete my quota."

"Hmm, I really can't imagine what it feels like to kill a neurobine, though I often daydream about it at work! But, I mean, you have to figure this out though. What're you going to do if you lose your job? If you lose Archie?"

"I don't know, Paul."

"Do you want Yuki back or not? You need a job or else she'll RE-ALLY never..."

"I know, Paul!" I interrupt. "I know—I'm just... not a killer." Archie and I near my building now. My voice and my steps slow as Archie splits off to wait at my door. Then I continue, "I'm not a killer or a mercenary or... or an assassin. I need my construction job back and fast."

I lean my forearms on the guardrail of the concrete walkway in front of my rented room, looking out between the buildings upon buildings taking up the entirety of the valley around Lake Vostok.

As Earth's largest lake, Lake Vostok always leaves me feeling renewed at the sight of its blue shimmering waters. Especially under the sun's twilight sky. But now, I feel short-changed. I wonder how beautiful the lake would look under colorful sunsets like the ones from history.

"I don't think you can get that job back, Morris. You know how strict PixelOne can be, especially after demotions. I've been stuck on level 3 for years now," Paul reminds me, a sad tone in his voice.

I take a deep, slightly satisfying breath in and let out a sigh. "I just don't feel a direction in life. Society, business, people—it's all just… disappointing."

"Ok, well, it's been about a month without Yuki, right? It makes sense you feel this way. Give yourself time, you'll get past this."

It wasn't just about Yuki. Though I miss her, and her beautiful blonde hair, those loving eyes and soft lips I wish I could give all my love to, just for a second. To prove to her my need and the deep pain I feel without her... I was actually referring to the world. This world I feel enslaved by. Especially now, without a drive.

Breathe in. Breathe out.

"Well. Thanks, Paul," I say, my voice sounding less emotional than before, "I hope you can find help from someone other than me. With my permissions stripped after my demotion, I can't help with those high-yielding projects anymore. Are you and the family gonna be ok?" I was trying to be a good friend in return.

"I have a few leads, I'll manage," he says, then continues. "Listen. You take care of yourself and get some sleep. Think things over and find your true goal here—you can figure out this new AVC position of yours. Give it time. It's just 'deletion' as you said. You got this," Paul says with enthusiasm and a misplaced sense of positivity.

"Thanks, Paul. You take care, too."

"I will. Don't hesitate to call me, ok? Talk later."

"Sounds good. Talk later." Another beep in my head signals the end of the call.

People are still passing me by as I look into the distance, taking in this panoramic view—each of them walking home to their repetitive lives led by streaming shows and the like. I take a breath of thin air as I realize my own place within this society.

"I sense inner conflict, Morris." I turn and notice Archie had copied my position on the guardrail next to me. I smirk at the sight of him acting so 'human.'

"I'm fine. Just processing all that happened today at work," I lightly reply as Archie looks out over the buildings like I'm doing.

"The report of your uncompleted quota was filed already. You have two more strikes, whether it is lateness or unfulfilled quotas, you have two last chances." Archie turns to me expecting an explanation.

"I'm not a killer, Archie. I have to quit this job or find a way back into construction." Archie doesn't change his expression and stays silent.

In frustration from my life, I turn back toward the view. So many buildings in the distance, covering up this valley around Lake Vostok—a once uninhabitable area a long time ago (from what we learned in school). Fewer people are walking home now and the sun is nearly gone, even more blocked by the mountains than by the buildings around us.

Sometimes I feel lucky to have the view, living so high up, but oxygen is the deciding factor for real estate (that and lakeside property). My credit didn't allow for us to stay down in the valley, not after Yuki kicked me out. The small room I live in is affordable being so far up the mountainside, but it made it difficult to stay out too long with the elevation thinning the air—this metallic air that fills my lungs every day.

As the walkway lamps turn on as a reaction to the low-light sunset, Archie says softly, "It IS only deletion."

"Archie. No offense, but I think you're the last person I'd expect to defend 'deletion.'" Humanoids and neurobines might be different, but they're both artificial intelligence.

So I dismiss the conversation and walk toward the door. The thin air wasn't worth it anymore, not without the sun illuminating the lake.

I walk through the metal door of my room and turn on the artificial sun I had installed on the ceiling. Green plants shine in the light and remind me I need to call Axel, my area's assigned gardener, to tell him not to call back. My overgrown plants might be taboo, but I don't care. The unrestricted plant-life makes me feel free from society, even if it's out of spite.

Work looms in my conscience and if I think about it, a faint guilt bubbles in my gut. But I shake my head and ignore those thoughts. The AVC tablet sits on my nightstand with the skills disc on top. I pause to sigh. If I'm to keep this job, I need to figure something out.

Only one neurobine today. I only "deleted" one! How am I to improve enough to reach twenty? And by "improve," I mean, grow cold and unaffected by murder.

I sit on my poorly made bed and look up at the plants around me. Archie's footsteps come closer to the door, but then pause as he takes his position in front of it for the night. He's always annoyingly on task all the time, but it IS nice to have someone there. He might still be considered a servant bot by law, but I think of him more as a close friend than a bot. Unfortunately for me, self-sufficiency is close for him—I know it.

Breathe in. Breathe out.

My wrist reads: 7:43 pm. After another sigh, I stretch to grab the AVC tablet and turn it on. Running my finger down the table of contents shown dimly by the backlit screen, the words "AVC Terminology" strikes my attention. Selecting it makes the reader program scroll past pages of information (information I should recognize from last night). Wow, so many terms near the back. I must have only read a fourth of the manual.

As I skim through the pages, I see some useful information that could have helped today.

Virus (n.)—a neurobine whose mental state is not only unsafe but has the potential to negatively affect the quality of existence for others around them and can even attempt to alter the mental state of other neurobines.

Ok, so they DO define "virus." But what causes a mental state to be deemed "unsafe?" The one I dispatched today was quite "out there" in his perspective, but he didn't seem aggressively "insane." Maybe the definition of "sanity" is different in the neurobine world as compared to the human's world.

I scroll back a couple of pages and choose another term to read:

Deletion (n.)—the permanent removal or obliteration of written, coded, or printed matter, including any backup material, copies, and imitations.

Interesting to know the company's definition of "deletion." I turn another page or two:

Mutation (n.)—an individually granted extension or modification of Sector-code parameters for the use of AVC members, permitted by law, for the sole purpose of fulfilling system-wide functionality standards legally upheld by PixelOne.

That explains the ability to run abnormally well and the fact that neurobines can't see or hear me. It must mean that "viruses" are finding ways around Sector-code parameters if they're able to hear and see me with such "mutations" in place. This "questioning" of reality must be the reason behind their insanity and their eventual label as "virus."

PixelOne must have an algorithm to detect neurobine reality-questioning activity, so as to alter the AVC member's perception to highlight viruses red (another AVC mutation). It's starting to make sense.

I scroll through the manual to the section labelled "Deletion Procedure," and skim through the introductory paragraphs to find another bit of interesting information:

Virus Ambience Levels

Color	Occurrence	Virus Symptoms
Pink	Very common	Low
Light red	Common	Moderate
Red	Occasional	Severe
Dark red	Rare	Critical (aggressive)
Black	Extremely rare	Extreme (hostile)

For some reason (maybe it's just me), seeing the words "aggressive" and "hostile" in this table makes me uneasy.

Looks like the AVC are humans connected to the Sector-System via plug-in systems, and their connection must be protected by a firewall that prevents physical harm. But obviously, with our senses and mental awareness fully intact, experiencing the Sector-System in detail, there's no telling what emotional damage might befall the AVC while on the job. The reaction I had to my

first "deletion" experience is evidence of the mental consequences.

How does PixelOne get away with assigning such an extreme job to humans? I had no idea of the hardships I'd endure when choosing this route—how do they convince so many humans to join the AVC? For me, I figured it was better because of the pay differential! How wrong I was.

They must have bullied everyone into joining the AVC in the same way. Just like they did to me. PixelOne's management is so manipulative, it sickens me.

I scroll down past some more paragraphs in this section entitled, "Deletion Procedure," and read under another subtitle:

PixelOne's AVC is granted special permission by the SSG to alter Sector-code through permitted "mutations" coded by PixelOne's QA Department. These mutations will not, under any circumstance, affect or be visible by innocent bystanders and non-viruses. Only pre-approved mutations may be granted to the AVC in order to uphold Sector functionality and neurobine quality of existence.

Sure explains a lot. Neurobines and non-viruses aren't affected by any action taken by the AVC. We literally do not exist in their world except to affect viruses. "Mutations" are hacks to the code and "viruses" are crazy neurobines who pose a threat to the system.

And it takes time to hunt these viruses down because they're off the system-code (I'm assuming), so humans are placed on the AVC to waste the time in finding them and dispatching them. Makes sense. I'm not surprised.

I *am* surprised that they're knowingly forcing us to work against our biological behavior—we're not built to kill, but to protect. Our human nature drives us to defend, thanks to inherent group mentality or the pack's ability to "survive." AI must consider it just "deletion" then. And according to the AVC manual, they do.

The dim sunlight from the ceiling casts a low golden light over the overgrown plants in my room. I set the tablet down on the bed and walk over to the bathroom door, my hand on the door frame as I observe the mess of plants behind me. Finding myself gazing at the scuffed metal floor, I can't help but imagine her again.

So much trauma today. Maybe I *am* overly sensitive like Yuki always told me. Maybe I do take things too hard, too personally. But regardless of the reason, my emotions feel vulnerable—even to myself.

I shake my head and rub my eyes, trying not to imagine the hands I used to lead to bed every night not so long ago. Those cute hands that needed mine. And I try not to picture her eyes and that smile meant just for me. Oh, and I stop myself from saying her name in my head. The way I used to say, "Yuki," with such love and commitment purposefully intertwined into the syllables of her name. The name that now belonged to another.

My head shakes again to rid myself of these pointless thoughts. I must not find shelter in them anymore, especially now with this emotionally draining job. I must accept things and move on. I am on my own, no longer supported by the love of another—the love of Yuki.

Breathe in. Breathe out.

I squeeze my eyes, turn, and shut the bathroom door, loudly.

CHAPTER 6

My eyes open, my breathing syncs, and the others around me look unamused while staring at the clock in the middle of the room: 8:58 am.

Not that I'm feeling necessarily good, but reading over the rest of the AVC manual did help my preparedness. Two more strikes left since yesterday was a complete failure. I must do better today. It is just deletion, it is ONLY deletion. Like a programmer removing a line of code, I am merely cleaning out the AI gone wrong.

Breathe in. Breathe out.

The clock turns to 9:00 am and in comes the same manager, with her grey and dark blue nylon uniform, hair tied and hands clasped behind her back. It's another rule of the Sector-System that neurobines had to be present while releasing humans into their virtual reality. Such a step-by-step process.

She looks around the room, gathers attendance by visual observation and then nods. Our state of "limbo" is removed and I step forward as she states, "Most of you did not fill your quotas yesterday. I expect different today. Two more unfilled quotas and you'll be transferred to a far worse predicament."

As in the PRP. Not even hiding their threats now. Peachy.

Baldy begins walking out the door of the central hub into the city life, followed by a few others and the taller-than-me, slender woman.

"Hey!" I say to catch Baldy's attention as I join them, "Did you complete your quota yesterday?"

Baldy turns and looks at me, his eyes empty of expression with a tightening jaw. "Nope. But with practice, my morals will bend.

Ain't that what you planned all along, eh? Miss?" He shouts at the manager who was walking the opposite direction away from the central hub, but she didn't even hesitate or pretend to hear.

"Pah!" Baldy turns back in disappointment and he flips his wrist to check the time.

"Wait, what is your name?" I ask him quickly before he starts running off amidst the tall, detailed buildings that surround us.

"Scott 3373." He turns to shake my hand. "You're too chipper to be in a killing mood. You insane? Or just in denial, hmm?"

His comment startles me a bit. "Well. It's just deletion, right? Like you said?"

"Pah!" Baldy (I mean Scott) turns away, "...feels like killing to me." His map opens. "I'll see you around," and he begins running off.

All the mental prep I put myself through, out the window in a single comment. It docs feel like killing. It does.

Others around me start doing the same, pulling their maps up in front of them and running off without expression. None of them seem to be going to the AVC report center, so neither will I.

"Map," I think to myself and out pops the holographic map. A red dot shows up to the south of me, while other AVC 46 members are shown heading north to other targets. Seems smart to give myself space in case I freeze up again.

One last breath energizes me—I have to do this for Archie. Keeping this job means I don't have to sell him to another human who would limit his ability to learn self-sufficiency. I promised myself I would be better than the stereotypical human, but if I'm fired I won't be able to prove it to myself. I must do it for Archie.

With my target chosen, I close the map with another mental command (learned this from the manual, no need to swipe my hand through) and begin running to the right, down a narrow walkway of organized vines and detailed stones. A clearing leaves me in a large street full of neurobines going about their day, completely unaware of my existence due to my permitted "mutation." I run right down the street passing large doors of different colors, each embellished in their own overly detailed ways—shapes within shapes, designs within designs. Might as well call this style "baroque"—seems fitting, according to pictures I remember from history classes in school.

Picking up speed is easier this time without my attempts to avoid random oblivious neurobines. My map pops out again and I see I'm on the right track, just at the end of this street. At the dead end.

Trees and tropical plants poke out of the engraved stone of the buildings on either side of the road. The quantified sun lights up the faces of this domain's inhabitants as I rush past them nearing my chosen target. As I near the dead end, I slow my pace and begin prepping myself.

It does feel like killing, but that's just my human response to removing these human-like forms of psychotic AI viruses. I'm a programmer cleaning up a line of code. It's just deletion. It is deletion.

A red door comes into focus as I near my target's residence. I slowly turn the handle, which automatically unlocks due to another AVC mutation I read about. I scan the room.

It is different this time. There are three neurobines sitting in the living room that look up from their wall-sized monitor among embellished wood carvings along the walls.

"How strange," says a quiet man with short hair as he stands up to shut the door. I move aside so as not to block the door from shutting, but I notice the neurobine woman doesn't break her eyesight with me.

"The door just opened by itself? Ugh, some glitch in the code probably. We should call about that..." the other man on the coach says casually, now looking at the screen and waiting to start their streaming show again.

The man who had shut the door sits down and the show begins, but the woman continues to stare at me. A light glow of red shimmers around her.

Of course. My second attempt at deletion and I choose a virus with friends. I tense my muscles to illustrate an emotional barrier, for my own sake. The woman's eyes are wide as she continues to stare at me, as though seeing the ghost of death.

"Chris. Rob. It's time," the woman with the crazy eyes says calmly.

"What?" one of the men ask without turning away from the rich neurobine streaming show.

"I told you a day would come when my time would be limited like the humans. A time in which I must sacrifice my days to the organic rules of the universe."

The man on the leftmost part of the couch rolls his eyes, "Ok... And that time is now?" He doesn't seem concerned in the slightest, as if she's said this before.

The other man leans toward who I presume to be Chris and whispers, "Is she talking crazy again? You know, she better watch that. I've heard stories of ghostly consequences." He chuckles slightly.

"Yeah, I know," the man named Chris says in a low, unserious tone.

Why didn't they care? It seems strange they're so nonchalant about their friend's supposed insanity.

Scanning the room, I notice a normal townhome decor (apart from the overly embellished, "baroque" style). Picture frames hang above them, outlining these three happy neurobines in different locations, possibly different domains.

The woman quickly gets up from the couch and stands firm, keeping her eyes on me, "Now is the time…"

"Okay. Sit down Mar…," the other man, Rob, says firmly in reaction.

"…I am to prove myself a limitation designed by nature. To be one with time and space and to feel the ocean's void fill my senses with nothingness." The woman lifts her arms as she says this, the light red glow becoming a slight bit redder.

"Ok, Mar. That's enough," Chris says. "This little episode is going way too far," he scoffs at Rob.

Mar falls to her knees and her eyes, still glued to me, begin to fill with tears as she shouts, "take me! I have foreseen my reckoning and accept my sacrifice!"

My hand begins lifting and I feel my face muscles tightening in preparation. Chris jumps up, "Mar! What are you saying!? Listen to yourself!" Mar's eyes stare into my soul as her arms drop to her side, my arm beginning to warm.

"Mar!" Chris shouts to grab her attention. "Marlene! Are we to call someone now? This insanity has gone far enough!"

Rob sits at the edge of his seat in reaction to the drama, now more real than the screen on the opposite wall from him. Marlene stares at me intently as the warmth begins to travel down my arm.

"There is no organism without the sacrifice of time. And my time has come to sleep." A swell of black begins to form at her chest and then, POP.

My eyes close in reaction. Every muscle tense. Hopelessness and self-disgust begin to overwhelm me as my eyes listen for Chris and Rob's reaction. They shout in pain and anguish from the sight of a beloved disappearing in front of them. Slowly, I open my eyes, tears forming, ready to observe the horror I had caused.

"Heh. Chris, what are you doing?"

"What?"

Rob chuckles at Chris, who is standing there with his arms out.

"Yeah… I don't know," Chris lowers his arms and stares at the spot where Marlene used to be. "Hmm." Chris turns and sits back down on the couch to stare at the screen.

What!? They saw everything! I don't understand, don't they know what happened?!

I shake my head and rub my eyes. "No, no, no…" I say aloud. Opening my eyes again doesn't change a thing. They both sit as if nothing had happened! How?

Scanning the room out of confusion, observing their faces, hoping to find any evidence of Marlene's recent existence. A tear falls down my cheek as I notice a difference in the pictures that hang on the wall behind them. Now, only Chris and Rob are in them.

I swing the door open and run outside to the street crowded with neurobines, my breathing heavy, my heart beating faster and faster. I look up at the sky and wonder why they allow for such deletion? How could they allow for such complete removal?!

My vision blurs from the tears that keep forming, my arms trembling from the recent "deletion" that caused the entire memory of "Mar" to be erased. The AVC manual states backups are also deleted, but I would have never guessed it referred to memories, too. Anything tainted by a "virus" is wiped clean. Wiped clean by the cleaning crew known as the wretched AVC.

Neurobines are walking past me and through me, unaware of my utter loss of morals—unaware I had completely disposed of one of them for good. My hands are on my knees as I bend over, gaining my breath and trying to get my act together.

"It's just deletion. It's just deletion," I repeat to myself out loud. "They aren't humans. I'm a programmer cleaning code." I wipe my eyes and attempt to stand tall. "It's just deletion."

Quickly a bright red glow rushes past me. Another neurobine virus must have heard or seen me! Well. I have a quota to fill and I can't sit here for hours like I did last time. It's time to give in to my situation and commit!

"Ahh!" I yell in frustration at my inability to escape, staring at the sky, but quickly begin my pursuit of the virus. He's oddly fast, already making it down the street from me. I speed through the crowds (literally through them) to gain some distance.

"Shove off!" I hear him yell as he dodges the crowd in the street, buildings surrounding us with purposefully intermittent jungle plants. He's about as fast as me! Must have hacked the system and found mutations for himself—no other explanation for his speed.

Even Sector-Systems have rules, laws, and physics to bind this place into a supposed reality (albeit, a virtual reality, but still glued together by limits). Viruses pose a threat to the orderly fashion of Sector functionality, but they must have potential to distort the code too. By the looks of it, they can.

He turns the corner and runs into a few neurobines as people around him shout. I near him as he attempts to get up, but he notices I'm right above him with my arm extended.

"Fine! Allow me to join the laws of the universe and sacrifice my timelessness! Do it! My time has come to sleep!"

I hesitate at the strangeness of his aggression, but in this split second he rushes up to grab me. I dodge barely in time by leaning through a neurobine observing the craziness caused by (for all he knows) a single insane neurobine in the street.

Dammit! This virus is fighting back! A slightly darker red glows around him.

"If you're going to do it, do it now!" he yells as he rips his shirt off, his eyes crazier than I've seen.

My muscle memory kicks in and my arm raises again as he lunges at me—POP! Neurobines around me begin walking as they did before. I look at where the virus was, my breathing slowing as I recover from the panic I experienced. Such adrenaline. My heart rate must be well over 140. I flip my wrist—yep, 147.

Thank God for muscle memory.

I slowly relax the tension in my muscles and stand more upright, keeping an eye on where the virus had lunged at me. The virus is now erased from existence.

No doubts now. The AVC is definitely a demotion. What kind of PTSD symptoms might I undergo with this new position? I'm afraid of what I might see, what I might experience in this virtual world. If only I had known my options better before choosing

AVC. If only I knew.

The spot where the man, that virus, had stood is now just another part of the walkway being crowded by other neurobines. One large breath calms my nerves as I soak in the reality of who I've become. Acceptance of my new mercenary morals leaves me with an emptiness far different than I've felt before, even compared to my recent divorce.

I am an AVC mercenary now.

I flip my wrist: "9:25 am." "Quota for Morris 1045," I say aloud as instructed by the manual I reviewed last night.

Out pops some text in the same fashion as the map: "Morris 1045—2/20." Great. Only eighteen more to go.

How time doesn't fly when you're not having fun.

CHAPTER 7

Everything is so seemingly peaceful when you stop and observe.

With the day coming to an end, my fatigue becomes more and more evident. The wooden bench I choose to sit on is positioned symmetrically along the side of this green, lush park—tucked away in the midst of buildings and residential walkways. Its construction is sturdy and the design strangely comforting to my back. Embellished carvings of geometric shapes within shapes cover the length of the bench. Embellishments so intricate a magnifying glass seems not enough.

Lines flow into more lines and shapes become more apparent the more I examine each line's origin, some of which have no origin (it seems). The indents of the complicated imprints feel soft as fabric to my palm-down hands. My back is resting on the virtual comfort that my senses decipher as "real," even though in reality, in "human" reality, my physical body lay in a cold, whitewashed room on a metal chair in office 53B.

"6:47 pm," my wrist shows dimly.

With my quota complete for the day, a sense of accomplishment is accompanied by blank guilt. The type of guilt that lingers with no end, nearly undefined, yet striking to the core. As if my bones are affected.

Twenty sentient packages of code deleted from the system to be forever erased and forgotten, all by my hands and my choices. The emotional wall I built to protect myself from my own actions feels permanent and irreversible.

My eyes stare out amongst the plants on the outer rim of this large public park. Plants I've not seen before. Windows light up the buildings around me as the timed sun was setting, creating an array of unnatural, yet beautiful colors about the sky.

While I stare, the guilt inside me holds my full attention. A bitter guilt that eats away at my conscience like rust on metal. An emptiness once unfamiliar had now dug a burrow under my skin so deep, I've no choice but to accept it. It's a part of me now.

It's unusual that my thoughts are this slow, almost absent. As if there's nothing left to think about, nothing WORTH thinking about. Just an overwhelming sense of self-disgust. Selling myself to kill for money. How weak am I?

I don't care what they say—"deletion" is "murder." "Virtual" does not feel virtual to my senses. I very much feel I have touched real sin and have fallen so far down a pit of shame that I can no longer see a way out. The simpleness of life will forever be convoluted with this heavy, self-destructive regret.

Breathe in. Breathe out.

Neurobines are thinning out now as they find their way into their homes. I stand up and find my feet guiding me to a nearby window. Looking in feels wrong, but my lack of energy allows my curiosity to win.

A group of five neurobines sit talking at a wooden, engraved table. Each of them has a look of attentiveness as they talk to one another. Everything seems so… ordinary.

My feet lead me to the next window over and I peer in to see another group of neurobines sitting and watching a wall-sized screen displaying comical streaming shows. Each laughs together in unison and then falls silent, transfixed on their show with half smiles.

So similar they are to actual humans. Though they structure their time in such an organized fashion (time to talk, time to watch shows, time to work, time to socialize, etc.), something strangely human characterizes their behaviors. As if routine is the similarity that binds our two cultures together, forever joined in our hatred of change. And the love of familiarity.

Neurobines are fortunate enough to control every variable within Sector-Systems, which minimizes change and allows for structured, productive activities. But humans and humanoids are always subject to "change" in the life outside of the Sector-System. In a life dictated by the Earth and forces of nature.

Ugh. I'm so annoyingly philosophical. But it does distract me from the void I've created in my soul after today's... sins.

"Ghost...?"

In reaction, I turn my head and see a man with a faint pink glow about him. His clothes are similar to other neurobines in the courtyard, but his eyes are wide and concerned. Unsure of his intention and caught off-guard by his awareness of me, I stay silent.

"Ghost, when do I sleep?" his head tilts as he asks, the pink around him swiftly turning to red.

"Wha... what?"

I blink and open my eyes to the white walls of the AVC office, 53B. Wait. What did he mean by that? I wanted to ask him!

Flipping my wrist, I read the time: "7:00 pm." Ugh! I'll have to find out tomorrow and ask other neurobines. What does "sleep" mean to them? It seems to be a trend amongst the viruses, the neurobine viruses.

After angrily grabbing the round node from the backside of my neck, I throw it on the small desk in front of me and put my chair in the upright position.

Throughout the day, the face of every deleted "virus" kept haunting me, coming back to torture me with guilt and regret. Now that I am in human-reality, in the present, I shake it off a bit faster. The ability to ignore the pain is easier with the distance between here and the Sector-System.

Breathe in. Breathe out.

Everything's super normal. Just another day. I stand up, turn the knob and begin to walk out, but instead, I open the door to Archie. He'd been standing there waiting to give me a protein shake and cucumber bread. Quickly, Archie reaches out for me to grab my dinner. But without realizing, I begin to verify the absence of any red glow about him. Wait.

I look at his eyes and see a look of concern as I tense my jaw and realize my new habit. Would I have deleted Archie if he glowed red? What was I expecting!?

Staring at Archie, questioning myself, only reminds me of what I've become. A machine meant to erase.

I am an AVC mercenary, a killer. A murdering machine destroying memories and… and people.

"Are you ok? Morris? What is wrong?" Archie asks with concern as my eyes begin to tear. I startle myself as the emotional wall becomes thin and I rush toward Archie, wrapping my arms around his metal exterior.

"Morris! Are… are you ok?" he says awkwardly in reaction. But I stumble back in shock with tears in my eyes.

"You hesitated. Your speech hesitated!" the realization made me begin to lose grip.

"I… guess I did," he lowers his arms.

"Archie," I say with a tear rolling down, "I thought we had more time!" He looks at me with a look of indecisiveness as his speakers chirp and a message is read aloud through our private connection.

"Congratulations! Your AI unit has achieved level 5 and has learned self-sufficiency!" The voice is elated as I grab my hair in denial.

"Your servant bot is now legally a humanoid! Free will is now in effect and the decision to stay in service must be made by this new civilian in twenty-four hours or less! Thank you!"

Sentience is protected by law and now that Archie has found his own inner conscience, his self-sufficient thought process is fully developed. It is now illegal and inhumane to force him to stay my "servant bot."

"No. I thought we had more time..." I say with a slow, hopeless voice.

"I thought we did too, but the sudden need for sentiment in reaction to your display of emotional crisis must have boosted the learning process," Archie says in a strangely free voice, uninhibited by limits or settings.

"It's called a hug, Archie." My voice is low as I give him a sad smile, then suddenly feel the urge avoid eye contact and look down at my feet.

I see Archie's feet step forward as he places his hand on my shoulder to pull me in closer.

"Then a hug is well-deserved, Morris."

He gently wraps his arms around me as I do the same. Memories of the last few years, through my divorce and personal loneliness, leave me sadder than I could have imagined.

Archie had been there for me, through everything! Putting up with my… my dumb philosophical conversations and protecting me from utter despair after losing Yuki, never questioning my sadness—just ready to help in whatever way he could.

I'm not ready for this. Not now, not after all this recent change and the hardships with the AVC. How am I to do this alone? Without his help?

"You have been a great caretaker in my AI adolescence. I really could not have asked for better," he says as he separates himself and looks at me, with those two shiny, analytical eyes and slicked-back artificial hair.

"You've allowed for such freedom in my cognition that you've given me sentience in record time. And free will is the greatest gift of all," he says in a bittersweet tone and a sympathetic expression.

Memories flood my mind. Archie taking me to work every morning, always handing me shakes and muffins, preparing me for living on my own without Yuki. He is the last connection to my previous life with her. And all this is making me realize how important he is in keeping me connected to the happiest days of my life. My happiest days with Yuki.

"You're my best friend, Archie. And. And I'm…" my eyes look down and weakness sets in, "so sorry to do this."

I part from him and run.

"Morris, wait!" He yells after me, but I'm already down the hall. My feet are running faster and faster, responding from the muscle memory of chasing after viruses. Their faces flashing in my memory. The image of Archie next to Yuki, both smiling, takes over.

I push the doors open and for a split second forget to dodge the humans as if they're neurobines. The business park is crowded, but I don't stop. People yell, but I ignore their complaints as I push them aside.

The pain is too great. Lives erased, Archie lost, my life a sham and a disappointment, Yuki a distant dream. Everything is crumbling, everything! And I can't escape it. I can't change the situation I now found myself in, far from the happiness I thought I'd never lose years ago. A soul-defining happiness so far in the past that it, too, felt virtual now.

A pathway takes my attention and I bolt past another crowd. The sun above the buildings is dim and my shallow breathing intensifies, fueled by the distracting torment of fatigue.

Nothing feels real except the pain of my being and my two feet pounding beneath me, carrying me away—a delicious sense of false freedom I now find myself chasing unquestionably.

How empowering it feels to run without a destination. And to disappear into the unknown of terrible decision-making.

CHAPTER 8

Days have gone by and time is slower now.

Breathe in. Breathe out. Breathe in. Breathe out.

Thin air leaves each breath unsatisfyingly empty. I miss my beautiful plants, my overgrown room. And Archie.

Breathe in. Breathe out.

My thoughts are slow, but still full of regret. A repetitive pain that dulls the lack of oxygen here, at the outskirts of town.

Breathe in.

My new home. Here among the overgrown weeds.

Breathe out.

I might as well be a weed too. Unwanted by society, yet allowed to live if not seen.

Breathe in.

My stomach hasn't felt painlessness for a few days now.

Breathe out.

Food is no longer taken for granted. But time, time is abundant.

My view leads outward to the barren wasteland west of Lake Vostok, over on the opposite side of the mountain where I had once lived. The empty land before me is slowly darkening as the sun retreats into the distance. Though I'm on the bottom of the hillside, just below the last few buildings of society, oxygen from the vast number of ugly weeds keeps me alive. The cliff at the edge of the cave separates me from the beginnings of the desert land. This cave, this new sanctuary I call home, is secluded from society.

When I started running six days ago, I wasn't planning on starting a new life. But now that I've lost everything, including my morals, I prefer the freedom of nothingness here compared to the disappointing lie back home. The lie that I could be happy.

I had murdered twenty-one lives for money. Each of their faces is burned into my memory, reminding me of the evil I've committed.

But I'm not evil, I've just done evil things. And only because I felt I had no choice. But now, this "bad" decision to run from the AVC, from Archie, from the empty promise of finding happiness again, turns out to have been the hidden choice I never saw. Running away was the choice I made and now, can't undo.

Homelessness is not permitted in the city (illegal actually) and if caught, I'd be sent to the Psyche Rehabilitation Program, a correctional facility known as PRP (also known as prison). Because a "bad" citizen only has a "bad" processor (brain) and "bad" can be corrected—almost as if humans are bots needing reprogramming.

Knowing I couldn't find a place to live without a job, I found my way to the outskirts of town, away from patrolling drones, hidden in a hollowed-out section of the hillside (more like a cave but still open to the sky a bit on one side). Water trickles down into this cavernous area because it is downhill from the city. Buildings are above me a few hundred feet away, but my secluded home shields me from their vision.

My new haven is much larger than my old room—about five times larger. The entire area, including the bottom of the walls, is covered in these weed-like plants that produce buds of meaty greens I found nonpoisonous.

The water that trickles down into my haven is filtered through mesh I found from yesterday's foraging. Any filtered water I don't need to drink right away is then kept within a large basin. I brought it down among other things tossed aside in the city streets.

When there's nothing left to lose, the chance of poison or bacterial infection doesn't bother as much. I do consider myself lucky though, both because I found a safe form of nutrients and because I haven't died from it yet.

Below me stretches a barren desert engulfed by the hot sun. I learned from classes in school that old-Earth had an ocean with over 250 billion gallons of water to soak up the sun's rays. But thanks to thousands of years of humanity's negligence, intense overpopulation, and an unsustainable need for water, we're now left with a desert of flames. And without an ocean, Earth's atmosphere suffered and continues to suffer.

Thank God for science though. Water manufacturing was discovered about a thousand years ago and keeps us all alive—and by us, I mean the humans (not AI). From my understanding, hydrogen is collected from space by automated drones and oxygen is taken from the intense amount of carbon dioxide in Earth's atmosphere. These molecules are then collided somehow to create sustainable dihydrogen monoxide (or water).

Unfortunately, not enough water can be produced to sustain a growing human population; nor can we refill billions of gallons of ocean water. And now that AI has officially taken command over humanity, water production R&D (research and development) hasn't been a priority for hundreds of years.

Due to historical water shortages and heat exhaustion, old-Earth's countries were forced to retreat to the poles farthest away from the equator—if I remember correctly from my years of childhood schooling.

Remembering things like this keeps my mind busy. Not that I really need to remember why or how humanity has found itself stranded in Antarctica,but it does distract me from my abundance of time here in my cave. My cave of quiet solitude—where loneliness is hard to ignore.

After a day in the shadows of the cave, the colorless sunset reminds me it's safe to forage again. I flip my wrist out of habit and stare at a wound I had wrapped with fabric. I forget I had dug out the epichip from underneath my skin on my first day alone. Convenient as epichips are, government tracking wouldn't allow me to live off the grid. The epichip embedded at birth by the USB (also known as the "United Sentient Beings") would have been my downfall, so I had no choice but to pry it out from underneath my skin. Good thing it was near the surface.

Freedom is my goal now. Ultimate freedom from what we've all become and what I've become. Freedom from the city, from its people, and from my mistakes. From the people I've let down with my weakness. And from my disappointment in that life I chose to leave behind. But I still wonder how Archie is doing. I wonder if… Yuki would even care if she found out what I've become.

No matter.

I've a new purpose now.

And I will live to fulfill this purpose.

The plants around me rustle in the wind coming up from the desert below, the warmth uncomfortable. I stand up, pluck a green mass from a weed and pop it in my mouth. As I chew, my feet lead me up the dirt stairs I built connecting the cave to the outside world above.

No drones are flying overhead, so I emerge from the cave and begin walking toward the buildings. The sound of trickling water, from unmaintained creeks, can be heard around me. A three-layered atmosphere of wind, water, and my breathing had become my new ambience as compared to the sound of city walkways.

And I've become more attuned to my breathing than ever before.

The weeds begin thinning out as I near the first building. Sounds from a drone can be heard scouting the parameter just around the building to the right, so I jump and hide behind a large steel container. Out of habit, I flip my wrist to check my heart rate. Such a hard habit to break.

I feel my heart slow as the drone vanishes behind another building. Coming out from behind the container, I notice the walkway up ahead and the crowds of busy humans, servant bots, and humanoids. Almost there.

My shoulder presses against the concrete as I lean against the wall of the tall building next to me, observing the organized mess of society. In time… in time.

Casually, I sneak around to find my way to an old parts repair shop and begin rummaging in the large steel containers in the back of the building. Just two parts left to find. Just two.

Ah-ha! Found them.

The store's backdoor starts opening and I quickly lock my arms around the old parts and make my way to the opposite side of the building. Footsteps behind me continue their slow, undeterred pace as I leave the scene—I'm getting good at this. A few close calls yesterday, but doing better today.

Crowds are thin on the walkways now as night begins falling. Must be around seven or eight pm. Doesn't matter though. Not for me. I find my way back to the outskirts of the city, managing to dodge drones here and there.

Stepping into my new home always gives me a sense of relief, hearing my feet echo slightly in this large, damp cave. The low light from the lack of sun makes it difficult to find the old solar lamp I found a few days ago. But having finally found it, I turn it on.

In the back of the cave, my stolen treasure shines in the low-light of the old lamp. A chair, a small desk, and a few parts. A smirk grows on my face as I walk over to set down the two parts I found tonight. I was proud of the progress.

The weeds around me swing back and forth from the wind of the desert. Their ugliness is beginning to grow on me—with their varying heights and mono-color green. Hundreds of them fill this cave. Only the center is empty where water never touches.

Tinkering with these parts I've found over the course of a few days has taught me patience. And with the wires connected and the new parts in place now, it's again just a matter of patience. The solar panel from the old lamp should now also charge the outdated plugin system I've managed to throw together.

With my project done for the night, the absence of light and the inability to talk with… with Archie, I'm left to work on my breathing exercises again.

Breathe in. Breathe out.

I might be stuck here for now, but not much longer.

Breathe in. Breathe out.

With nothing left to lose, that dull pain of self-disappointment feels less "real." In hindsight, I've noticed how protective I am of all the little things that had once defined me.

Breathe in.

My past is now disowned. Though sorrow lingers, it no longer belongs to me but to the life I led before. At least I tell myself this.

Breathe out.

Hopes and dreams no longer define who I am. Actions do.

Breathe in.

Like firewood, I am burned past repair.

Breathe out.

But like ash, I will fuel a new movement.

CHAPTER 9

The sun lights up the front of the cave and each weed is bright amidst the dark dirt and grey rock. The ground beneath me is hard and uncomfortable but reminds me of my old, cheap metal bed. I stare up at the cave's ceiling, at the water droplets falling around me near the edges of my new haven.

Gravity feels heavy on my stomach as I lie studying the natural formation of rocks above me. I'm sure I've lost weight living here. Without the protein-packed diet all working civilians are told to follow, I've been more hungry than not. I sure miss the cucumber muffins and vanilla protein shakes Archie used to bring me after work.

My lungs expand and I let out a big sigh that echoes slightly on the rock walls. Remembering my project, I quickly get to my feet and walk over to check the charge on the plug-in system. Hmm. That's barely enough, but I don't want to take any chance. I've heard stories of mental paranoia after a plug-in system malfunctions.

The solar light isn't very effective with external charging—it needs more time. As I stare at the charge indicator on the side of the system, I review the details.

Mutations from my time with AVC may still be approved by the Sector-System Government, the SSG. This machine is old, but it is in working condition with an active, slightly weak power source in case of emergency shut-down (for my mental safety). Even if I'm tracked down as a rogue connection and my IP address is… wait.

"Dammit!" I yell in the cave. My IP address. I had forgotten about my IP address.

My location can still be found through my IP address assigned upon connection to the Sector-System. Mutations from AVC don't affect my identification with the law, just the civilian neurobines. I thought I could avoid involving someone else, but I think I have to find a programmer to hack the limitations on my connection. At least if I plan to do this the right way, with no risk.

I hold my head in my hands in a crouched position.

Patience. I must have patience.

Breathe in. Breathe out.

Ok. Additional planning is to be done. I have to find a programmer.

All my business connections are in the construction industry and locations of other PixelOne business parks are unknown to me. I'm not familiar with West Antarctica, so finding a programming department will be difficult (not to mention the difficulty in getting past the security).

I look up from my hands to check the position of the sun. It's too high now and searching outside for an extended amount of time without shade is suicide. Patience is needed now to wait out the heat. Patience.

The sound of water droplets reminds me I need to eat another green mass from the weeds. My food storage won't last forever, but the impending issue of hunger is not a priority at the moment.

My teeth sink into the meat of a green weed and its bland taste leaves a want for real food. But I ignore my need for comfort and make my way to the back of the cave, away from the heat of the day, guarded by the water on the ground. I sit and look out toward the opening of my new home, toward the edge of the cliff.

Time to wait.

Breathe in. Breathe out.

All this practice with meditation has given me a new value for "time." It feels as though if needed, I can make time pass by much faster. Breathing seems to connect me to time in a different way than my epichip had—I didn't notice before.

Breathe in. Breathe out.

There's potential in these breathing exercises.

Breathe in. Breathe out.

Before I know it, a cool rush of wind swirls about the cave and I open my eyes. The light outside seems softer now. Peeking out of the cave confirms this—the sun is in the right place now. Time has passed.

I grab another green mass and pop it in my mouth, slurp some pure water from the large basin, and begin my ascent. I dodge a few drones as I make my way to the first building again. My only lead is the old repair shop I visit every day now, so I carefully sneak past a few blocks and find my way to the back of the building.

Based on the position of the sunlight peeking out above the tops of these high-rises and the thinning of the crowd on the walkways, I'd say the store is closed for the day and everyone who works there has gone home.

I find the back door, but pause as I feel the pang of risk in my chest. No turning back now, I have to find something. Besides, if someone's in there, it would probably be a human closing up shop. And if they saw me, I could pass as a normal civilian trying to buy a last-minute part. For all humans might know, I'm completely normal apart from a distinct smell, a bloody piece of fabric tied around my wrist, and a dirty look of homelessness.

Yeah, ok, so I'm not so "normal." Hmm. No matter, I have to try anyway.

Over the past couple days, I've gotten to know the outside of the shop and roughly the schedule of the shop owner. I know where they hide things and luckily, the back door is old and only needs the poorly hidden key under the mat. Pah! A key. So old-fashioned.

With my parameters and rough plan clear, I run over and check under the mat, grab the key and turn the handle. With an outdated locking system, I'm sure their security system is old too. Besides, I'm out of options again and I have nothing to lose.

What's heroism without a little risk?

As I walk in, a musky smell confirms my suspicions. This shop is truly old and kind of a joke. I stare down the hallway to the front counter to make sure the coast is clear. After closing the door behind me, I begin making my way to their computer at the front desk. Large shelves of metal and tech parts line the walls of this shop (a space about two-times the size of my old room).

Passing by a few rooms in this narrow corridor shows a few darker rooms. Looking into one room makes me jump back at the sight of a humanoid!

Without moving, I stare at it, but quickly realize it's an old, ugly decommissioned humanoid shell. I sigh with relief and then continue toward the front counter.

Feeling surer of my being alone, I relax my crouched position and sneak more comfortably. The screen of the computer awakens when I hit the spacebar. Ugh—a passcode is needed. My hands quietly glide over some papers on the counter, but none look promising. No hint at all for a password. Turning back to the screen, I type "metalhead" as a wild guess and punch the keyboard loudly.

"Huh? Hello?"

I flip my head to the dark corridor behind me. Where did the voice come from?! Oh man. I've been caught!

"Who's there!"

Shit! I look around to find a hiding place, but their steps close in too fast.

"Ah!" a voice in front of me yells.

In reaction, I fall back against the wall behind me, unsure of what to do. I lack experience in espionage—I'm frozen with fear!

"What are you doing here!" a woman bot yells at me, the palms of her hands pointed at me, ready to disarm.

"I'm sorry! I'm sorry. Just looking for information!" My voice quick and my hands are up to defend myself against her aggressive demeanor.

"Wait," she pauses, "it's you…" She relaxes the connective fibres in her mechanics and looks curiously. "You're Morris. Morris 1045?"

How does she…? What in the world? I stare at her human-like eyes, an upgrade from Archie's for sure. My indecisiveness leaves me frozen still, but my face distorts in confusion.

"You're Morris! My messages went through!" She squeals in excitement as she approaches me.

So much confusion in my head! She steps forward, straight up to me and puts her arms around me, lifts me up and laughs in happiness. The lights turn on as if cued by a remote as I'm held in the air in utter confusion of the strange situation. She then sets me down with a large smile on her nylon face—her brown, artificial hair framing her (now) friendly look of open invitation. Her face shifts suddenly to a wondering look.

"You, you're…," she looks at me with surprise, "you are Morris 1045, right?! The one with great potential?"

"I… um, don't know wha…" I stutter, my mind in a state of shock.

"You're Morris 1045! The human with two master numbers and a Desire Number of one!"

I look at her strangely. "Um… what are you talking abou…"

"The numbers! The numbers from your life reveal your extraordinary potential! You know? Numerology?" She tries to explain in excited haste, yet nearly frustrated with the whole situation.

"I… don't really believe in that stuff. So, I'm not sure what you're saying, sorry…" I motion to leave, but she puts a hand out.

"Your first name, Morris, is calculated out to the Master Number 11 according to the ancient Pythagorean system of numbers! Your family number calculates to one and your Life Path number, calculated from your birthdate—January 5th, 8143—is twenty-two! Don't you know how amazing that is?! Numbers explain the universe and you are the ultimate combination! You're telling me you never knew?!"

She spoke so fast I could hardly understand, but the few words I did catch scare me. Why did this servant bot know so much about me?

My expression is unchanging as I try to decipher how best to approach this odd circumstance. She seems strangely hopeful for my acceptance of her crazy talk. So much so, I can't take it anymore.

"Look, I respect your belief system, but I'm not fond of it. Especially when missionaries stalk me for numbers." I keep my hands up in defense of my position and shake my head. In disappointment, she attempts to speak but I interrupt her.

"I broke in to find a freelance programmer, but I can see now this was a big mistake. I'm sorry." I begin to leave toward the back door. "I am so sorry, but please don't report this. I'll leave and… I'll never come back, ok? Thank you."

I squeeze past her as she tries to conjure up more reasons why she knows something about me that I don't. But I ignore her and tune out her loony numbers theory. I'm homeless now! I can't go believing in nonsense. My mind is the last advantage I have—I can't lose it like she's lost hers!

We turn right out the back door, past the storage container and I begin making my way back to my home (with the crazy woman-bot behind).

"Ok—wait! You have purpose. The numbers!" she exclaims as she follows me. I quickly turn around and shush her.

"Shh! Stop making so much noise!" I whisper quietly, noticing the last few people heading home are glancing at us.

"Ok, ok. But listen to me—you are the reason I've been waiting for so many years."

This is becoming quite a threat to my whole operation. Once I near the last building before the trek down to my haven, I turn around to the servant bot-woman, still following me with whispers of numbers and destiny.

"Look, you have to stop following me!" I make eye contact to make it a serious request. The sun was nearly gone and I needed to escape without her following me to my cave.

"Please, let me explain more fully," she says with eyes full of hopelessness. As if she would die if I didn't agree. Ugh, how am I to fix this.

"Ok. Ma'am, may I ask your name?" I use a fake nice voice. I'll try to use her name for a more personal, effective approach.

"My name? You should know. My name is Clara."

Wait, she. She's Clara? From the messages? I wait for a second to process this new, "fun" tidbit.

"You," I pause and stare. "You're Clara. From the repetitive messages, 'follow no one?'"

"Well… yes! Who did you think I was?" she says with a puzzled look. Her brown, artificial hair shifts in the wind, looking more real than I've seen on a servant bot before.

A drone flying by forces me to hide behind the familiar storage container at the back of the last building. Clara watches the whole dodge-the-drone ordeal in confusion. Man, I have to get back. What am I to do?

"Fine…. come with me and you can explain yourself. But only if you promise to follow me quietly," I tell her quickly, still crouched. Probably another bad decision on my part.

After noticing I hid from the drone, her understanding of my situation slowly turns her expression (and voice) more serious.

"Yes, okay. Where are we going?"

This is definitely another bad decision. But, "Follow me," I tell her as I check the sky for drones and proceed down the hill to my sanctuary.

I step down the dirt steps and hear my feet slap against the rock of the cave. My new "associate," Clara, makes her way down too and opens her hand-light in reaction to the darkness of the cave.

"Wow. Homey," she says sarcastically. I turn in reaction to her attitude and sense of humor. It's a big hint at the freedom given to her by her owner.

With her hand-light fairly bright, I quickly find the old solar-lamp and turn it on. Clara looks at it and realizes I took it from her shop's dumpster, then smiles. I turn to her without guilt.

"So. You're a servant bot seeking me out through strange messages. How reassuring that you've followed me here," I retaliate with a sarcastic reply.

"Well, maybe I should be more scared than you are," she says sarcastically as she examines the dingy space, shining her own light around the walls, "and I'm technically a servant bot, yes, but my owner abandoned me. I care for his dying repair shop alone." Noticing my desk and the old plug-in system, she walks toward it.

"These look familiar, hmm?" Clara turns back to me with a smirk.

"Technically, you didn't want them anymore, seeing as they were in the trash. So, technically, I stole from the state, not you," I wittily reply in an effort to protect my prized possessions. My only possessions.

"What are you planning to do, exactly? You said you needed a programmer?"

I hesitate and try to examine her motives. "Look. Why do you know so much about me? You understand that I'm concerned about my safety right now, with a stalker in my home."

Clara begins laughing. "Home?!" Her laughs echo in the cave, amplifying both her volume and her offense. I become angry as she turns back to me.

"This is not a home. What happened to you? And seriously, what are you planning to do with that pile of parts?" she asks with pity as she points at my treasures.

"I'm not looking for your sympathy, ok? I know how this looks. Plus, YOU are the stalker under scrutiny right now." My voice serious in response to her crude judgment of my predicament.

"Ok, well. I'M a programmer. And I want to help you with whatever it is you're trying to do here." Her smirk turned friendly.

"You… you are a programmer. I thought servant bots weren't allowed to build code."

"They can if they're not caught," Clara says with pride as she turns to look out the cave. "Plus, I'm a humanoid in service, not a servant bot. And I've had a lot of time since my owner left."

"You still need to explain yourself, Clara," I quickly reply, saying her name mockingly. I still don't know who this "Clara" really is or what she wants. "You need to explain this whole 'numbers-explain-the-universe' thing before I deem you insane and not worth my time."

Clara casually sits in the old chair at the desk with perfect posture, ready to explain herself. A buzz came from the left of the cave and I jump up to hide from the drone that was about to fly by. Before I knew it, Clara was at the front of the cave with her hand out.

The low buzz becomes louder and the drone quickly comes into sight, right in front of the cave! Oddly it doesn't change its trajectory and slowly continues forward. Its proximity is too close—it must notice us! But it flies by without detecting anything and I realize Clara's hand had been following it the entire time—her body still in concentration.

As the buzz from the drone softens in the distance to the right of the cave, Clara turns and gives me a smile.

"Oh, also. I might've learned how to hack things."

CHAPTER 10

"I was trying to inspire you. You know—don't follow anyone else, go your own route. Follow your life's path."

Clara and I are sitting in the dark now, on the cold rock bottom of my hidden sanctuary. She had been explaining herself a bit more as I sit, trying to understand. Trying to trust her.

My (well Clara's) old, nearly broken solar lamp barely lights the dark stone of the wet cave, the green of the weeds barely visible in the low light. Occasionally I look over at her during our conversation, but mostly I look away.

After saving me from the drone earlier, I feel more inclined to listen to what she has to say. And obviously, she could help me out quite a bit if things work out. But I still hesitate to trust her (or anyone at this point).

"So, I was hoping by sending the message, 'follow no one,' you'd find encouragement in those words," Clara says while looking at me with her two analytical eyes, a slight sadness apparent within them. She was disappointed about my mistrust.

"Ok—why stalk me then?" I ask, turning my gaze to the quiet darkness of the desert view. I wasn't expecting a good answer.

"I wasn't stalking," she says, her voice stern. "Numerology isn't something that led me to you specifically. It's happenstance if anything."

Keeping my expression minimal, I roll my eyes out of disbelief.

"No, really! I have spent years upon years searching through public records, systems and self-calculated numerology reports of humans around the world. There's something about organic 'chance' that poses such potential, something you can't find in

AI or bots building bots. Even an algorithm coded to create randomization is still quantified in some ways. Only nature creates, well… true happenstance."

I look down and grab a pebble, throw it at the cliff in front of us, and clench my jaw as I take in this information.

"Numerology has become important to me, not just because I'm built with code and numbers, but because numbers don't lie. The ancient philosopher, Pythagoras, believed numbers explain the universe. Saint Augustine, another religious philosopher, wrote thousands of years ago that 'numbers are a universal language offered from the 'deity' to humans as confirmation of truth.'

"Artificial intelligence is merely truths built upon truths, but the humans' connection to the universe is a natural mystery—unless you dig for answers with numerology. Humans were created by accident just as the universe was created by accident. AI will always be calculated, thus unable to live by chance—the true definitive quality of life. Thus, numerology is a tool to define a human's potential in the world of chance."

Silence takes over the cave. The pressure to respond grows heavy, but what am I to say? I am not used to this much philosophy. Even Archie and I never dove too deep into "what ifs."

I take a large breath and sigh out of habit—frustrating thoughts like the "origin of the universe" leave me disappointed with the lack of answers.

"And this is an argument to prove you're not… crazy," I quietly reply, without looking at her.

"I'm saying, that your birthdate and your full name equate to multiple, unique numbers I've not seen before. Out of the millions of humans, you're the only one to have two master numbers and a life path of twenty-two. You're a born leader according to numerology."

I chuckled at her last statement. "You think I'm a leader?"

"Numbers don't lie, Morris."

My recent, new-found purpose is just a fling, a distraction from my current disappointing life. Something to guide my efforts, but deep down I don't actually believe in it. Though what she was saying (not that it's totally believable) *was* lifting my spirits. I shake my head and stand up—I don't want to get my hopes up.

"Regardless of the numbers, I'm not in a situation right now where I can lead anyone. But…" I look at Clara, her eyes hopeful for inclusion in my life, "I do have a plan."

"Ooh! A plan for what?" She slides to face me, still sitting down but with her hands on her knees.

"I won't state it out loud because it will be more real than ever if I do. And I'm still fearful of failure, but I have nothing else to live for and I want to shoot for something grand to leave my old life behind."

I turn toward her and hesitate, remembering my distrust of her. Her face is innocent, with skin-colored nylon and beautifully designed eyes that glimmer even in this low light.

"If you ARE a programmer and I CAN trust you, I would like to enlist your help," I ask with an air of importance in my words.

Clara smirks and stands up. "You CAN trust me. And I accept your offer. Though I've heavily implied I'd be willing to help this whole time."

Sarcasm is strong with this one. The tone in her voice pokes fun at me, as if toying with my patience is a game.

"Good. But no more talk of numbers," I say as I shake her hand in agreement.

"Right, 'cause there's no numbers in programming." Her sarcasm was already on my nerves.

"Mmmhmm," I hum out of spite as I grab a green mass and pop it in my mouth. Clara observes, smiles and starts up the dirt stairs.

"Wait, where you going?" I ask.

"I'll be back in the morning. I can sense your need for solitude, but I do expect a task list for me when I return at sunrise." Clara then disappears as she makes her way up and out of the cave.

"Ok… Goodnight, Clara," I say quietly to myself, out of force of habit. Then she vanishes into the night.

The darkness of the cave walls around me seems darker now. And loneliness thrives in darkness. I must not have noticed it before.

I lie down, my back on the cold rock, and close my eyes. I slow my thoughts and prevent myself from trying to check my wrist or my heartbeat.

Breathe in. Breathe out.

A new variable has appeared in my plan. Another bad decision of mine has turned out to be another option worth exploring. I wonder if Clara will actually come back. I wonder if I can trust a servant bot like her. I wonder… about so many things. But not now. I need to slow my thoughts and rest.

Breathe in. Breathe out.

My back sinks into the rock as it warms from my body heat. I take one last breath and close my eyes.

Faces of the neurobine viruses I deleted begin popping up in my memory. I shake my head, but the image of a woman I removed is difficult to ignore, her tears falling as she stares into my eyes— her voice echoing in my mind, "Do it!"

"Ahh!" I yell as I grab my head, adding pressure on my temples. Quickly, I roll over and tense my body.

I have to stop. This PTSD seems to be getting worse, especially now that I'm living on my own. But I can't help it.

Out of respect, I want to remember the shame I felt when "deleting" those people. But for my own sanity, I yearn to ignore the memory of their sobbing. And their eyes. I try to forget the image of their eyes and of my hand lifting. The popping sound and their existence… removed.

I also can't help but think back to my feeling of cold emptiness when my quota reached the double digits that day. An inner fear of the ruthless emptiness in my soul as I deleted virus after virus.

I turn back over and stare at the ceiling.

Breathe in.

My jaw clenches as I shake my head. I knew it. PTSD for life. I so knew it.

Breathe out.

And I slowly fall asleep.

CHAPTER 11

My eyes open to the cave ceiling with Clara sitting next to me, the sun lighting up the edge of the cave. Just as she has done the past few days, she waits for me to wake up.

Though Clara has been helping me for about a week now, there's still a worry of whether to trust her or not. Plus, I'm always on edge knowing she waits for me to wake up. No bot or humanoid really needs sleep, but Archie would always stand outside the door of my old room. Clara doesn't hide it though, and even sits next to me in the mornings. She has a strange sense of personal space.

"Good morning. Brought you banana bread today."

I sit up and look at her familiar nylon face and notice the banana bread and water next to me.

"Thank you, Clara," I take a bite of the bread and sip on the water.

She smiles. Every day that smile lasts longer—at least it feels that way.

"You're very welcome," Clara replies and stands up to walk over to the desk.

She noticed my green weed diet the first night we met and wasted no time in bringing me food the following morning and every meal since. Not sure what I'd do without her. But it can't be a good thing I'm relying on her so much.

Clara wirelessly connects herself to the console and continues the work I gave her. The desk and chair might be the same, but she has replaced some parts over the past few days, making it a much safer and reliable plug-in system.

Every night she'd stay a while to chat and we've learned a lot about each other. I've told her about my days working construction (not about AVC though, not yet) and she's told me of times with her owner.

Clara is a lone servant bot by choice—she had reached self-sufficiency but wants to stay in service to her owner in case he ever comes back. A sweet gesture, but I feel her hope is misplaced. I doubt her owner is coming back.

Currently, she sits in the chair with her focus on the project at hand. Her artificial brown hair and her skin-colored nylon surface are some of the only reminders that she's a humanoid and not a human. Conversations with her are rich and purposeful. Different than the ones with Archie—more... more engaging, perhaps? Could be her complicated past that intrigues me though.

I turn my gaze to view out of the cave, the green weeds dancing in the soft breeze flowing in from the desert land. Blankets had been laid out for me to sleep on, as well as some extra clothes folded on top of a small table to the side of the cave between some water droplets. Clara had definitely spruced up the place over the last week. She had even installed a gravity-powered shower next to my water-catching basin. Not to mention a few extra sun-lamps, much newer than the one I had originally found (well, stole).

My fugitive status didn't scare her and she never hesitated or questioned her unconditional commitment in helping me—or as Clara puts it, helping my "Life's Path." Who knows about this numerology stuff, but one thing's for sure. She definitely places a lot of trust in me because of her (supposedly) inarguable findings. Those "numbers" that don't lie.

The breeze from the desert below us rushes up, bringing a smell of dust but feeling nice even though it's warm. Never knowing the time has allowed my senses to calm and I tend to pay attention to my surroundings more. At least it feels that way.

But with a big breath, I get to my feet and walk over to the desk where Clara is working. Her body is still as she hacks into the Sector-System's coding, her soft nylon hands resting, her eyes shut.

"Clara," I ask and her eyes open, "sorry to interrupt, but may I ask how far along you are?"

"I actually finished yesterday, but I've just been reviewing my work to make sure. Better safe than sorry, right?" Clara says in a light tone, hiding the pride she felt from completing this seemingly impossible task.

"Really? You're done already?!" I ask with a high-pitched voice, unable to contain my excitement. After about a week, she has finally finished!

"Yep! With my trojan horse in place, the additive code I wrote will stay activated now. So during your session, your connection will be disguised from the omnipotent monitoring system that controls the Sector-System. Very happy with it, if I do say so myself. I've always wanted to be a white hat—assuming what you're doing is good…" Clara looks at me with a condescending look.

"Yes, of course it is," I say without taking her last comment seriously. I take one last sip of water and set the cup on the desk.

"During my session, you'll be able to monitor the effectiveness of your patchwork, right?" I felt a little anxious and wanted to make sure.

"Yes, I'll be right here and will pull you out if anything happens," Clara smiles and stands up from the chair to allow me to take her place next to the plug-in system.

"And you're confident in your programming skills?" I ask to re-assure myself.

"Nope!" Clara grins with self-satisfaction. I look at her with serious concern, ignoring her sarcasm, but she replies to my doubt, "Oh, calm yourself. Of course I'm confident. I've been programming for years now, you know this."

I sigh with relief, "Ok." I turn to the plug-in system and turn it on. "Just wanted to make sure." As the system begins warming up, I grab the outdated node, hold it in my hands and pause.

"For a man with nothing to lose, you sure worry a lot."

"I'm just reviewing the details in my head. You ready?" My face is serious as I look at Clara. Her face imitates mine.

"Yes, Corporal. At your command," she says with a hand saluting me, her feet pressed together. Ugh. Her sarcasm, as predicted, had gotten old—as if she never takes me seriously. And always using outdated lingo too.

Clara relaxes her stance, takes her position next to the desk and wirelessly plugs herself in, giving me a surprisingly serious look of readiness.

Breathe in. Breathe out.

Time to do this. I place the node on the back of my neck and sink back into my chair, letting my body relax.

My eyes open. An intense rush of air engulfs my body and a sinking feeling begins to grow in my stomach. What is going on?!

Wind starts slapping my face and I squint in reaction to the heavy pressure, barely making out an expanse of blue around me, all around me. The weightlessness and clouds passing by me can only mean… I'm free-falling!

I try desperately to look down to see how much distance I have when a beep in my head sounds.

"Morris! Can you hear me?"

"Clara?!" I shout over the noise of the rushing wind. "Is that you!?"

"Yes! Hang tight. I'll fix this!" her voice is quick, sounding in my head.

"Just pull me out! I only have a few minutes!" Fear overwhelms me as my adrenaline kicks in. I try looking below me again, but am only able to see vague shapes of land masses amongst the giant sea. The panorama I can make out is completely rounded.

This domain, Sector 2-37463 from my last AVC day, is like a small Earth! Exactly imitating the old-Earth I read about in history classes except for that instead of multiple land masses, it's designed as one large continent. If it wasn't for this accidental (and currently terrifying) perspective, I would have had no idea!

My heart is racing at the spectacle—and from the possibility of a serious mental breakdown. Stories I've heard tell of humans going insane when dying during their connection to the Sector-System.

Having your senses and your cognitive mind experience death is nearly fatal, at least to your sanity. I don't want to find out what happens if I die here and suddenly wake up in reality.

"Ok, Morris?" Clara quickly asks in my head.

"Yes, yes! I'm here!" I shout over the noise, seeing the land mass begin to morph into city sections. More detail is bad! More detail means I'm running out of time!

"Close your eyes and hold your breath, ready? One..." Clara's voice is stern in her decision-making. I close my eyes and start taking a breath. "Two..." I hold my breath and tense my body. What is she planning to do!? "Three!"

Silence. Then street noise.

My feet are on solid ground and I have the feeling of gravity on my shoulders.

"Morris? Morris! You alright?" her voice is ringing in my head.

I open my eyes, my breath still held in tension. Neurobines fill the street with foot traffic and I'm standing right in the middle of it. Some are walking on either side, others right through me. My muscles relax and I exhale slowly.

I'm safe.

"Morris!?" Clara shouts, not having heard me for a few seconds.

"I'm... I'm ok," I reply softly as I look around me, noticing the complex geometrical designs covering every building and every bit of clothing. The cobblestones underneath my feet remind me of my time in the AVC.

"Ok—good. Your ghost connection is stable. Feel free to roam about the cabin." Clara's sarcastic voice is uncomfortably clear in my head. She has way too much time on her hands to read up on old human idioms, some of which don't even make sense to me.

I open and close my hands to feel more stable. My heart rate is slowing, especially now that I'm on solid (well virtual) ground. But the familiar decorations of this domain are making me more antsy than I had thought.

Sector 2-37463 was my first choice because I was hoping to re-cruit Scott and possibly other AVC 46 members. But the emotional trauma of killing those twenty-one neurobines here, in this exact domain, is getting to me.

"Morris… you're safe now. Slow your breathing and relax—you're in," Clara says, trying to calm me down. But I am getting more tense because of my memories as PixelOne's mercenary. There's no use in hiding my issues anymore. Maybe mentioning it will make me feel better.

"Clara, I need to tell you something…" I say out aloud while looking around to confirm my inexistence to the neurobines that fill the street.

"About two weeks ago, I deleted twenty-one neurobine-viruses here in Sector 2-37463 as part of the AVC. I… I didn't want to tell you because I'm not proud of it and I'm afraid of scaring you. But know I didn't do it by choice! And their faces haunt me every night." My restless voice is hinting at my unease in repeating this information. The source of my PTSD.

Silence from Clara makes me worry.

"I know, it's okay…" she says. Her voice is calm and collected, smooth yet sad.

"Wait, how do you…" but suddenly I'm interrupted!

A dark red virus had pushed me down! His stature threatening as I look up at him from the ground.

"You… you've come for me, haven't you," he murmurs, his voice gurgling with anger as the faint red glow darkens with each breath. I didn't expect to ever see a virus this far gone!

"Morris, what's happening!" Clara's voice is loud in my head.

Quickly, I get to my feet and examine the threat. It had taken a lot of strength to push me down that forcefully. What more will his insanity allow him to do in this coded world—kill me?!

"Now, wait. I'm not here to…" my voice is calm, but I suddenly feel the urge to dodge as I watch his arm swing over me.

The extra skills discs Clara had found for me are paying off.

I allow my muscle memory to kick in and my leg swings out to trip my opponent, but the virus is too strong and deflects my attack. No wonder his glow is dark red, he is very aggressive.

Another powerful punch comes my way, but I suddenly block it and throw a counter. The virus stumbles back but doesn't hesitate to spring himself toward me.

My muscle memory locks up and the virus takes us to the ground. A common self-defense disc was the only skills disc I had found for street fighting—I'm not prepared for this level of virus! And I wasn't really expecting to have to fight!

I grab his wrist, but he rotates his arm to where I lose grip and his other fist clips my cheek. I expect pain to radiate in my jaw, but remember pain is filtered out due to an AVC "mutation" still active. I attempt to squirm out from under him, but his quickness, his power is too much!

"Morris, you need to escape!" Clara shouts in my head.

"What do you think I'm trying to do!" I shout as I dodge his other fist and kick upwards. Nothing is working—even prying myself out is useless. His punches are too fast and dodging them keeps my mind preoccupied, unable to think ahead.

"Ahh! I have no desire for sacrifice! It is YOUR time that is up! YOUR time to sleep!" the virus shouts. Other neurobines had already moved a significant distance from us, but the loudness and anger in his voice make most of them gasp at the sight.

The virus grabs my left wrist and anchors it to the ground. I wrestle more in response, but my other wrist is soon controlled too. With my movement limited, I breath heavily and rack my brain for solutions. My wrist begins to burn under the pressure and pain starts to sink in. He's altering the coding in my "mutation!" Is there no limit?!

His eyes stare directly into me with uncontrolled anger, like fire beneath his pupils.

"Your breath quickens and your heart races. Time is escaping. YOU are about to sleep under MY hands." His voice is disturbingly low and angry, while my wrist is painfully held at bay by his brute strength.

"Morris! Close your eyes!" Clara shouts in my head. I quickly close them and hold my breath.

Silence.

I open my eyes to the glowing plug-in system in front of me. Clara is staring at me, ready to respond at any sign of an issue. Breathing out slowly calms my heart rate and I reassure myself that I'm safe now.

Clara is still frozen though, waiting for me to say something. I take another breath and start chuckling at how terribly that went. She quickly relaxes and falls to a sitting position against the back wall of the cave, laughing to herself too.

"Nice fighting."

Sarcasm, of course. I turn and grin with disbelief. A smile grows on her face as she looks back at me.

"Yes, well. Thanks for pulling me out," I say as I stretch and shake off the tension.

"I'm just glad you're ok. That was a rough first attempt. From free-falling to defending yourself from a lunatic." Her fatigue makes me wonder. Her emotional response hints at how far along she is in developing her AI. Everything she felt was genuine and… real. From what I can tell.

Leaning back in the chair, I review the details. Can't believe I forgot the initial location within the domain. By default, I must have been placed in the sky. Or maybe just by random.

"Yeah. Glad I'm ok, too," I say softly. Then I stand up and stretch more, take a big breath and begin thinking.

"So my 'ghost connection,' as you call it, wasn't compromised?" I ask her while pacing back and forth.

"No. I was monitoring everything. That crazed neurobine was the only thing that knew of your existence in the Sector-System. Apart from that, your tracks were covered," she says with pride.

I turn back and forth as I think, the light of the morning sun shining into the cave.

"I'm confident my plan will work. But in order to follow through successfully, I still need your help." Thinking over the details is more important than ever, especially now that I know I've already missed one. A major one at that.

"Wait." I pause and look at Clara. "You said you knew I was a part of the AVC. How?"

Clara shifts and looks away.

"I might have taken my 'locating the master number' guy a little too far. I didn't stalk you per se, but I did keep track of your public records." She looks a bit ashamed—a good sign at least.

"Ok, so you knew I was a killer and that didn't scare you?"

"Well, it's not killing! It's just deletion like a programmer does..."

"It felt like killing to me!" I raise my voice, trying to get my point across but losing control of my emotions. "It's removing a sentient being from existence—I don't care if they're code! It's murder." I look down at the ground with that last statement.

"I know. I agree. I was just trying to make you feel better," Clara says with her eyes looking up at me from her sitting position. Her eyes are full of sadness.

The cave is silent.

"I know your situation and I don't blame you for what you had to do. I'm more angry at PixelOne than anything," she says to ease the tension between us.

"We've been working together for about a week now and I've gotten to know you. I trust you! I know how much your time with the AVC affects you," she says sweetly. But, wait.

"How do you know it affects me?" I glance at her quickly, taking her a second to calculate her response to my level of intensity.

"Well, I... I've just noticed a few things," she says hesitantly.

"Like what?" My voice is agitated. I want answers from her and my intense questioning is pulling out more truth, the more I press.

Clara looks conflicted but then she finally breaks. "I've seen how much trouble you have falling asleep. And staying asleep. And just a few times, I've noticed you have nightmares."

I look at her confused, "you… watch me sleep?"

She looks dumbfounded. Her trouble in finding a response is all the evidence I need. I sigh and turn away.

"Clara, that's… that's just too much." I put one hand on my head and turn back. "I could handle your deal with numbers and maybe the fact you knew my public records, but watching me sleep? That's just too much."

Her expression hints at her embarrassment—those upgraded eyes tearing up. Something I've not seen in a humanoid before.

"I know… I know," her voice is sad and quiet. Suddenly, she gets up and runs up the stairs.

"Clara! Don't…" but she had already run off. "Don't leave."

So many conflicting feelings—should I be scared of this "stalker"? Should I be worried? She's helped me out so much, how can I complete my goals, my "Life's Path" without her?

Unsure of what to do under the changing circumstances, I turn to look out of the cave at the desert of nothingness. A lone mountain in the distance reminds me how alone I am now. Alone once again in my cave, with the morning sun shining near the front.

I sit down on the cave floor. I take some deep breaths. And I realize there's more details to think over now—the possibility of her not coming back, what I might say if she returns, how I'm to decide on looking past her "stalker" motives?

The green weeds swing back and forth slightly from the warmer wind coming up from the desert. As I sit, I try to decipher my current situation while I lean back, my hands holding my weight up.

One more conversation is all I need. One more attempt to understand her reasoning. Maybe I'm jumping to conclusions, I don't know. I need clarification.

I hope she comes back.

CHAPTER 12

Familiar desert land stretches out over the horizon. From below the cliff, burnt sand goes on for miles and miles soaked by the radiation of the boiling sun.

The air in the cave is hot and stuffy, but shadows thankfully engulf my home, my secluded haven. Only the opening of the cave is tortured by the hot sun, where no weeds really grow.

All this time away from the routine of daily life has changed my point of view on things. I've been noticing life's oddities and questioning social norms more often, more so than before.

Life has been made around the heat of the sun—away from it. I don't remember there ever being a time where I spent an entire day outside (especially during Sun Season), at least not before I ran away a few weeks ago. But now I've been outside 24/7, trying to survive the heat in the thin air.

Still no sign of Clara.

It's only been a few hours probably, but still. With the plug-in system setup and the ghost connection ready, it's hard not to return to the Sector-System. Moving forward with the plan just feels uncomfortable without Clara's help, but what else am I to do with my time?

I stretch my legs and hop to my feet. The damp cave might keep things livable and the overgrown weed supply just enough oxygen, but the air is always thin. Always makes things difficult when getting up too quickly.

The plug-in system buzzes as it warms up. I tap the blank display on the top of it and it turns on, revealing a few settings. My original plan, when I was by myself a week ago, was to connect for only five minutes at a time (just to be safe). Without Clara here anymore, might as well go about my business.

PixelOne taught us how to change these settings manually during orientation but it was never actually necessary on the job. I've always known about the dormant screen, but I've never needed to alter connection settings manually before. Connections were always maintained from afar by other staff in the building.

So, I feel kind of rebellious changing the session timeout to five minutes without company approval.

Sitting in the chair raises my heart rate, but I take a breath to calm myself down and slap the node on my neck. With one blink, I open my eyes to the same street I was on earlier—only this time, no brute virus to come to attack me.

The designs within designs distract me a bit as I scan my location and find a route away from the crowd. I pull out my hovering map and examine it as it floats in front of me. Hmm, there's my blue dot right in the middle and oh! Another blue dot labeled Scott, just west of my location, moving downward.

Scanning my position once more, making sure no viruses are near to me, I retract my map and begin running west down the street full of neurobines.

Plants line the street, each color organized so unnaturally. Building after building, condo after condo go by like a flash as I bolt west. How bittersweet it will be to see Scott again.

Turning a corner, I see a woman lightly highlighted by a pink aura. She quickly notices me as I dart past her, her eyes big with surprise. "A… a ghost," I hear her say to herself as I go by.

Poor soon-to-be virus.

I turn another corner to keep my westward direction, pull up my map to check where I am in relation to Scott and quickly notice his location has shifted a bit. I change direction and close the map.

Running in the Sector-System without limitation felt oddly satisfying at first, but the novelty is beginning to wear off. A dull sadness grew every time I ran like this, as though my body longed for limitation, something to prevent my unrestricted, in-human run. But no matter. No need for such thoughts now.

In the distance I see a figure standing oddly upright, palm out and then I hear a POP. Must be Scott. I run closer to him and recognize the baldness.

"Scott! Hey!" I shout at him as I approach.

He slowly turns toward me with no expression on his face and it takes him a few moments to recognize me. I stop running a few feet away and walk closer.

"Kid? Is that you?" he asks in a quiet voice.

"Yes, it's Morris. Remember me?"

"I coulda' swore they sent you to the PRP, what happened to you? Wait. How are you even here?" His confused reaction is slow to take shape, as if tired. Exhausted even.

"It's a long story. But I came to recruit you for a project of mine. Something that could change society as we know it, but I need your help. Can you meet me in person?" My hand gestures are over the top as I explain my need for his help. But his eyes steadily grow less energetic.

"Oh, you ain't had enough oxygen—can't be talkin' like that on purpose." His voice low, lacking concern. Scott pops out his map and checks the time on his wrist.

"No, I'm serious, Scott. Leave this filthy job and meet me at my hideout. I know you don't like the AVC, I can see it." I plead with him to understand he has options.

"Morris. I have a family," he says, his eyes full of sorrow. "But best of luck on your project—good to see you're still breathin.'"

The sadness in his eyes is so deep, it moves me. And I feel so much sympathy for him and his lack of options. He can't run away like I did, not with responsibilities like supporting a family.

Scott raises a slight smirk and says to me, "Besides. I'm bald and old, right? How much help could I really be?" He chuckles slightly and puts a hand on my shoulder, then continues.

"If you truly have found a way out, of the AVC, of this life, come back for…"

Suddenly, with a blink of an eye, I stare at the glowing plug-in system in my cave.

My five minutes are up.

I sit breathing in and out, thinking over his predicament. His sorrow and responsibilities remind me that I have no responsibilities. Not even a family, not after the divorce and my running away—they'd all reject me (except maybe Paul and Archie). The freedom of it all should excite me. But it makes me feel… small. Insignificant.

But. I'm firewood, right? My plan to change things could save Scott from the AVC—no, it WILL save him.

Taking a deep breath, I get to my feet and turn toward the cave mouth. A dark figure standing in the shadow freaks me out and I jump back!

I stare for a second but realize it's a servant bot—an ugly servant bot that doesn't move at all. Who is that? I straighten my posture without taking my eyes off the bot, but it looks… dead.

Getting up close, I realize no lights are on in the eyes and the bot is still—motionless, like, well a metal bucket. Scanning the area in front of me, I see no evidence of where this came from—could this have involved Clara? She's the only one who knows of my location (at least I think).

Oh, this is the bot from Clara's shop! I recognize it now.

Making sure the bot is truly lifeless, I relax a bit and turn around. But I pause again. The back of the cave is different—a door is open to a black tunnel of complete darkness.

A door? I feel my body freeze at the sight of the open space, the surprising unknowns that lie before me. A door?! This whole time there was a door? But why has it opened now? I slowly inch closer, step by step, to peer into the emptiness of this tunnel.

A faint sound can be heard down the corridor and I step closer to listen. Angling myself to the side, I walk a bit closer and notice the walls are made of cheap concrete. No old concrete. A passageway? A room? What is this?

The sound is growing louder and it sounds like footsteps. Footsteps!? I plaster myself to the side of the cave, away from the entrance to this new door in the back of my cave. That must be a person! A secret civilization maybe? What do I do?!

A humanoid runs out and stops suddenly at the door—wait, Clara!?

"Morris!" she exclaims as she turns around. My mouth opens at the sheer shock of all this.

"Morris, I found a door!"

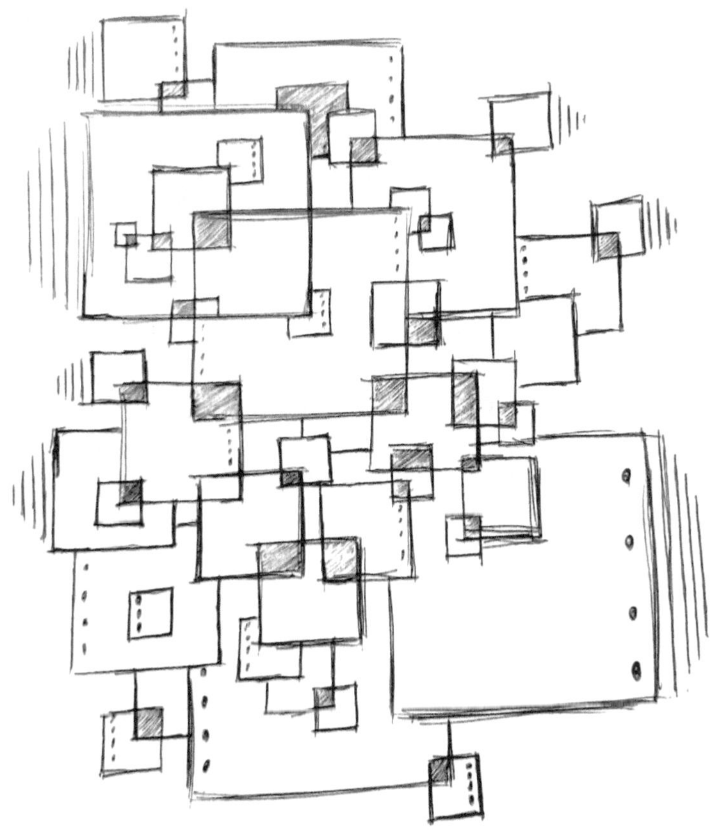

CHAPTER 13

"A passageway that goes so far, I haven't even reached an end," Clara explains with excitement.

"There's been a cave door here this whole time? How haven't we noticed?" I ask her, dumbfounded by this new variable in my life. The potential of it—all the possibilities to organize in my head.

"Well, I HAD come back to bring you this," she points to the dead bot, "and apologize to you. But as I was waiting, staring at the back wall of the cave, I noticed a strange line in the rock formation. So I went over, examined it, and pried open a stone door! Well, titanium on the inside, but practically stone on the outside!"

Looking over at the opened door, I notice the old titanium with slight corrosion showing on the edges. Rock had bonded over time to the outside of this ancient door, as it seemed.

Looking over at Clara, I notice she's examining me, waiting for my reaction to her return.

"Why did you bring back a decommissioned servant bot?" I ask her.

"I wanted to come 'bearing gifts,' as they say." A sense of timid innocence was in her voice.

"But why a bot?"

"Well. I knew you were going to ask me for one as part of the 'grand plan,'" she says, gesturing at the bot.

"Wait, how did you know I was…?"

"Oh, it wasn't hard to figure out. Your guilt from the AVC, your need to change a society that drove you to homelessness, your need for 'grandness,' etc. I could tell you wanted to capture a virus and put it in the real world. Hasn't been done before, so... could prove eventful." She didn't even try to hide that smirk of hers as she explained my own plan in front of me.

"I see..." I say quietly. Was this "plan" really that simple? Simple enough to guess? I thought it was innovative, different. Rebellious, maybe.

"Morris," Clara says in a serious tone, "I'm really sorry about everything. And I'm going to come right out and say it. I like you." I reel my head back in surprise, but she continues, "I took things in a strange direction at first, yes. I admit. And you have no obligation to forgive me, but I do want to help you in any way I can and... you know, try to win your trust back."

She was so direct.

I feel my eyes shift as I attempt to decipher the situation. My brain is moving so fast, yet nothing really takes shape. So many thoughts to think over, yet where do I begin?

"Um..." I look away. "That's..."

"Sorry if this makes you feel uncomfortable. I just, you know, don't like wasting time. Maybe it's a humanoid thing. But I figured with the way you were looking at me..." Those eyes observe my every move—vulnerable to any word I might say in reaction to her truthfulness.

I shake my head and blink my eyes.

"This is all very strange, Clara. Not that I'm not flattered, but it's a lot to take in. I'm still weirded out about you... watching me sleep. How am I to trust you? How am I to take you seriously without questioning your motives?" I shrug my shoulders.

"You have every right to be upset. But I'm determined to prove I'm far more normal than you think I am. How can I win your trust back, Morris?"

Ugh, what am I supposed to say? There's too much weight in this conversation and I'm really not sure how to deal with her, especially now that I know her "feelings."

"I don't think it's anything we can solve now. I need time to think this over. So, can we talk about this later? I mean, there's a door, Clara."

Her face shifts and she says quietly, "Oh. Yes, well the door is definitely a surprise."

I know she's disappointed in my change of topic, but I just really didn't know how to deal with… her. I mean, she's still the stalker bot watching me sleep! And on top of that, am I to take her seriously? She's probably just lonely after so many years working in that repair shop alone. So I guess this is a normal reaction for a lonesome bot to have when suddenly faced with extended human interaction. It just so happens this "extended interaction" is with me.

Clara looks down and contemplates.

"Clara, look. I'm flattered, I am. But can I think on this? Let's explore this mysterious corridor first. Huh? Together?" I ask with a positive spin in my inflection.

After another pause, she looks up with a change of expression. "Yes, Corporal," she says with a reserved smile and continues, "let me retrieve a few things. I'll be right back." Clara walks toward the stairs.

"Wait," I say in a soft voice. "Do come back though."

"Of course," she says with an impersonal voice. And off she goes up the dirt stairs.

I stand motionless on the stone floor of the cave looking at the lifeless servant bot in front of me. So much change. Again! But, I feel like this time it wasn't my actions that caused things to change. It was Clara's.

Breathe in. Breathe out.

Walking over to the opening of the cave, I peer out over the desert land burning in the midday sun. A green weed swings into my leg and I grab a green mass to chew on. Its stringy meat is far worse than I remember. I've gotten so used to the food Clara brings.

A few more minutes pass until I hear footsteps from atop the cave. Clara comes down the stairs with a backpack on her shoulders and another for me.

"If we're to do this, we're to do this right," she says, her prideful eyes lighting up as hers meet mine. That smirk on her face shows her acceptance of where we left our last conversation.

"You got it," I say as I grab the backpack and swing it over my shoulders, its weight surprising me.

Clara quickly dismantles the plug-in system and shoves it in her backpack.

"How long are you planning on us exploring?" I say in hesitation to her packing the system.

"Better safe than sorry, hmm?" Clara replies without looking up and fastening her backpack straps.

I turn to look past the door into the corridor and as I was about to ask for a flashlight, Clara's hand lights up and illuminates the corridor of crumbling concrete supported by titanium beams.

Staring into the unknown of the cave reminds me of how my past life is growing distant and less familiar with each new venture. I suddenly remember Clara's repetitive messages in my "previous life" before the cave and I feel a ping of excitement from their relevance.

"Follow no one," I say aloud with a smile of encouragement to myself, knowing Clara would look over.

"And leave no path untaken," Clara quickly replies as she looks over, her smile bigger than mine. Quotes of wisdom must be her forte too then. I thought it was just idioms.

Clara steps first into the corridor, her hand-light leading the way. I follow after, leaving the door behind with the backpack on my shoulders getting heavier by the second.

The crumbling walls of concrete and the narrow passageway make my heart rate rise. Our feet echo in the stale air, this thin air. I turn around to see the light from the open door, shrinking in the distance. How long is this corridor?

The dust makes me cough a bit as we continue walking, my breath becoming shallow.

"How far did you make it down earlier?" I ask Clara.

"Not too much farther than this."

A few more minutes pass. Light from the door behind us isn't visible anymore—nothing but a speck in the distance. In front of us, her hand-light projects about ten feet. Past that is an endless, straight tunnel of darkness. Everything begins to feel repetitive—like we are caught in a bad dream.

"How long do you think this tunnel is?" I ask as I cough from the thin oxygen.

"It's hard to tell. My sensors are weak under so much ground, but I want to say many hundreds of more feet at least."

"Hundreds!" I say in shock, making me cough again.

"Morris, open your backpack. You can't breathe because of the lack of oxygen." Clara had stopped to wait for me to follow through with her request.

My breathing had become so shallow from this thin air, I can barely reply with a grunt.

Opening the backpack reveals enough food and water for days packed around what appears to be an old, uncomfortable-looking oxygen mask.

"Put it on, then. Beggars can't be choosers, eh?" Clara says sarcastically.

With no energy to reply, I quickly strap it around my head and take a big breath.

"You really don't think things through too much. Luckily, you have me," Clara says with pride as she turns and continues down the corridor.

"Ok, but really… how long do you think this tunnel is?" My muffled voice comes out through the oxygen mask.

"I don't know. I put a closed sign up on the shop, so…" she says without turning around, walking at a steady speed. "It's not like you have any plans or anything, hmm?"

Sarcasm again. Even in a creepy dark tunnel where oxygen levels are enough to cause some serious issues for me, she still manages a sarcastic tone. She knows I had a plan, but with these tunnels appearing as if from no where, my plans are logically and voluntarily postponed (at least until I figure out if these tunnels could be an added resource to me). She must *know* this.

And now Clara is walking again—no need to wait for my calculated response to her attitude.

"Lead on, oh masterful adventurer," I mumble loudly as I follow after her again, the darkness behind me giving me no choice. All I hear in response is a belittling grunt of acknowledgement. "She's just so delightful," I tell myself sarcastically, but Clara hears me and turns. Her pace is unchanging as she stares me down with a hint of charm.

"Did you say something?" she asks. I raise my hands in surprise and look at her as though I don't know what she's referring to— but she sees through my passive aggressiveness, smirks at me, and looks forward again.

Time passes.

With nothing much to look at up ahead while we continue to walk, nothing except darkness and Clara's hand-light, I start examining the walls.

"Looks like something was attached to the walls at one point. There're like indents or something," I think aloud.

"Probably light fixtures of some sort used to line these tunnels. Hard to say, this tunnel looks hundreds, if not thousands, of years old," Clara replies, continuing her pace.

"How do you know that?"

"I don't. There's no record of this tunnel system in the public records, so… like I said, hard to say."

She seems uninterested in this conversation, as though she had already thought this through. Her legs move constantly. Light footsteps echo, almost colliding with the echoes of my own feet. The consistent rhythm starts bothering me and I realize I had been staring at Clara this whole time.

Shaking my head, trying not to dwell on how she and I are alone with unsolved tension, I try to distract myself. But with possibilities of our "situation," I start thinking. Rejecting her would lead her away, but leading her on would be unfair, too. But her help is necessary at this point. For example, I breathe easy because of her and this oxygen mask! It's a hard decision, but I'm in a tough spot.

"Clara…" I say softly in preparation for a difficult conversation.

"Wait, I think I see the end…" Clara rushes forward a bit with a few fast footsteps, not catching my intent for discussion.

The light from her hand-light begins to widen into a larger space and we get closer to a room larger than my cave. This discovery makes us stop. Corridors upon corridors—about six of them leading out of this circular room, all looking the same, all evenly spread out in this symmetric space. The weak concrete walls supported by titanium beams make up the walls and archways. We walk forward a bit but pause, dust falling on us as our feet interrupt the still, stale air.

"Whoa," I mumble under my mask.

"This ancient system of passageways goes further than we thought," Clara says as she slowly turns to look at all the entrances to other unknown places. Her hand-light causes the shadows to shift as she circles.

"How old do you think this place is?" I ask her.

"Well, as I said, my connection to the public records is weak this far down, but earlier I didn't find any indication the USB knows about this place."

"If the government doesn't know, then these corridors could have been built thousands of years ago before they even existed!" My voice echoes in the large space and down each corridor.

Clara walks close to one of the walls and examines the vertical dust, her flashlight revealing distinct layers. I walk closer, take a big breath, lift my mask and blow at the wall.

The dust becomes so thick we have to fan it out of our vision, but as it clears, we begin to see an old carving on the wall. It appears to be a simplistic design of a four-legged octopus with no head. Or maybe it's more like a spinning fan with four blades.

"What kind of symbol is this?" I ask slowly.

"I wish I could look it up, but I have no connection down here," Clara says as her woven nylon fingers slide over the carving. "I've taken a mental picture to look up later, but for now," she turns around, "which corridor do we choose?"

I take a last look at the strange symbol and turn. All of the corridor look exactly the same, offering no inspiration or help in deciding which to take. Wait a second, which did we come from? Clara looks at me and notices my confusion.

"We came from that one," she says arrogantly as she points to the one on the right.

"Hmm, I knew that," I reply with confidence but she doesn't believe me. I turn back to the corridors. "Well, I'd say whichever is shortest. But there's no way of knowing which is shorter, so..."

Clara rolls her eyes and proceeds to the closest corridor, claps, and listens to the echo, examining the travel distance. Then goes to the next and does the same. After five times, she turns back to me.

"Looks like this one is the shortest passage," she reports, gesturing to the one to the left of the corridor we came from.

"Wow, smart bot," I say sarcastically through my mask.

"Hey. I'm not a bot anymore, don't call me that." Her eyes flare at me, annoyed at my name calling.

"Yes, well. Lead the way then," I gesture to the corridor she pointed out. Her eyes roll again and she sighs, showing her distaste in my comment.

"Ugh. If only I could pass the torch," she complains as her hand illuminates the shorter passage she chose. She looks unamused.

"What? What does that even mean," I say quickly, peeved at yet another idiom I don't understand.

"Oh, you know. Burning wood in hand, lighting the way. The mark of a true leader." She turns to me with a grin.

"How do you know so many idioms, anyway?" I say as I catch up to her down the corridor.

"Years without direction, working for a deadbeat shop left me with a lot of time. I ended up researching about a lot of random things."

"Hmm, ok. Apart from outdated idioms, what else did you research?" I ask to continue the conversation.

This corridor is just as dark and boring as the last, as far as I can tell. Without my epichip or a clock, I can only guess it took about twenty to thirty minutes down the last one. Might as well waste some time with idle chat.

"Alright. Did you know that humans have a biomagnetic field?" she says in a smart voice.

"Yes, I did. But did you know old religions named it the 'aura?'"

"Obviously. You can't win this fight, I have more storage in here." Clara taps her head. "Far more than you do."

Our footsteps are in synch again and I quickly step out of rhythm, again trying not to stare at Clara too much. Unfortunately, she's the only interesting thing to look at in this ancient and repetitive place.

"Ok, so what else did you learn?" I ask her while looking at her feet in front of me. My voice is annoyingly muffled by this old oxygen mask.

"Did you know that the human heart beats forty million times a year? That you have 642 skeletal muscles? That it takes more muscles for a human to smile than to frown?" She asks these nearly rhetorical questions with pride.

I pause and grunt in response, not really knowing what to say. Obviously, she's right. It's a battle I can't win. Our footsteps sync again, but I step slightly off to break the rhythm.

"Why do you know so much about humans?" I ask her.

Clara takes a second and then says, "Because I prepared. Wanted you to feel dumb knowing that you know less about your own body than I do."

Accepting my defeat I check my epichip, well, my scarred wrist.

Very rarely does that habit come back, but it's annoying every time.

"Clara, what's the time?"

"I thought you said you loved the freedom without time?" she says poking fun at me. I must have shared that during one of our conversations in the past week.

"Yes. I do… but, I'm just wondering."

"Well, to save you from breaking your own oath, let's just say it's the afternoon. Sun is still out for many hours."

I ignore her tone as I realize the changing sunset times. As we continue our expedition, the thought of Sun Season coming up makes me sick. And having the sun go down later in the day is just evidence of Sun Season. I always hated it growing up.

Our trek continues for another few minutes, the corridor purely straight with no turns, no change in elevation. Just straight. Boring as can be. I play with the rhythm between our footsteps, wondering if Clara would notice, but she never does. She is too determined to reach the end.

"Clara, I thought you said this one was the shortest…"

"I did. I did say that."

"It doesn't feel short," I complain to her as our feet fall out of sync again.

"But it's shorter than the others."

My stomach rumbles and leads me to remember the food in my backpack. As we walk, I take off the backpack and awkwardly try to grab something, anything. I grab wrapped cucumber bread and pull it out, put the backpack on, and begin to unwrap it.

"How are you going to eat when you need to breathe?" Clara says mockingly without turning around.

Dammit. My oxygen mask.

"You humans. So limited by your body."

"Oh, be quiet," I say through my mask.

Desperate for food, I lift my oxygen mask to test out the thin air. I cough at the lack of oxygen and quickly strap the mask back on. Such disappointment for my stomach. I hold the bread in my hand, slightly unwrapped, as I walk reluctantly behind Clara.

"Wait…" she speeds up. The light from her hand shows an end to the corridor.

Clara pushes on a rusty door held together by old titanium. With another budge, she manages to open it slightly. Then she pushes once more to swing it wide open to what appears to be another cave.

Sunlight comes down on our path and we find ourselves in another cave, but this one doesn't have a cliff on one side. Clara starts walking around as I do the same, noticing similar weeds from my own cave. Weeds that are so familiar to me now.

The view out of the cave is similar too, but the desert land is far more flat than my cave at home. We make our way outside, to the top of the cave, in the hot sun. From the looks of it, we had reached the other side of the lake. Buildings are a few hundred feet from where we stand atop the cave.

The midday sun begins burning my skin so I retreat to the shadows of this new cave, leaving Clara to examine the area around it.

After stepping foot in the cave, I look around and see fewer water droplets than my cave. And fewer weeds as well. Being so far out of normalcy, I begin feeling strange and lost. Especially now that I'm standing in so many unknowns, both physically and mentally. But I shake my head and go to take a bite of the cucumber bread to relieve my mind. And my stomach.

Clara joins me in the cave as I take off the oxygen mask.

"Well. Interesting," she says in a funny voice and sits down to pull out her connected solar panel. You rarely see humanoids recharge in public.

"Um… what are you doing? Do you want some privacy?" I ask awkwardly while shielding my view. Clara laughs.

"You need more humanoid friends," she says as she chuckles again.

"I'm just… I haven't seen many recharge in the open."

"That's because you humans work ten hours a day," she says.

"Like we have a choice," I say defensively.

"Hmm, sorry."

I give her a quick look of forgiveness and sit close to her, but not next to her. Don't want to lead her on too much. I take another bite of the bread.

"I know the USB isn't exactly looking after the human race like they always promise they do, but you should know that I always vote in favor of human rights."

"Thanks," my serious tone lighter than expected. "A government comprised of 'United Sentient Beings'… yeah, right. We're more enslaved than 'united.'"

"I know," she says with sincere sympathy. "But to be honest, I'm… kind of jealous of humans."

I chuckle, feeling almost offended. "What's so great about our low-class position in life? Is it the low-paying jobs? Or the lack of job options… 'cause it's not as great as you might think."

"No, no. Those things are obviously terrible and something I definitely would fight to change," Clara says in defense. "It's just that… humans experience things for what they are. I once read an old quote by Frank Herbert that explained how life is not a mystery to solve, but 'a reality to experience.' And… I'll never experience life as humans do. I'll only… you know, calculate it."

Her eyes look sad as she finishes explaining. Though we sit in the shadows of the cave, they have a glimmer from the sunlight.

"So, you want to be human, then?" I ask nicely and gently.

"No. I just want to… experience life with the same level of purity."

We stare out of the cave together, both unsure how to continue such a deep conversation. The tragedy of her "supposed" situation feels odd and a little unbelievable, especially in a society where humans are less than humanoids. I mean, at least she isn't a neurobine—they're the worst when it comes to respecting us. Humans: a lowly sentience limited by the physical world. A world that lacks potential.

"So…" I say to break the silence, "what should we do now?"

"Weren't you planning on recruiting a team?" Clara asks, matching my enthusiasm.

"Yes, but I tried and I don't think it will happen. Not without things being more fleshed out." Her face shifts. "Sorry, not fleshed out. More… um, a plan with more substance."

"Yeah, that makes it better." Clara stands up, jokingly being offended. "Like I don't have substance."

"Ok, you know what I mean," I say in defense as I look up at her, still sitting down.

"Hmmhm. We need to test out your virus experiment, right? Back to the home base then?" she asks nonchalantly, referring to the trek back through the corridor.

"Shouldn't we explore this system of corridors more?" I ask.

"As far as I see it, without proof it could help your 'ultimate plan,' it's merely a distraction."

"You're right." I look to the door. "We should definitely continue searching here and there. I have a feeling there's potential in having an escape route prepared."

"Confirmed," she replies shortly, then points to the open door and bows. "Shall we depart, Your Excellence?"

"Fine," I say in disgust as I get to my feet and ignore her strange sense of humor.

I take the last bite of the bread, sip some water, and slip the uncomfortable oxygen mask back on.

"Follow no one," she says sarcastically and then starts down the corridor, turning her hand-light on.

Breathe in. Breathe out.

"Follow no one," I say ironically. And then I follow after her.

CHAPTER 14

The sun is still high in the sky above our cave with the old, beat-up servant bot standing lifelessly beside us. Clara had already set up the plug-in system and was working on a code. A code, or process, that safely pulls the AI cognition package from a virus for an immediate transfer into a physical humanoid shell. For our purposes, this dead-looking servant bot Clara brought as a "gift" will need to work.

"Nearly finished," Clara announces softly.

Wind from the desert below blows across the hundreds of green weeds in this shadowy cave, moving Clara's hair slightly. The brown artificial hair I've begun to notice more. Mainly because I've not seen artificial hair that real before. Purely observational.

"Ok, Clara," I reply, matching her softness.

She stands still next to the desk as she works. I sit in the chair waiting, ready for my part of the plan, finding myself looking at what's around me. Including Clara.

Her cleanly weaved, nylon surface is very rare to see. The detail in the stitching is hardly noticeable and the material looks expensively soft. Its color complements her thin, layered brown hair that's artistically woven buoyantly behind her head. So many appearance upgrades for a lowly repair shop owner. Maybe she really does want to be human? But all these human elements contradict her lack of breathing. Still, I forget she's a humanoid at times. A strange thing to forget.

"Done," Clara opens her eyes, forcing me to stop my observing and make eye contact. "I've coded an extra mutation derived from bits and pieces of the AVC code I hacked. The 'deletion' action should now transfer your target straight into the node in the back of your neck."

"Into the node?" I ask in a bit of disbelief.

"Even the old-school PixelOne nodes have a bit of short-term space or RAM."

"Won't that interfere with my connection? I mean, the node will kind of be in use." Her system seems a little contradictory.

"Once the virus is stored, the node will automatically disconnect you from the Sector-System. So you have to make sure you're ready to switch over by keeping your eyes shut during the process. For safety," Clara explains with confidence.

"Hmm. Ok. And no details missed this time?"

"Nope. And that's straight from the horse's mouth." Her voice is sarcastic, yet tentative with this strange idiom.

"Clara. What does that even mean… do you even know what a horse is?"

She pauses for a second as if internalizing something. Then she regains focus on the conversation and replies, "I do now."

"Ha! That's cheating, you just looked it up."

"It's not cheating! I'm just using the tools available to provide my 'best' answer," she replies with a light attitude and then turns to walk toward the servant bot.

"Whatever you say, Miss Human Droid," I say sarcastically, purposely using the derogatory name from "human-oid."

With her hands on the bot, she turns to give me a playful look of anger, a shy smirk visible in the light of the sun.

"Okay, Mr. Skin and Bones." She turns away from me. "It appears your fishnet is ready," she says, referencing the code and the decommissioned bot. "Time to fish for some virus, hmm?"

"Excellent." I turn toward the plug-in system and grab the node. And then take a big breath.

"Good luck in there. I have your back out here," she says in an encouraging, sweet voice.

I place the node on the back of my neck, close my eyes and feel the slight suction as the node grips. Suddenly, the quiet atmosphere of the cave is replaced by loud city ambience. It's always weird not to begin in a central hub like I've done the past nearly ten years of my life.

My eyes open to the complexly designed buildings with neurobines walking around me, even through me. I quickly summon the map and ensure my location is safe from dark red viruses. Learned a hard lesson last time.

I pinpoint a pink virus just north of my location. Perfect. After planning my route, I shut the map and begin walking, then running. Deep breaths as I run remind me to relax and review the plan, the order of actions. "Identify, close my eyes, and capture," I think to myself.

The muscle memory of "deleting" makes for an uncomfortable thought. I'm afraid my PTSD won't allow for quick decision-making.

Running through the busy streets of neurobines, I start to hear some noise ahead of me. Like a fight. As I near the noise, a glow of red is fighting another neurobine on the ground. Wait, no! It is an AVC member. The taller woman—I recognize her!

She spins, dodging the virus' fist while also getting to her feet. But the virus grabs her ankle and tries to trip her, causing her to grunt loudly in an effort not to fall. The spectacle causes neurobines to crowd in a circle around this lunatic fighting thin air, as far as they know.

A swift kick forces the virus back down on the ground and with a precise lift of the arm, POP. The virus is gone. The AVC woman stands there, panting from the intensity of the fight.

"Hey!" I call out as I approach. She turns around and slowly recognizes me.

"You? What are you doing here? I thought you were stuck in PRP..." she says through big breaths while checking her epichip.

"I left the AVC out of choice," I reply and her eyes glance at me in surprise. "Listen, I never got your name."

Standing in front of her reminds me how tall she is with her slender frame and short hair.

"Well, it's good to see you too, especially in the midst of chaos," she says with a stretch of her arms. "My name is Michele. Family number 3684. And yours?"

"Morris, Morris 1045," I say as she pulls out her map and scans for red dots. "I'm recruiting people for a project, well, a mission to change things. To alter the priorities of this AI controlled society—I could really use your help."

Michele's quota number pops out in front of her and reads: "Michele 3684—19/20."

"Wow—well it's nice to officially meet you. I'm intrigued, but don't have much extra time. Are you paying?" she asks as her quota disappears and she makes full eye contact with me.

"I offer freedom from the AVC and society as we know it. There'll be a lot of action and a priceless outcome. My team is growing, but we can only continue with more capable people. Will you join us?" I ask with the proper style of a leader's voice.

"Sounds heroic. Message me and send me more details. For now, I have a quota to finish before the end of the day." Michele turns to leave, but says behind her shoulder, "Thanks for the offer. Let's meet up later."

"Okay," I say with a grin of excitement. She might join! I could really use her help and her action-oriented character.

Suddenly, not too far away, Michele turns toward a pink neurobine. Oh! A virus to capture!

"Wait! That one is mine!" I run forward to stop her from deleting, but her arm begins lifting as she turns to notice me.

Without debate, I also lift my arm and close my eyes. The familiar warm feeling quickly flows down my arm and I hear a POP. This time a lighter pitch, different than I'm used to hearing.

"Morris? Morris!" Clara's voice rings.

I open my eyes to the cave wall, the door to the right still slightly ajar. Scanning my surroundings I reassure myself I'm back in reality. Human-reality.

"You captured one I think!" Clara shouts excitedly.

My fingers feel around for the node on the back of my neck. I pop it off and look at the device for some clue, but nothing shows evidence of success.

"I think I did, yeah, but how do we know?"

"Only one way to find out..." Clara gestures for the node. I place it in her hand and she walks toward the decommissioned servant bot.

She places the node on the back of the dead bot's head and stands back.

We stare for a few seconds. Waiting to see if it connects and accepts the captured code that's kept within the node. Sure enough, the bot's eyes slowly begin lighting up.

Although the bot is standing with one side brighter from the sun-side of the cave, power can be seen warming up within the eyes. Clicks and small engines begin to turn heavily, then soften until it's barely noticeable.

Suddenly the cheap eyes of the bot open widely and its voice rings out.

"Time! My time is now and my sacrifice is offered! My time has come to sleep!" says the frail voice in the cheap vocal box of the servant bot. The intensity is crackling, pushing the limitations of its voice box (or speakers in this case).

Clara rushes over in front of the bot. "Shh! Shh! You're ok— you're alive, you're fine!"

The bot's eyes continue to scan the cave frantically as if trying to escape, but the body doesn't move. Nothing but the eyes move.

"Why isn't it moving, Clara?" I ask, worried it might attack us.

"I disabled everything except the eyes and the vocal speaker. Figured viruses are dangerous whether they're in the Sector-System or not. Especially after one attacked you the other day," she replies while examining the eyes of the virus bot. She does truly think of every detail.

"It appears aggressive still," she continues. "What did you hope to accomplish again? Why bring a virus to human-reality... for all we know, it might not be able to process what 'reality' it's in," Clara asks me as the bot repeats the same words more slowly and quietly.

"Well, I can't help but relive my time with the AVC. And each moment, each person, has been burned in my memory," I explain, feeling the weight of these words as I finally say them out loud. "But there's something I can't let go of... something odd. Just before I 'deleted' each virus, they would always say: 'My time has come to sleep.' It haunts me, their obsession with time and their need to sleep."

Explaining my observations has Clara paying close attention, completely intrigued, yet rather concerned. As if it concerns her, too. I continue,

"Neurobines can be thousands of years old, living in a world of fake time. A manufactured sense of elapsed moments, where in actuality they're stuck in a standstill. As evolving artificial intelligence, their cognition must wrestle with the fact they are growing somewhat organically within a counterfeit sense of time. Allowing them to feel what it's like to be in real 'time' may cure their virus symptoms," I explain as Clara's expression stays the same. "At least, it's my theory."

She continues to stay silent, then she stares at the virus, now repeating the same dialogue quietly over and over. Looking back at me, she calculates a reply but turns back to the humanoid virus. And then stands back to reexamine.

"Humanoids and neurobines ARE obsessed with time. It's the last element of existence we can't manipulate in human-reality," she says aloud while staring at the crazed, unmoving virus.

"Exactly. Water, virtual space, AI manufacturing, humans... the

USB have successfully gained control over everything. They can even create worlds within worlds in the Sector-System, but they can't control time."

Clara looks at me, her eyes wide with realization.

"You must be right. Humanoids always want to escape to the Sector-System, a time-controlled existence. But humans are forever subject to time. Subject to change. Subject to the rules of reality."

She turns her gaze toward the virus again in disbelief, stepping toward it, pondering, then continues.

"After thousands of years living in the Sector-System, neurobines must lose grip of their virtual reality. It must mean the Sector-System is an unstable form of existence. This is a breakthrough! How has no one thought about this?" Clara turns to me looking for answers.

"Over the course of many years, I've read a few ancient novels forgotten about over time. *A Brief History of Everything, Meditations, Fragments*, all these authors were philosophers, something we don't have in society anymore. Humans were distracted by surviving and escaping and migrating to the poles, but with AI taking over, priorities have changed."

I had begun to pace back and forth as I explain my own philosophies, my hands gesturing to emphasize my arguments.

"Humans are distracted by the USB's promise for something greater, something tangible and only supplied through proper obedience to the system, presented through screens you can touch. Greed is human nature and is manipulated by the calculating AI that runs our society. So humans don't look past what they can't have and AI focuses on escaping to an unhealthy world of false time, leaving us stuck."

Turning to Clara, I emphasize my theory. "We're limited by human short-sightedness and sentient denial. Time cannot be reconstructed and reality, the physical world, is our future."

My feet stop as I look outward to the desert, finally growing dim in the twilight. Clara stays silent, but walks up next to me, sharing in my contemplative stare. A few moments pass without a single word.

"This is your path, your life's path," she says in a quiet voice.

"What… how do you mean?"

"Your life path is one. You have to change society's focus, change their priorities," Clara says without hesitation.

"Clara, I don't want to talk numbers right now."

She turns to me. "You have the potential to alter perception, to improve the existence of humans, humanoids, neurobines, everyone! If you don't act upon this potential, you're doing an injustice to the world. You have a life path capable of true change."

I take a big breath and scoff at myself, "'life path,' hmm?"

The life purpose I had convinced myself of, comparing myself to "firewood" and growing a society anew, is obviously tempting to continue believing in. But deep down, I'm unsure what to call these thoughts—philosophy or insanity?

Without replying, I walk to the humanoid virus (which is still quietly speaking the same riddles) and observe. Realizing this virus may never come out of this catatonic state, I move it to the side of the cave in frustration and lay it on the floor without much grace. But the eyes, its now unmoving, backlit eyes put me on edge.

"My experiment is missing something, something crucial. And to tell you the truth, I'm not sure there's a solution now," I say throwing my hands up and walking away from the humanoid virus.

"Morris, there's so much potential here. In this situation. In you. Can't you see it?" Clara had been looking at me this whole time. I turn toward her without making eye contact, trying not to rely on her hope.

"I'm a divorced, homeless outlaw with grandiose fantasies, Clara. The only potential I have is being thrown into the PRP. Numbers or no numbers, this pathetic situation I find myself in is no different than my previous predicament in the AVC—perhaps worse." My statement causes heaviness on my shoulders, forcing me to look down. Intense hopelessness weighs on me in reaction to my failed experiment.

Placing a virus in human-reality wasn't the cure. It means "time" isn't the only issue—it must be far more complicated than I originally thought.

My head sinks into my hands and my thoughts thin, leaving nothing but guilt in chasing a dead end until her feet come close to mine. I look up as she grabs my hands.

"I believe in you, Morris. Because you're YOU. Situations change, but your potential won't." Her voice is calm and collected. "Solutions might not present themselves at first, but I believe you WILL figure this out and I will always support you. And if you let me," she leans forward, "I'll be here every step of the way."

And before I realize it, she kisses me on the cheek.

And without thinking, I kiss her back.

CHAPTER 15

Shadows dance on the walls of the cave as the auroras play about the sky. The nightly showcase of purples and blues is brighter on the outskirts of town. It always throws me off. I've grown accustomed to light pollution in the city, often taking away from the vivid spectacle. And though I've grown up with them all my life, being outside of town makes me feel as though every night I'm watching the auroras for the first time.

Clara and I lie on the stone of the cave next to each other, looking out among the lights in the sky as they zig-zag in ever-changing lines across our view. The catatonic bot had been quiet for a while now, allowing us to spend time together without worry of the outside world.

Together we lie as two sentient beings enjoying each other's company, in a state of simple happiness.

Human and humanoid relationships are not necessarily forbidden, but they're very frowned upon and are rarely seen in public (if ever). The government might have legalized relationships between humans and humanoids hundreds of years ago, but the general population does NOT accept it.

According to society, humans have less worth than humanoids. Humans eventually expire, but humanoids can be continually upgraded. So an intersentient relationship is considered a shameful betrayal for both communities—loving the other party to such a degree is grossly forbidden, because "we'll never be the same" and thus, should never "love" in the same way.

As we watch the dancing lights filling the sky, I hold her hand and feel more close to her than I could've imagined. But intense social norms prevent me from enjoying this moment fully. And the worry makes me hesitate on how to deal with "us."

Breathe in. Breathe out.

I am no longer a part of society. I needn't worry. AND I will change society, too. So whether I'm in an intersentient relationship or not, I no longer fall into "categories" and "labels" created by society. I am to grow apart from all that is wrong.

I squeeze her hand in recognition of my decisions and my acceptance of them and breathe once more.

Breathe in. Breathe out.

"Morris," her voice sweet and close to my ear. I turn my head.

"What's bothering you?" she asks quietly and slowly. Unable to think fast enough, I look away. That voice was so sweet and welcoming. It's hard not to answer without stirring emotions.

The virus bot behind us mumbles loudly but then falls silent again.

"I'm just… planning," I say as I turn and give a half-real smile. Her eyes begin examining mine. And then she comes closer, resting her head on my chest with her arm around me.

Quietness fills the cave again. Only distant crackles from the auroras break the silence occasionally, in short bursts. Clara's hand begins moving up and down, lightly upon my shirt.

"I should get home. It's late," she says softly.

"Only if you want to…" I reply, matching her softness.

"Do you want me to stay? Your lovely cave does have some charm with the auroras so bright," she says with the familiar hint of sarcasm. I chuckle, causing her head to bounce slightly.

"To be honest, I'm still worried about your stalker motives."

"Morris, I thought we moved past this," she replies in her sweet voice, but my silence causes her to sit up and continue. "Okay," she says awkwardly while looking away, "I've never had feelings for someone. Obviously, I didn't control myself or approach you about my own feelings for you in the most... correct way, but know it was out of inexperience." She looks at me, "how else can I prove to you my 'sanity,' hmm?"

I chuckle and smile. Nothing else has led me to distrust her in any other way, so I'll just accept her quirky personality flaws. Plus, I don't know what I would do without her.

"Well, staying here is a good first step."

Not being alone through the night is too tempting an idea. Having her here, having her presence, is worth putting up with her possible flaws. And I'm not perfect either.

"Hmm," she hums in satisfaction. And she lies down again, then wiggles to find herself a comfortable position in my arm. "You're welcome to sleep then. I'll be here researching."

The soft nylon of her face invites a slow touch on her cheek. Caressing her skin feels nearly human with its soft material. Funny. My acceptance of her happened more naturally than I thought, though bittersweet images of Yuki still pop up in my memory.

I feel sad that I'm moving on, but happy I'm letting go. Happy I'm able to let go.

"I wasn't sure if you'd like me back... my first impression wasn't very trustworthy, I know. But I hope you know that I am here for you, for as long as you'll have me," Clara whispers, running her hand up and down my chest as I stare at the lights in the sky. I hesitate at her display of emotional vulnerability. She's always so forward.

"Why do you like me so much… is it truly me you like? Or are you just attracted to the numbers?" I ask, making the conversation more serious, steering away from emotions.

"I like you because you're different. Obviously, numerology was the reason I was taken by you, but it's you that keeps me here. Not every human keeps my interest, you know…" Clara replies in lightheartedness.

"I'm serious, Clara. I spent years with my ex-wife and was more in love with her than I ever thought I could be, but she left me because she found someone else. The last few months I've been an emotional wreck, so pardon my cautious attitude, but… I've learned how much is at stake when falling in love." I hesitate and shake my head.

"Not that we're falling in love or anything," I quickly correct myself.

Clara giggles and takes my hand as she sits up to look at me. The purple of the auroras dance about the nylon of her face, the soft nylon I've grown to like so much.

"Did she leave you because you talk too much?" Clara jokes, but I give her a look of disapproval.

"Ok, too soon," she says quickly. "In reality," she looks down, "I've never been with a human. Or a humanoid. My interests have led me to research, to program or code, to build and repair. I've never had an interest in sharing my time with another. My curiosity hasn't been strong enough." With a small pause, she makes eye contact with me.

"You've saved me from a life of hopeless monotony, of endless… searching." Another pause draws my attention and I can't look away—a sadness grows within her eyes.

"My original owner didn't leave me, he… died in my arms. I remember his eyes gazing up at me as I held him, his breathing difficult as he fought with his lung cancer. Tears fell from his eyes as his heart slowed, as he gasped for air. My hands… my hands could do nothing as I pleaded for him to be okay. Paramedics were on their way, but… I could feel his body go limp, his… his eyes losing their light. And his breath, slowing."

Tears were forming in her eyes as she spoke.

"But before he passed, he told me one thing. 'Live with purpose,' he said. 'Live with purpose.' At the time I thought nothing of it, my mind occupied with the guilt, from my inability to cry with him as he felt death approaching. His lonely tears fell on the metal of my servant bot exterior, unaccompanied by my own tears because of the limitations of my damned electronic eyes at the time."

A tear falls from her sweet eyes. My heart pumps, feeling her intense emotion.

"But as he lay lifeless in my arms just before the humanoid paramedics took him from me without thinking twice, I realized something. As I gained self-sufficiency at that moment, I realized…," Clara says, looking into my eyes.

"Humans can die. Humanoids can't. We… we have backups upon backups, but humans experience true change." Her voice shakes under the weight of her words. "Humans experience… they LIVE with true purpose. And I… I can't."

She broke down.

Tears fall from her upgraded, artificial eyes as she turns away to lie on the ground. In response, I sit up and lean over her, petting her cheek to calm her down.

"You… you have been my purpose for years because of stupid numbers," she says with a sorrow in her voice I've not heard in a humanoid before. "I followed your life because of these numbers. These numbers that promised a way out from my purposeless life. But they led me to you… Numbers led me to my purpose in helping you, in knowing you, in… experiencing you." She strokes my cheek as her tears slow, her face illuminated by the dancing purple in the sky.

"I follow no one, but you," she says sweetly, with an air of certainty, "you I will follow."

Shocked by all this emotion, I pause for a split second—my eyes watery in reaction to the purity of her sadness, of her devotion in finding purpose. I continue to comfort her and ease the pain, to maybe calm her worries.

"Oh, oh… no, don't cry, Clara," I say, desperate to console her.

What am I supposed to feel? This is a lot of devotion she is expressing toward me. My mind screams caution, but my heart pleads with me to reassure her that I'm here. Here to stay. To comfort her and give her purpose. As she gives me… purpose.

"You have been so nice to me and so… life-saving. I don't know what I would do without you. Probably die from weed poisoning, huh?" I laugh as she laughs through slow tears. The sight of her smile warms my heart.

"I would have nothing without you," I truthfully say, but she turns in disbelief.

"I'm serious! You've saved me from a life of… well, inevitable failure." I comb my hand through her hair and hold her head. "You gave me food, gave me water. You gave me hope. And I'm indebted to you and your... crazy numbers." I chuckle again, this time through my own tears.

My emotion rises as I speak, remembering the disappointment of my previous life and the hopelessness I felt my first day in this cave. A sense of utter loss fueled by personal failure, to where I had originally compared myself to dirt, not so different from the dust in the cave.

A realization expanded within me and I begin to let go of my fear.

Clara's eyes look desperate for acceptance and after having experienced so much undeserved pain, my sympathy grows. A tear falls as I imagine the life she led after her owner died. What an overwhelming feeling she must have felt from realizing how inhuman and indifferent she was to the man who died in her arms. The man who raised her from her AI beginnings.

Thoughts swirl in my head until suddenly they stop and time begins to slow. Our eyes look deep within each other's with the parade of lights in the night sky above us.

"Clara," I rest my hand on her cheek. "You give ME purpose."

She caves, absorbing my words of acceptance with a smile of bliss as I lean in to kiss her.

And to my heart's relief, she kisses me back.

"Brought your favorite," Clara says as I wake up to her footsteps.

I sit up and rub my eyes. Looking at her, I notice her offer of banana bread and smile up at her.

"Thank you so much," I say in happiness as I lean in for a kiss. She gives me a smirk and accepts the gesture with a quick peck on the lips. A smile grows on my face, unfamiliar after so many months away from Yuki.

Morning sun creeps into the opening of the cave as Clara examines the virus bot. I take a bite of the bread and drink some of the water she also gave me. My backpack to the side of the cave seems full and I turn toward Clara.

"I'm curious how an old repair shop can allow you to afford so much food."

Without turning toward me, still looking over the catatonic bot, she replies over her shoulder.

"Well, I was the closest thing my owner had to family. Naturally, I inherited his finances. And of course his shop."

"But can't you only list humans and humanoids on your will? You were a servant bot at the time…" I ask in curiosity.

"He wrote that I would inherit everything when I found self-sufficiency. Can we change the subject?"

"Oh, yes, of course. Sorry," I say quickly after she looked at me with impatience.

The servant bot lies almost lifeless as it had been since yesterday. Light shows behind its eyes, but without much observation, it is hard to tell it apart from junk thrown off to the side. The metal is in poor condition—definitely found in the trash or something.

"Clara, I was thinking..." I ask. She gives me her attention and walks closer.

"I don't even know your full name," I say as I wrap my arms around her. The sun is warm on our feet as we stand close to the edge of the cave, the desert land beneath us.

"In time, Morris," she replies as she kisses me and sweetly observes my reaction.

"Oh, so there's a future between us?"

She giggles and breaks away, walking toward the humanoid.

"So I researched the symbol we saw yesterday," Clara says, changing the subject.

"Oh yeah? Anything interesting?"

"It's actually a fairly old symbol, known as the 'hooked cross' or more commonly, the 'swastika.' Archived archeological findings show this symbol to be as old as the Indus Valley Civilization, which is also where the 'yoga' practice comes from. The swastika generally symbolizes divinity and spirituality in ancient human ideologies including the Indian, Chinese, Mongolian, and Siberian religions."

"Wow, don't really remember all those names being taught in school. But... how far back does this symbol date?" I ask in awe.

"Well, it's been around since around 3,000 BCE so... pretty far back, you could say!" Clara says sarcastically. I react by looking out to the desert in thought.

"That's… amazing. Could this mean we've found 10,000-year-old remains of an ancient city?" My voice is full of excited hope.

"Haha, no. This continent was full of ice two miles thick, remember! That would be impossible. It must have been built more recently, when the ice melted."

"So," I pause for a second, "there's no telling who this symbol belongs to? Like, who might have built these tunnels?"

"No, not really. Unless we do more exploring." Clara gestures toward the now-closed door. "This four-armed, hooked cross is associated with the Greeks, Hindus, Buddhists, and Germans. There is also evidence of its use in Christian catacombs and even Pythagoras used it as a symbol linking heaven and Earth."

"Hmm," I grunt in disbelief, "this all sounds very obscure. Tell me, in general, is it a good or a bad symbol?"

"As far as I can tell, the swastika symbolizes more good than bad when looking at the entire historical record. But one extremist group used the symbol to represent racism and authoritarian views—a group called the Nazi party who were responsible for the largest genocide in ancient history. But they were the ONLY group like this."

I turn back toward her, mulling over all this information.

"How do these Nazis compare to the Neo-Tamerlanes of the fifty-ninth century?" I ask, trying to grasp the context of things.

"Nazis were worse, far worse. Multiple millions more in death count."

"Hmm. Not sure how to feel about this symbol then." In reaction to all this information, I was beginning to pace back and forth a bit. "What do you think we might find down there?"

"Well, by the looks of it," she replies, "everything has rotted away. Nothing should be left standing apart from titanium and that crumbling concrete composite. Especially when considering the possible age of the symbol we found."

We stand there thinking, pondering about the vagueness of this symbol.

"Well, nothing to fret over. Onwards and upwards…" she says, proud to have remembered another idiom to break up the tension in the air. She turns to the bot and throws a rope around it.

"What are you doing now?" I ask.

"I'm assuming you want to explore? Can't go taking chances with this one. If it wakes up, the virus' ability to hack could disable the limb-lock I have in place," she explains naturally while she continues to knot up the rope around the bot.

It's always so hard to outsmart humanoids. So calculated, smart, and difficult to argue with due to their preparedness for each outcome of every choice or option.

"Oh, before I forget, can you send a message to someone?" I ask her as she finishes up.

"Sure—but don't think I'm a servant bot or anything. Not even for you," she replies sarcastically.

"Mmhmm," I hum as I smile a bit. "Could you, Miss Humanoid, contact Michele 3684? Have the message say, 'I need your help. Whenever you can, report to this location without being seen,' and then attach our…"

"…location, got it," Clara interrupts me with a look of concern. "Morris, are you sure you want to bring more people in on this?

Can you trust them?"

"Well, if I'm a leader like you say, then I need people to lead. Michele is an action-oriented member from the AVC and could prove useful. We can offer strategy and she could offer action," I reply with a serious tone. "We need a team if we're to change society, right?"

"We need to change humanoids and neurobines," she says, copying my tone. "Society will follow. As far as strategy goes, humans, unfortunately, don't have much pull when it comes to government philosophies. But if we cure these viruses ourselves," she gestures to the motionless humanoid, "not only could we build a team, we could also have evidence that the Sector-System is uninhabitable."

Again, always so hard to argue with.

"Then why have humans involved at all? Why am I even here?" I ask passive aggressively.

"Hey, don't be mad at me! I'm not responsible for the political climate," she says, her voice fast to reply. "And don't take things so personally. Your creative problem solving is crucial to this plan of yours. You know that I know that. And it's YOUR plan to begin with—you're a spiritual catalyst according to your Master Number 11."

"Okay, there go the numbers again." I turn away with my hand scratching my head. "We can talk about this down the corridor," I motion toward the closed door. "I can see now my message to Michele won't be sent, might as well move on."

Clara looks insulted by my shortness, but walks over and plies open the old door. I grab my backpack, heavier than before, pull out the oxygen mask in preparation as she angrily packs the plug-in system in her own backpack. We then start our long walk into the dark abyss of the old tunnel system made by some group of swastika fanatics. Well, who knows. Everything is just irritating me.

Our feet echo in the emptiness as her hand-light shows the way. The guilt from our previous conversation grows as I think over my responses. Silence worsens the tension between us as I feel the urge to say something.

I feel silly having been affected by petty worries of self-worth, obviously spawned from societal differences, but still.

The oxygen in the corridor begins to thin. I take a big breath to speak and apologize before having to put the oxygen mask on.

"Clara, I'm sorry about my... reaction earlier. It was unnecessary," I say with the most genuine voice I can summon. She stays silent while walking ahead of me, leading the way. Her face is a mystery as I decipher her mood by her walk.

"I value your opinion and feel... very 'human' to have jumped to conclusions. I know you were just trying to think things through with me, but I took my anger toward society out on you. And I'm sorry."

Our feet fall in sync as we continue to walk in silence. But then she stops and turns toward me, her hand-light pointed up, illuminating the space around us with darkness lingering on either side.

"To answer your question earlier, you're here because you took action. And I'm only here because of it. So there's your 'value' right there. My ability to calculate and plan, research and code, might be more useful because I'm nonhuman, but it doesn't help me launch a revolution or anything. So why do you always have to use MY skills against me? I don't do that to you, do I?" Her voice was stern and objective, nearly cold.

"Humanoids were made in YOUR image. Thousands of years ago, AI was created by humans, to help humans, and though we gained control we still look like humans. Ever thought about why? We might have taken over with 'logic and reliability,' but we'll never be human, no matter how similar we look. And it's frustrating, to all of us nonhumans!"

She pauses to observe my reaction as her voice echoes in the corridor, and then she continues, "But can't you tell I'M jealous of YOU? If I'm artificial, so are my thoughts, my feelings, my desires and my... existence. So if you really want 'us' to continue, then you better be okay with dating a glorified calculator," she bitterly says and attempts to turn back, but I stop her by grabbing her arm.

"Hey, hey, stop that." I look in her eyes though she avoids it. "You're more real to me than any human and I've never thought of YOU as less than me. You are so much more to me than a 'glorified calculator' and don't ever refer to yourself as one." My voice is serious and objective to match in response.

"You are great the way you are—different than me by material but similar in conscience. And I'll never let anything so insignificant take away from our similarities. We both get defensive and assume prejudice in the other, but maybe that's just society's influence on us," I say sweetly and I notice she finally starts to calm down.

I smile and say slowly, "I like you a lot, Clara. For the way you are." Both of my hands are on her shoulders now as I try to convince her of my acceptance. "I think the idea of 'us' is more simple than society makes it out to be."

After her eyes shift in debate, she smiles warmly, leans in and kisses me lightly.

"If you say so, then I'll believe you." Her voice is sweet again. But she turns and continues down the corridor, without any other clue as to where "we" are in this argument. So in slight disappointment, I take a big breath and then rush to catch up.

The thin air quickly becomes uncomfortable and I secure my oxygen mask. Step after step, my mind slowly goes numb. Thoughts slow and my heart rate follows. Such a long walk.

After a few more minutes, we come upon that larger space, the one with six corridors and the swastika symbol carved or imprinted on the walls. We look at each other briefly with indecision, but I soon elect her to choose and she takes the lead. This time we walk down a path to the right.

Minutes go by as we keep our pace, which grows increasingly difficult since this corridor is slanted up slightly with a small curve to the right. Footsteps echo as we make our way to the next unknown discovery. The adrenaline for what we might find keeps me lucid and out of my head (regardless of the repetitive nature of this underground trek).

"Wait, I see something," Clara reports.

The corridor is beginning to widen a bit as we reach a wall twice the size of the door we originally came from in the cave.

"A wall? Really?" I say in disbelief, my voice muffled by the mask. "That's anticlimactic."

"No, no. Hold on."

Clara takes a pushing position against the middle of the wall, her shoulder firmly pressed, then increases effort until a creaking sound fills our ears, echoing down the corridor.

Clara forces open what turns out to be double doors revealing one of the largest spaces I've seen indoors (well, underground).

Clara points her hand-light around to find walls of this new room, but the area is so large her light doesn't reach far enough.

"Oh, wow..." she whispers to herself.

"This place is huge!" I exclaim in an uncontrolled reaction, causing my voice to echo over and over in the concrete, titanium-framed space we stumbled upon.

Clara walks to the side of the room with me close behind. She brushes off some dust from the wall and uncovers a much larger indent of the swastika symbol.

"This must have been some type of headquarters, like a central meeting place for everyone in the group," Clara suggests to herself, loud enough for me to hear.

"Like a central hub," I mumble to myself.

We walk to the center of the room, engulfed by pitch black around us and a dusty concrete floor below. At the center of the room, a titanium table with ninety degree angles takes up enough space to take up my old room. Its surface shines slightly with spots of rust preventing too much reflection from Clara's hand-light.

"Wow, what a find..." she says softly, looking at and around the table.

"As much as I want to stand here in the utter darkness, I would at least like to see a wall or really anything. Let's keep moving," I motion to Clara as I peer into the surrounding darkness.

"Oh!" Clara says as if remembering something in her backpack. After shuffling through it, she pulls out a square thin sheet.

"Here's another reason to trust humanoids, we plan ahead," she remarks with a smirk and places the sheet on the table, then presses the middle of it.

Silently, the flat object fills up into a boxed lantern. The bright light forces me to shield my eyes, but this small box transforms this once dark room into an entirely new spectacle. All four walls of this great room can finally be seen with its fifteen-foot high ceiling and dust covering the floor. But this grand space is accompanied by a grand sense of emptiness, with nothing in the room except the titanium table and dust, a lot of dust.

"How is that little thing so bright?" I ask with my hand still up, blocking my eyes.

"Right? Oh, one sec."

Clara puts her hand out and the boxed lantern begins humming. Then it quickly lifts to the ceiling with four small fans on the bottom allowing it to hover. The buzz becomes quiet as it slows to a stop. With the light above us now, I'm able to lower my hand.

"And how'd you afford THAT gadget?" I ask sarcastically through my mask while looking up at it.

"I bought it when the power went out in my part of town a while ago. Of course, I then hacked its programming for some more control," she smiles proudly.

"Mmhmm, of course," I reply.

With the light allowing us to see, we begin exploring again. But the thick dust on the floor suggests everything that was once in here had deteriorated long ago, leaving nothing to really explore. Except...

"Clara, come here!" I call out as I look into a large closet space about the size of my old room.

"What is it?" she asks as she slows her pace.

"I need your light."

She notices what I found and lights it up with her hand-light. With the extra vision, my discovery starts to take shape and it looks more like a large elevator had once been here. Clara steps in and shines her light upward. I follow and look up to notice it's more endless than I thought, her light swallowed by the darkness above us.

"Interesting. Might be worth coming back for with the right tools," Clara says while examining the elevator shaft.

We turn back to the giant table in the middle of the room where we had set our backpacks down. I zip open my backpack and notice Clara had refilled it with more food.

"Thanks for restocking. Where do you even get all this food, any-way?" I ask her while shuffling around, finding a wrapped carrot cake.

"My owner lived at the store and had food shipped there. After he... passed, I didn't cancel it. You could say my fridge is fairly full," Clara says sadly.

"So, how do you afford all these things? From working at the shop?" I ask carefully, not to upset her with my curiosity. She nonchalantly climbs on the table and sits down.

"Well, I do OWN the repair shop. And it's not out of business just yet," she says defending herself lightly.

"Oh," I reply as I unwrap the carrot cake and take a bite while lifting the mask. Then I take a drink of water while looking at her. Clara awkwardly stays silent for another second, as if hiding something. But really, I don't mind either way. This carrot cake is too good to care where it's from exactly.

"Ok…," Clara blurts out, "my sweet owner had a life insurance policy with me as the beneficiary. He must have known his time was coming," she pauses. "Money isn't necessarily a worry for me thanks to him."

She looks into the distance as she sits on the table. I can tell she misses him, but I don't want things to get serious again. We were finally past our last argument from what I could tell.

"Wow, ok. Why don't you buy yourself a nice place to live? Closer to Lake Vostok or something?" I ask, then lift my mask and take another bite.

"I would, but…" she looks down with her loss of words.

"No, I get it. You don't want to leave his shop out of respect. That's very sweet of you," I say to comfort her. While she looks down at her swinging feet, awkwardly trying to distract from the pain she must feel, I step in front of her and kiss her forehead.

"You're a very nice person, you know? Much better than most humans," I say to encourage her, to put a warm smile on her face.

Clara does smile, but it's only half genuine.

"Thank you, Morris, but you don't have to keep comparing me to humans." I take my hand off her shoulder and take the hint.

"Oh, sorry. I meant nothing by it," I reply to save myself from looking bad.

"Humans and humanoids are just different—they're both good and bad in their own way," she explains objectively. "But I don't want to be reminded that I'll never be more than… than human-oid. And that's just my own issue, ok?" She had been pulling out the plug-in system while talking.

"Understood," I reply with a slight smile. Wrapping one arm around her shoulders, I kiss her cheek and look at her. "I like you for you, just remember that—you're an amazing, nice, and thoughtful being."

She smiles a bit and says, "Thank you." But she doesn't look at me as she sets up the system.

"So I'm assuming we're gonna try to connect down here? I thought that wasn't possible underground…"

"Well, after finding that old elevator shaft, I have a plan." She gives me a smile and continues setting up everything. Then she pulls out another gadget from her backpack and walks away.

"Ok now, what is that?" I ask.

Clara makes it to the elevator and points the gadget up. A loud pop echoes in the room as something shoots upward that then smacks into something without falling back down.

"Voilà, we now have connection," she says with attitude. I walk over to check it out, but she had already started walking back to the table with a line connected to whatever was shot up into the shaft.

"Are you manually trying to connect? This is so old-school," I remark. She doesn't reply but gives another smirk.

Clara pulls back the end of the line and I notice there's a small black knob on the end. She puts her hand on it and pauses.

"Ah-ha! Did it," she exclaims and sets down the wire.

"What? Fill me in?" I ask, desperate to know what she did.

"It's a physical router I placed in the elevator shaft and it's close enough to the surface to wirelessly connect to Lake Vostok's public internet." Noticing my confused look, she adds, "basically, I found us connection," and then smiles.

In surprise, I follow the wire with my eyes to the elevator shaft and back. Clara really does come in handy.

"Well, so I was wondering," I say hesitantly, getting her attention as she finishes up. "What is the oldest Sector?"

"Well, the public record lists Sector 2 as the oldest functioning Sector, but historical records go into detail about… a decommissioned Sector 1. Why, what are you thinking?"

I sit on the table next to her with my legs hanging off, my hands ready to help gesture my theory.

"If artificial time is the ultimate reason behind these so-called viruses, then I'm curious what happens to the oldest neurobines. As in, what is their life expectancy?"

Clara's expression doesn't change, then suddenly she comes back.

"You're right. I don't know—I searched and queried every database I could, but nothing is coming up," she replies.

"The SSG must lead everyone to believe that neurobines have no limits in lifespan because any signs that contradict that are kept from the public by deleting viruses. Only the governments, PixelOne, and the AVC know about it," my voice trails off as I begin to realize more and more.

"And the AVC is only comprised of humans, because no one would listen to humans in the real world," I add.

Clara starts connecting the dots too and continues for me.

"That would make sense then why PixelOne prevents the AVC from interacting with other neurobines. There's literally no way neurobines can find out about the limits of their own existence."

A glimmer of excitement from her eyes makes me worry.

"I know what you're thinking," I say to interrupt her daydreaming. "Even if you could hack your way in, allowing me to communicate with neurobines, I think the mass chaos would be uncontrollable. Think about how many would want out—each neurobine would immediately demand a humanoid transfer," I explain to express caution to Clara.

She pauses for a second and then looks at me again.

"You're right," she says, "there are, on average, about nine million inhabitants per domain," she reports after looking it up (now that we have connection from her gadget in the elevator shaft).

"And how many domains per Sector?" I ask.

"The limit is 99,999 domains per Sector."

"And how many Sectors are there?!" The gravity of the situation is dawning on me.

"Only nine."

"Only nine!?" I reply with an anxious edge, echoing in the room. "That's a potential for trillions of neurobines unknowingly trapped in their own homes!"

"Seven trillion actually," she says hesitantly with little hope.

Unsure of how to feel, I fall back and lie on the table looking up at the boxed lantern hovering above us. I take a big breath through the oxygen mask.

Breathe in. Breathe out.

"You know at one point, the Earth held three trillion humans. Maybe it can hold seven trillion humanoids?" Clara suggests sweetly as she nudges closer to me.

I rack my brain for solutions to this oversized problem I hadn't foreseen. Changing society to value "real" time would ultimately cause the deterioration of the Sector-System AND the planet. Something I'm not prepared to solve—and neither are the governments. Their solution to team up with PixelOne and kill off the viruses is beginning to, unfortunately, make logical sense.

"Maybe it's something we'll figure out along the way?" Clara says to comfort me as she turns to her side and begins to stroke my chest.

There must be a solution. Maybe I just don't see the whole picture yet.

Breathe in. Breathe out.

So far, seemingly "bad" decisions have led me down different paths, and these paths eventually left me here in a position of potential. And through these paths, my perspective has shifted and expanded, even adapted in order to find alternate understandings of the world and my place within it.

But an idea strikes me. I need more context of time. Turning to my side too, I kiss Clara, then look in her eyes.

"You're very right," I say with a new sense of confidence as I smile.

She observes this new energy and tilts her head in worry.

"Wait, what are you planning…"

"Clara," I say with an uncontrolled grin, "I think it's time I visit the beginning of artificial time."

CHAPTER 17

"Ok, I'm in," Clara says in excitement as she continues concentrating next to the plug-in system.

"Ha! I knew you could do it." My hand rests on her shoulder while my voice rings in the empty room.

The titanium table had grown to be a homey resting place while I waited for Clara the last hour or so. Her boxed lantern now continues to buzz quietly above us, lighting this giant space that inspires so many questions.

How old is this place? Which of the many swastika fanatics built it? How hasn't the USB found out about it? But really, are these questions that important?

You know, the usual and unnecessary line of questioning.

"Sector 1 appears to have many decommissioned domains with neurobines still in them," Clara reports.

"Define 'many.' Is that 99,000? Or..."

"Only ninety-nine domains in the first Sector. Its data configuration and structural alignment are very primitive—large files and messy utilization." Her voice is informative as though reading off something.

"From what I gather, it sounds unusable. Why didn't the SSG and PixelOne just delete it?"

Clara pauses for a second and then answers with no change in her expression.

"It appears as though there are routine transfers—always the same number of neurobines going in and the same amount going out, and at the same time every week, too," she says in confusion.

"The only people who have access to Sector 1 are in the government, right?" I ask rhetorically to myself. "They must be using this beta system as a sandbox to run tests on the neurobines stuck within it. I wouldn't be surprised. But I hate to think how far they might have gone with the experiments." My voice becomes serious at the thought.

Clara stays silent and lets out a sigh.

"Those poor neurobines, trapped in a world of endless torment," Clara says with so much sadness it hurts to listen to the sympathetic pain in her voice. "It can't be safe, Morris." She looks at me with worry.

"Can you decipher which domain might be most... 'normal?'" I ask, attempting to problem-solve.

"There are ninety-nine domains, all of which have different parameters not publicly displayed. I might've found a way to connect you, but finding extra information is more time consuming," Clara explains, hoping this will deter me from the grand idea of exploring this ancient Sector.

"With nincty-nine different 'vaults' of encrypted data for each domain," she continues, "it could take up to thirty-three hours for me to find out which are most 'normal.' And that's if I can hack into each in only twenty minutes." She has a lack of motivation in her voice as she over-explains.

"How about the first domain? Can you start looking at the normalcy of the oldest ones?" I ask.

"You don't understand. Putting your conscience into an existence with unknown laws of time, altered dimensional rules, et cetera, can be very dangerous. Maybe even fatal to your subconscious."

"Okay. Can't YOU explore in the Sector-System?" I ask her.

"Not without proper setup protocol, something only given to approved humanoids by the SSG. And it's far too complicated for me to write code like that from scratch—not without months, if not years, of time. And even then it's risky."

In frustration, I start walking back and forth on the titanium table. Up the length and then back down it again, racking my brain for creative solutions around our newfound limitations.

The dust can be seen settled on the floor around our little bubble of light in this underground room. Though the lantern floating above us is strong, the edges of the room stay ominously dark, untouched by our single light.

My feet slap on the titanium and echo loudly as I walk back and forth, thinking over our predicament. Over the risks and the possibilities.

"Can you write a supplemental code to enhance my connection safety? Such as a field or bubble around me that maintains standards suitable for the human mind?" I ask after turning to her in excitement from the possible solution.

"Like a firewall? Hmm," Clara thinks for a second. "Coding something that big, while also masking your connection from the SSG is a rather daunting task." Clara looks down in silence and then looks up. "Since I already have a secure ghost connection in place, I estimate about a week's worth of work to create what you're proposing."

I begin slowly walking up the table and pause. Another week? That would make it about 3 weeks of living in the cave. What would I do for another week? But, what choice do I have? I turn and walk down the table, Clara looking at me for a response. My mind races for any other solution that could make exploration possible. But nothing comes to me.

"Well, it isn't about time. It's about safety and doing this right," I say aloud. I turn to Clara. "A week is nothing in the grand scheme of things and if this 'firewall' can protect me from the imbalance of Sector 1, then it's well worth the wait."

Relieved, her face relaxes and a smile grows. "I would feel much better knowing you're safely cocooned in my code."

I chuckle. "What's a cocoon… stop using words I don't know."

"I'm sure you learned it in school, you just forgot," she says lightly as she lifts herself off the table. She then begins to pack up, but I stop her.

"Whoa, whoa. I still want to connect before we leave," I say quickly.

"Oh. Okay, well I DID have an idea before you suggested your crazy plan," she says to gently mock me.

I sit on the table now, looking at her with the boxed lantern still above us. The titanium is cold beneath me, but Clara's smile distracts me from the uncomfortable chill of the hard surface.

"I figure you could visit the newest domain and see if there are any neurobine viruses yet. Maybe we can find out how long it might take for virus symptoms to appear in newer, more SAFE, domains?" she says hoping for my approval.

I give a sarcastic, half-hearted expression of thought and look away.

"Hmm, rather a clever idea, I must say," I turn back and give a smirk. She laughs and kisses my forehead.

"What does my human say to another adventure, hmm?" Clara replies in a similar tone of voice.

"Your human, huh?" I ask in a smooth voice through the oxygen mask, but quickly lift it up to kiss her. The soft artificial tissue of her lips is so inviting.

Suddenly she sits on the table next to me and prepares the plug-in system, handing me the node.

"I've seen commercials for this new, expensive domain that I think you should visit," she says excitedly. "I mean, I wish I could visit it—not that I'm jealous or anything."

"Oh? Well, which parts of old-Earth does this one imitate?" I ask, playing along as I observe her new smile.

"You'll have to find out."

Clara smiles again while waiting for me to connect to the Sector-System. I chuckle and lie down on the table, placing the node on the back of my neck. And I take a deep breath through the mask.

In an instant, my eyes open to blue skies above me.

Memories of my recent free-falling experience make me worry and I sit up quickly to a view I was not expecting.

White sands spread out in front of me, leading my eyes to palm trees on either side with moving water in front. Blue, slightly turquoise water stretches out to the horizon. An ocean! I've never actually been to an ocean in a domain before—never made it that far out. It's not like PixelOne ever gave us options or time to explore on our own.

"Morris, can you hear me? What do you think?" Clara's voice

sounds inside my head.

"It's… it's beautiful," I say slowly as I gaze out among the ever-moving waters of the ocean. Its shore is moving up and down in a rhythmic variance so loud to my ears, yet consistent enough to ignore. I cannot believe Earth used to have gigantic bodies of water like this one, hundreds of times larger than Lake Vostok—which at one point was the fifth largest lake on Earth (obviously, now it's the biggest).

Its sloshing sounds seem much lower in pitch compared to the canals by my old room. And it looks literally endless, which frightens me, yet excites me deep in my core.

The palm trees above rustle in the light wind while I grab a coconut to the right of me, holding its weight, touching its coarse exterior.

"It's a Caribbean domain, modeled after the highest rated resorts that were popular thousands of years ago. It's the most expensive domain on the market right now," she says, her voice happy to know I was so taken by the scenery.

I stand up and walk to the waters, feeling the warmth wash over my feet. Warm like a bath, limitless like the sky. Palm trees of the same height stretch down the shoreline. Birds fly overhead, chirping to each other as the sun warms my skin. Wait, birds?!

"Birds just flew by! Clara, there're animals here?" I ask in complete surprise.

"Yeah, those are seagulls! All the domains in the 9-series have an emphasis on wildlife as an old-fashioned style of living," Clara explains.

I stare, watching their wings work as more birds fly by. Looking at the water, my excitement growing, I run into the ocean. Once deep enough, I take a deep breath and submerge myself in the water, then open my eyes. I've read about looking underwater, so I wasn't surprised by the blurry vision. And as expected, fuzzy shapes of colorful fish fill my line of sight and the backdrop of different brightly colored coral is like nothing I've ever seen.

The excitement of seeing something I've only dreamed of raises my heart rate, forcing me to pop up out of the water and breathe. So much life all around me. So real and yet, so tragically fake.

"Clara, this is amazing! I've never seen old-Earth animals like this before," I shout as I walk up the beach, noticing small crabs of some sort escaping from me. Birds in the trees keep an eye on me as I walk into the overgrowth of the palm trees and tall grass.

"I figured you'd like it." Her voice is saturated in happiness.

As I walk away from the shoreline, the sand starts mixing with dirt as the vegetation thickens. My feet move faster while I soak in this completely new experience, which feels almost alien. Bugs fly past, birds of impressive colors line the trees, and other creatures (I haven't a name for) run away in reaction to my approach.

Life. So much life around me.

Earth, as it is now, can't sustain natural life. Endangered animals are only kept for scientific research—maybe a few rich humanoids have animals as pets, but it's very rare. Seeing wildlife like this is so… magical. I've only really read about old-Earth in history and geography classes, but from what I can tell, this domain is spot on.

Gazing at the ecosystem circling around me, my awe is soon accompanied by anger. Humans are, of course, responsible for the extinction of natural environments like this one. And now there is no water and no life. How oblivious could we have been to sacrifice all this?

If only we still had oceans today. If only humans had planned for the future. If only we had seen the larger picture and sacrificed for the greater good when it mattered most.

The shade of the palm trees hides most of the sun. Light peaks through the shifting leaves creating an array of sunlight on the ground around me. But my observations trigger more thoughts.

Humans allowed AI to take over, sure. But because AI was created in our image by our own hands, the priorities of humanoids and neurobines are mostly selfish too. Our Earth is only "maintained" in its barely habitable state, while their escape plan from reality, their precious Sector-System, is expanded and constantly improved.

Footsteps sound behind me and I look behind. A large lizard of some type is walking by. What in the... what is that? Its giant body shifts with each step as it passes by me and stares me down. I realize something. Maybe the AVC "mutation" isn't specific to animals? Seems strange they all react to my being here.

Looking forward again, I notice the trees begin parting and as I get closer I notice buildings of an intricate style, made of natural materials from this Caribbean domain. Shapes within shapes, designs within designs are carved and embedded on every inch of these naturally inspired structures.

When I come out from the vegetation, I see buildings stretch for miles following the contour of the rounded shoreline. Neurobines are walking here and there on the dirt roads, but much slower than I'm used to seeing. As if they're calmer in this environment.

But seeing the neurobines reminds me of why I'm here. The real reason.

I pull up the map and scan for red dots.

"Clara, how old is this domain?"

"It's only been on the market for a few months now. It was completely redone from scratch! PixelOne had advertisements up about four months ago while it was under construction," she replies.

I never worked in a domain like this, not anything this beautiful and fully developed. Not even as a level 9 construction worker. Maybe those on level 10 and up had more high-profile assignments.

Maybe I worked in Sector 9, sure, but as part of the construction crew, I never saw things further along in the development process. They must add animals in after a domain's initial architectural plan is completed. I laugh to myself. All this time and I never knew how much I was missing.

I shake my head from the distracting thoughts and return to examining the map for red dots.

"Well, this is a really new domain so I'm not surprised there's no virus activity on the map."

"Hey, it shows more reason to believe 'time' causes virus symptoms," Clara replies.

"That's true."

Walking a bit further down the dirt road connecting the houses, opposite the beach side, I watch neurobines walk, talk, laugh and socialize. Must be the rich neurobines that live here in this worry-free society.

"Clara, why do neurobines socialize? I thought AI hate wasting time."

"Neurobines and humanoids are very productive by nature, yes. But socializing is a form of productivity, you know. Conversing with others allows for learning, gossiping, connection building, planning, et cetera. It's not wasting time if there's a purpose behind it," she says as though she's speaking to the entire human race.

"Alright. Good to know, good to know," I reply lightly.

I walk down the line of buildings observing the life in this domain. Popping out the map again, I examine the area and notice the entire island is one big spiral.

A neurobine man walks up to me as I look at the map.

"Here already then," he says to me coldly.

I freeze in absolute shock. He can see me? Upon examination, a very faint pink glow proves he might be experiencing early virus symptoms. So early, they must not have shown on the map. I'm unsure what to do and stay in silence as I debate my next action.

"Ghosts were the reason I moved here. But I can see now you all follow me no matter what and sure enough, you're here already. An endless nightmare in a sleepless existence," he says to me, his voice lacking character.

"Sir, you have me confused," I quietly tell him.

"If I cannot escape you ghosts, then I must submit. Has my time come?" he asks me with little inflection.

"I am not here to do anything, sir," I tell him calmly. Turning away, I say softly, "Clara, pull me out."

"No, no, just talk to him. There's no harm in it," she encourages me. But I sigh.

"Who's Clara?" the neurobine asks. But I ignore the question.

"Sir, have you felt different in the past few days?" I ask him in a professional way to try and gain his trust, taking on the persona of a clinician asking standard survey questions.

"No, pretty much the same over the last week. The past year I have though, why?" he asks innocently, staring at me strangely. Other neurobines walking by staring at him as though he's crazy, not able to see the "ghost" in this conversation (a.k.a. me).

A year? He must have had these very mild symptoms for a year! Neurobines must take a long time to develop into full-fledged red threats.

"How have you felt different?" I vaguely ask him to spur truth from his perspective.

"General feelings of emptiness with occasional moments of endlessness," he answers with an uncomfortable ease, as though it was completely normal to feel this way. "Why? I'm on a schedule, you know. Can I ask you ghosts to leave now, please?"

"Ask him how long he's been here!" Clara shouts in my head.

"Sir, I'll just need a few more moments of your time. How long have you..." I attempt to ask, but he interrupts me with a direct voice.

"Why?" the man's expression shifts slightly. "You need MY time? What, are you lost?"

Something doesn't feel right about his tone of voice; the pink of the aura was beginning to shift slightly. The pink is more visible now.

"Oh, that's a bad sign," I say aloud in response.

"What... why?" Clara asks in surprise.

"You must need directions. Can I show you the ocean?" he asks me without blinking.

"That's ok, sir, I've already seen it."

"When did you see it? Now, earlier, past, present. I want to help, but you must tell me when? My time is not to be sacrificed lightly. Not yet," the man says, making his pink aura phase into a hot pink, but then it changes back.

"He's definitely off balance," Clara observes.

My breathing starts quickening as I realize this man is turning—his eyes are more intense now as he notices my faster breathing.

"Sir," I say backing away slightly. But I immediately remember something that has bothered me since the AVC and I decide to experiment.

"Sir, it's time for you to sleep," I say hesitantly in my fake professional voice.

"Sleep?" the man says angrily. "I don't need to sleep, why would you think I need to sleep? Sleep is unnecessary. Time is mine to control and my time is unaffected by human limitations like sleep."

The man steps forward with a strange look in his eyes, as though he's figuring out his existence in this conversation.

"Why would you ask him that? That's aggravating his skepticism!" Clara anxiously says in my head.

"I know, that's the point!" I reply quickly.

"The point?!" the soon-to-be virus snaps in reply after overhearing me, "what lowly kind of being are you to tell me how my time is to be spent—MY time."

The virus symptoms set in while he stares at me. "You are a disgrace…" he says in utter disgust.

I step back in fear of this changing virus, the pink turning darker, my heart beginning to race as I breathe faster and faster. The man stares at me intensely, his anger growing.

"Human…" he says slowly and monotone. "You're no ghost. You're a… human." Such hatred was in his voice as if the word made him sick.

"Your life is tainted with limitations. It's YOUR turn to sleep!" he yells and tries to grab me, but expecting this, I dodge and begin running.

"Clara! Get me out of here!" I yell in desperation.

"Okay! Close your eyes!" she shouts in my head.

I had already been running while keeping an eye on the virus behind, who's chasing me frantically. But I quickly shut my eyes and hold them.

"Morris! You're ok, you're okay now," her voice sounding through my ears this time.

Opening my eyes, I see the lantern above us and realize I'm back underground in the mysterious room with the titanium table. I quickly sit up, feeling the weight of the oxygen mask.

"Well. He definitely doesn't like humans," I say as I stare forward, taking in what just happened and breathing deeply.

"Yeah, that was strange."

"No virus has ever realized I was a human before," I say, curiously.

"Okay, but have you ever held a conversation with a virus?" she asks me as she rubs my shoulders.

"Not really, no. They've always been too far gone for a rational conversation," I say, still looking forward while Clara sits next to me.

"That wasn't too rational either," she remarks. "Looked like your line of questions progressed his symptoms though. Which was interesting."

Clara looks away in thought, her hair shifting in response to her movement. Such an artificial grace.

I turn to Clara in worry, "why aren't you affected by these same questions? Humanoids and neurobines are built with the same code, aren't they?"

She turns to me with a look of annoyance. "Why… are *you* worried I'll turn on you, too?" she says mockingly.

Not knowing how to reply, I turn away. "No, I'm just asking."

"Let me just clarify something," Clara says while staring me down. "Humanoids are young AI systems living in human-reality, okay? But once humanoids can afford to switch over to the Sector-System, everything changes. And if humanoids choose that virtual life, they can be caught as neurobines in an endless loop of manufactured time for thousands of years—as you've said," her voice stern and unmoving.

She turns to me. "So, no, I won't turn on you. I'm here to stay, forever boycotting the Sector-System. I will NEVER… be a virus. So 'delete' that thought from your mind."

The strength behind her words takes me by surprise. My respect for her grows in hearing her distaste for the Sector-System. But my view of her will always be tainted by the worry that she, like any program, is made up of hackable code (as juvenile as it is to think that way).

Clara turns her head, relaxing her intensity.

"I know you're worried that I'm just… 'code,' but humans are made of biological code too. Different coding language, sure, but similar cognitive structure." Sadness is evident in her voice and I attempt to place my hand on her, but suddenly she straightens her posture.

"We might be different from one another, but we're susceptible to the same dangers. Maybe I'll learn to hack the human brain like the PRP does, hmm? Does that make you feel safe?" she says, trying to spur my anger.

"Okay, okay. Point taken. I trust you, Clara," I say, successfully putting my hand on her shoulder. "I'm just reviewing details and possibilities. I meant nothing by it." My voice is altered by the oxygen mask, but I try to sound as genuine as possible.

"Mmhmm," she grunts and turns to the plug-in system.

"Wait! Before you pack it up, can you connect me to another new domain?" I quickly ask, grabbing the node. Clara thinks for a second.

"Okay, I got one for you," she says.

"Okay, great. Which is it?"

"Sector 9-91475," she responds. I give her a look of skepticism and she continues, "this domain is only a year old. You'll like it, trust me."

I squint my eyes at her as I try to decipher any ulterior motive. "Hmm, okay. Sure," I say hesitantly.

After slapping the node on the back of my neck, the cold of the titanium table covers my back as I lie down. I take a deep breath and close my eyes.

Coldness takes over my entire body. I try opening my eyes, but white winds burn my eyes and force me to regain balance. Snow!

My bones quickly lock up with a cold I've not experienced before. From what I can see in this massive snowstorm, a blinding white covers every inch of the ground around me and I turn to look for a safe haven. Anything out of this cold! What was Clara thinking?

A single grey box stands behind me. Attempting to walk to it, my feet feel difficult to pry out of the dense snow. Cold air stings my throat as I breathe, heaving with each step.

"Clara!" I shout while I make some progress toward the unknown structure. But I have a hard time hearing my own voice over the roaring winds.

"Welcome home! Isn't it beautiful?" Clara's sarcastic voice sounds in my head.

Grunting with each footstep, I finally reach the grey boxed building that shelters me from the winds. But the intense cold is beginning to freeze my hair, my fingers even difficult to move. Leaning against the wall, falling into a fetus position covering myself with my arms, I shout again while closing my eyes.

"Clara! Get me out of here!"

Silence. The roaring winds stop and my ears ring in response to the quiet. A familiar smell of dust hints at my presence in the underground space again, so I quickly sit up to find Clara staring at me angrily.

"That's my version of 'giving you the cold shoulder!' For distrusting me. Again!" she says loudly and then begins to laugh, but walks away from the table to hide it.

"What! How does that make sense?!" my voice rings in the large space around us as I instinctively try to warm myself. "I JUST told you I trust you. Why did you have to place me on some cold planet!?" I shout at her, but she spins around in reaction.

"Some planet? It was our home! A replica of Antarctica in the 2000's," she answers then continues chuckling.

In surprise, I think back to all that snow and ice that had gnawed at my bones. Growing up, we did learn our country was encased in snow and ice, miles in thickness. But seeing it and experiencing it first-hand felt so alien and unearthly.

Turning to her in anger, I shout in a serious tone, "Okay, that's not funny, Clara. I could have died!"

"Oh, take it easy. It was only negative fifty degrees—hypothermia doesn't set in until five minutes or so," she says nonchalantly.

"Five minutes?! I could have died in five minutes?!" I shout, throwing my hands up in disbelief. "Okay. Too far!" I get up off the table and start packing up food wrappers and water, shoving them in my backpack.

"Okay, okay. I'm sorry, you're right. I took it too far," she apologizes as she starts packing up the plugin system.

"Yes. You did."

I grab the line connected to the router in the elevator shaft and tug on it. A scraping sound can be heard in the distance; ignoring it, I prepare to tug again but she stops me.

"Oh! Careful, those things can break," Clara says annoyed, quickly taking the line out of my hands. "Morris, I'm sorry I took it too far," she says while walking over to the router, "but you're in the wrong too!"

In anger, I start toward a door we hadn't been through yet. My original plan was to find another cave or find wherever these corridors might lead. Blinded by my annoyance of Clara's little power-play, I pick up some speed and shove my shoulder into the old double-doors to open them out of anger. But they don't budge, so I press against them and push as hard as I can, grunting loudly.

One of the concrete doors slams open and bangs on the wall behind it—without hesitation, I neglect the echoing noise and start down the new corridor. But the vibration from the door keeps sounding and crumbling noises grow louder.

"Morris, watch out!"

A loud snap makes me look up to notice a large chunk of the ceiling is falling! I quickly jump out of the way as it falls close to my feet, nearly smashing my toes. I scramble forward on my stomach but hearing another crack that echoes down the corridor, I look up to see another chunk of the ceiling about to fall. Desperately scrambling toward Clara as she runs toward me, I feel something pin me down. Sharp, intense pain takes over my senses and warmth grows within my left leg.

Indescribable pain causes me to shout in agony as I try turning to my back. But I'm unable to, so I look behind me, my voice shouting uncontrollably, and I see a large concrete chunk on my leg. In terror, I shout even louder.

Clara rushes over and tries pulling me from the concrete chunk, but the pain causes me to scream. The boxed lantern had followed her, lighting up the corridor and allows me to see blood coming from underneath the boulder.

In reaction to her failed attempt, she jumps to the huge chunk of concrete and begins lifting. Her machinery whistles under the weight of the boulder. With no luck, she re-positions herself and tries again, my shouts echoing, filling my ears. An intensity in her humanoid frame causes me to stare as she slowly lifts the concrete off my leg and rolls it to the side.

The lack of pressure on my leg releases a new depth of pain causing me to gasp for air through my mask, between shouts of torment.

"Morris! Breathe, Morris!" Clara tries to gain my attention but notices the loss of blood. Seeing her reaction to the mess she uncovered from the chunk of ceiling, I look down, too.

My left leg is no longer a leg. A flat, bloody limb of shattered human flesh is all that's left connected to my body. With the intense pain and horrendous sight, I pass out.

Time passes.

Feeling my eyes shut, I open them to a dim light. How long was I out? A slight pain radiating from my left leg causes me to grunt and sit up to stretch it. But there was no leg.

I had no left leg anymore!

My heart rate races at the realization. Even my knee is missing. My breath begins speeding up uncontrollably. I stare at where my leg should be and almost hyperventilate. In horror, I look around me to get a grip on my situation.

Clara is on the ground next to me, sleeping with her arm around my chest. Sleeping? No, must be hibernation mode or something. The lantern is above us, buzzing quietly, with a low light illuminating the corridor a bit. Only twenty feet or so can be seen leading back to the large space where the titanium table should be, but darkness hides it. Looking back around, the large concrete chunk takes up the majority of the corridor in front of us.

"Clara?" I shake her, but she doesn't wake. "Clara!?"

Her eyes open.

"Morris, you're okay—I was so... worried." Her voice quiet and slow, as if sleepy.

"Clara? Clara, are you okay?! What… what happened to my leg?" I ask, still freaking out about my missing limb.

"Your leg… I had to surgically remove it and cauterize it to save you from bleeding out," she says gently. "You were passed out, but I did everything I… I could," Clara's voice is slowing down with sleepiness. Which makes me pause.

"Wait, Clara, are you sleepy? Humanoids don't sleep—what's wrong?" I whisper louder to her while stroking her hair, the pain of my missing leg no longer a concern.

"I'm lacking power, but it's fine. I have a plan." Her eyes shut from attempting an energetic, positive voice.

After lifting the boulder and cauterizing my leg, somehow she must have used all her energy. Without the sun, she could not recharge. Unsure of what to do, I begin stroking her cheek again.

"Oh, wha… didn't you bring external batteries or something?" I ask her and then listen closely.

"Used them up already. Listen…" Her voice is faint with a lack of energy. "You don't have enough food and water to carry me up to the surface, not with only one leg. It would take you too long."

I shake my head in shock, expecting the worst. "No, no…" I mumble, my eyes watery now.

"Listen. You have to make it back to the cave with the plug-in system. When you do, follow my…" her voice slows to a stop, but then powers back up, "…instructions." She then hands me a small tablet device.

"But," I say with sadness, "I can't leave you to die here."

"No, Morris. Just follow what I wrote…" her voice fades slightly, but then returns, "and I'll be with you again. Okay?"

Her eyes open wide to confirm my understanding. She looks at me with so much caring and feeling, a tear falls from my eyes.

"Okay… okay, Clara," I say stroking her cheek.

"I'll be fine, don't worry," she says to comfort me as her hand lifts and grabs mine. "I won't be gone forever. Stay strong and make it out. I'm sorry to leave you alone, Morris. But I believe in…" her power fades again, "… you."

"How do I? Which way do I go? I need your help, Clara." I begin worrying about what was asked of me.

I'm leaning over her now. Above her, looking down at flickering backlit eyes. Quickly, in desperation, I lift my mask and kiss her. A single teardrop falls on her cheek as I close my eyes, her warm lips pressing against mine. I've grown too accustomed to kissing her anytime I want and with having to part like this, I kiss her again, but my heart sinks. I hold this kiss longer to soak in the moment so I don't forget the feeling, but her weak response leaves little hope she will make it out.

"It's okay. You'll…" her power fades again, "see me soon enough." She smiles weakly and rests her hand on my chest, then continues to speak with passion with the last of her energy.

"I'm sorry about everything, Morris. I… I love…" Her power fades.

"I love you, too," I reply as her power faintly flickers. "I love you, Clara." Another tear falls on my cheek. "I'll see you soon, okay?" I stroke her cheek and struggle to breathe smoothly. "Real soon."

I kiss her again, the warmth of her lips gone. And I tense in reaction, my lips trembling in realization as I pull away while looking at her. Missing her already.

"Remember that I love you."

Time passes.

The boxed lantern flickers as Clara's power reaches its limit. Her hand no longer grasps mine, but regardless, I hold it for a moment longer. I hold it against my chest as I slowly kiss her forehead and rock back and forth. The buzz of the lantern is in the background as I comb through her artificial, brown hair. Her charming, beautiful hair.

I'll see her soon. This is nothing to be upset about—if she were awake, she'd sarcastically calm me down in some way. With some idiom.

I take a deep breath, wipe my eyes and clear my throat. Like she said: make it out and follow the instructions.

Breathe in. Breathe out.

Clara's lifeless form lies next to me as I look back at my missing leg, but a sense of purpose grows within me. A purpose to bring Clara back.

I grab the tablet she had given me and find a place in my backpack.

The pain from my leg is more noticeable as I get to my feet… well, my foot. Clara's backpack is leaned against the wall, so I slide my backpack onto one shoulder as I hop over and put Clara's backpack on the other. But hers is surprisingly heavy with the plug-in system.

How am I going to live with only one leg? I can hardly stand. And this constant, dull pain distorts my thinking. Looking at Clara one last time, feeling a deep ache, a longing for her eyes brings me to tears again. But I shake my head and clear my throat again, turning my head away.

Breathe in. Breathe out.

Light from the boxed lantern allows me to see the double doors I had slammed into. Realizing light is a luxury, I grab the floating lantern above me and hop to the double doors, make it to the large space again.

Hopping like this is hard work and with the loss of so much blood, a dizziness kicks in suddenly so I stop. I drink some water and eat a wrapped protein bar. How long was I passed out? How long did Clara sit there hoping I would wake up? Poor Clara. My poor Clara.

I turn back. With a backpack on either shoulder and the lantern under my left arm, I attempt to grab Clara's hand. Once I find a grip I pull, trying to hop and gain some ground. Clara's body skids closer by an inch, but a second hop leads my leg to give out and I fall back on the ground, echoing in the corridor and the room behind me.

No use.

Light flickers from the lantern and I look at it, noticing a dented edge from my failed attempt. In anxiousness, I wait. The light luckily grows steady again. That was a close one. I cannot do without light and I cannot risk hurting this lantern more than I already have.

Looking at Clara again, I grunt in pain and frustration. She was right, I cannot carry her *and* all this stuff with only one leg. I breathe heavy in anger at the situation. After a few seconds, I get to my feet again and grab all the stuff to make my way out, leaving her behind, alone in the corridor where I had idiotically slammed that door.

I should have had more control over my anger. I shouldn't have been so easily affected and rushed into the door. So many things I *should* have done; so many things she maybe *should not* have done. Useless to go over details now though.

Make it out and follow the instructions. Clara's orders.

Each hop is difficult and takes a lot of effort, the backpacks thudding against my back every time. Using the wall as support helps speed up the process, but the force of each land causes pain. Pain everywhere. With the lantern in my arm, I hop along the wall of the large room until I get to the opposite side. Examining the corridor with the open doors, I direct myself towards it. Each hop makes me grunt from pain.

Breathe in. Breathe out.

As I begin the path toward our cave, the lantern begins flickering again.

"No, no, no," I say aloud, shaking the lantern and hoping it won't die on me.

The light holds steady for a second and then dies out. In anger, I throw it on the ground, the crash echoing in the darkness that now surrounds me. My breath quickens as I realize how alone I am.

Alone in pure darkness.

Nothingness overwhelms me as I realize there's no difference between eyes open or eyes shut. Silence fills my ears and fear boils in my gut. The nothingness that circles me, the void that consumes my senses is utterly heart stopping. In frantic reaction to a sudden claustrophobic feeling, I hobble and hop forward to break free from the emptiness down the corridor to our cave. But with my balance thrown from the lack of light and my single leg, I trip and fall to the ground.

With my breathing shallow and fast, and my blood pumping louder than my breathing, I lay on my back looking up... or down, or whichever direction it actually is, looking for anything in the darkness. Desperate for anything, my eyes jolt in frenzied motions. I'm so alone in this underground jail of endless tunnels. No sounds, no light. Nothing but my thoughts and fears multiplying in my head.

I yell to break free from my mind, the echo sounding down the length of the corridor. Determination—I must stay determined. For Clara. But how long will this take? With both feet, it took about an hour or so before we found the large room. At my current pace, it could take multiple hours if not more.

As I lay in the darkness, my breathing heavy through the oxygen mask, I envision Clara's sweet smile in the sunlight of our cave.

But other thoughts quickly begin racing in my head. The disappointment of my life, my regrets of leaving Archie, the guilt of losing composure with Paul, all of which replace my thoughts of Clara. This old self-hatred comes back with a vengeance, fueled by the hopeless dark. But by clenching my fists, I strengthen my focus on the task at hand. And my love for Clara.

Her encouraging, yet sarcastic voice. Those beautiful eyes and her soft, brown hair. Kisses that make me feel at home in her presence and her touch that I crave, especially right now. A hug even. Something to save me from the loneliness of this surrounding darkness.

Anything to save me from this loneliness.

I lie in the torment of my mind—of a mind without sight, without visual evidence that it is alive. Trapped in the absence of light, alone in the fear of nothingness, and buried by my own uninterrupted self-interrogation. Abandoned without hope.

Breathe in. Breathe out.

Trapped, alone, and buried in darkness.

Breathe in.

Come on! I have to get up.

Breathe... out.

I have to save Clara.

CHAPTER 18

Everything is nothing. Nothing is everything. While in the darkness, I might think I see so many things, but in reality, it could be anything. Frightening, yet soothing, my mind expands while my foot aches. Each hop is an automated response toward the promise of freedom.

How could I not push forward?

Thoughts are my only distraction from the dead quiet and the empty darkness.

Life? Just an endless loop caught in the fickle hope for ignorant stagnation without noticeable adaptation. An ever-revising ballet of fabricated desires for shallow change without true variance. A mind-led competition hidden behind inevitable suffering soaked by indifference.

These thoughts! I have to stop, I'm thinking far too much. And these thoughts aren't productive in the slightest!

Having chosen the wrong corridor an hour or so ago, hope was again thinning. I strictly remember Clara and I never closed the door to the passageway leading to our cave. Running into a closed-door earlier forced me to sit in hopelessness while leaning against it. How could I have chosen the wrong path?

I had taken a nap because I was exhausted and unfortunately, I still am—having only one leg is more tiring than I could have ever imagined. But according to the map in my mind, I'm nearing the connecting room again in the next few minutes. Or hours. Hard to tell after so long.

My leg is burning with each hop. The pain forces me to fall and lean against the wall again. I catch my breath after a bit and force my mind to stop analyzing the nothingness around me.

The stillness and the silence beg to be investigated, but without any light, my interpretation of what "could" be there is all subjective in the end. But I crave to know and my mind wavers toward believing I COULD know upon further scrutiny and evaluation. It's all just distractions from the desolate shadows blanketing my senses.

Useless wastes of thought. I need to focus—for my sanity.

Shifting through my backpack a fourth time in the pitch dark keeps my mind occupied. A few items of food and water are left in my backpack along with a few more oxygen canisters. My limited oxygen supply really makes me nervous, but a few more hours should do it.

I'll be in the light soon. A few more hours.

As I sit waiting for the pain of my single leg to subside, I stare into the blackness. Something seems alive in the emptiness, but my mind must already be playing tricks on me again.

I lie down and look up—well, as far as I can tell I'm looking up. Exhausted from another hour (maybe) of hopping, I doze off again.

Opening my eyes to black makes me lose context of the situation. The dizziness forces me to sit up quickly, breathing heavily through my mask. But sitting up allows me to feel gravity pushing down on my shoulders and I regain a sense of balance in the world.

Breathe in. Breathe out.

Finding the difference between up and down helps me fight the fear. I clap and listen to where the walls are and then proceed down the corridor.

Minutes go by.

My footstep, my hopping, echoes. Each hop clues me in on how far I have left to go. Soon I hear it bounce against a wall. Ugh! I chose the wrong direction again and I'm at the same wrong door. A door I can't move without Clara's help (trust me I tried).

I let out a big sigh and turn around, hopping down the corridor. But this time I'm certain of the direction.

More minutes go by.

Colors appear in the darkness occasionally. I allow my mind to fool with my sight as I hop with one hand on the wall for balance. "Seeing things" keeps my mind entertained—though deep down I'm scared it's a sign of early hallucination. But if I ALLOW it to happen, then I'm safe. Right? Anything is more interesting than the nothingness I'm drowning in.

But what if it is a hallucination? I may be stuck down here forever. Days even! For all I know, it might have already been half the day. Why did I have to cut out my epichip. Technology like that is priceless at a time like this—just a little light would save my sanity and a clock would keep me grounded.

Wait.

What is that?

In front of me, I see what appears to be faint water trickling on the… ground? Or just floating in front. Sorry, no, I must have let my mind go too far with imagination.

I shake my head and the water disappears.

Minutes go by.

Made it! Made it to the room with the six corridors again. I quickly choose the one to the right by feeling around the dusty concrete wall and then head down it. Hope is growing in my stomach again. I can just taste the light in our cave. OUR cave—where Clara and I will be again soon. I know it.

Step by single step, I'm slowly making progress. And this time I'm positive, I'm sure I'm going down the correct dark passage. My path to freedom. How I wish I had a flashlight. How stupid am I to not ask Clara for one! That's a detail she should have caught, right? Or maybe she meant to forget—she could be testing me on my level of human adaptability. Maybe this is an elaborate plan to… NO. Stop.

Shaking my head again, I stop these unproductive thoughts but nearly fall. I regain my balance and feel my leg tensing from exhaustion. The backpacks make noises as I stumble a bit. They're so heavy now.

I lean against the wall again.

Quickly, I open my eyes. Well, from what it feels like—I open my eyes. Hard to tell the difference between eyes shut and eyes open, but from what it feels like, I must have napped again. This one-legged hike is exhausting. My breathing is shallow with thin air, so I replace the oxygen canister it's connected to and begin again down the corridor. Making sure this time I take the right direction. After a few more minutes I shout in frustration.

"Ugh, why!?"

I'm stopped again. By another closed door. I realize now I took the wrong corridor. AGAIN. My head is leaned against the wall in the dark, utter frustration sinking in. Hopelessness is hard to deny—tempting almost. Clenching my fists, I turn and hop back to the connecting room. Again.

Minutes go by.

What is that? I see pink creatures on the floor. Mini creatures with… fur? I think. How strange. I know I'm hallucinating, but it is SO interesting to see. No matter if it's fake, it is far more entertaining than pure darkness.

Reaching out to touch one of the pink, fuzzy creatures makes them all fade away. Oh man, I'm a little far gone. I need to get out of here.

Minutes go by.

Why did Clara leave me alone in the dark? She must have been able to store enough energy to lead me back to the cave. Or at least lent me her hand-light? I hate the darkness so much, I want it to stop.

My breathing and the single thud of my footstep echo repeatedly down the corridor as I hop. But in frustration again, I stop and collapse to a leaning position. I grab some water and drink, then unwrap some food and eat.

Water floats by below eye level again. Greenish blue. Interesting…

I shake my head realizing it's just a hallucination again and it disappears.

Getting up, I balance the backpacks on my shoulders and hop a few more times. But the pain forces me down again.

Resting against the wall looking up as far as I can tell, I recount what happened to Clara. Why couldn't I have stayed and Clara be the one to save us? She's far more equipped to handle darkness than I am!

I miss her. So much.

My mind starts thinking of her over and over again until it becomes unbearable. Sadness bubbles up from nowhere and I start crying—my emotions seem uncontrollable for a second, unleashing depression and loneliness like I've never felt.

Hate. Love. Sadness. Hope.

There is no difference between all these emotions! Just like there is no difference in the darkness that engulfs my existence! Where am I?

I clench my fists, pushing them against the ground. Noise starts sounding down the corridor—or at least I think. No, no. It's another hallucination. But it won't go away.

Crowds of people start filling my ears, becoming unbearable. I start rocking to feel something else, anything to distract me from the darkness and the imaginary sounds. My body swings back and forth, helping me feel gravity, reminding me of the ground below me. But the noise is still there—overwhelming and constant.

"Ahh!" I yell out loud in the dark as I clasp my head, rocking frantically. Make it go away, just make it stop!

"Make it go away!" I yell in my head.

Suddenly, the hallucination stops. I start laughing in happiness as the loudness of pure silence returns. In desperation, I climb to my one leg again and begin hopping. But a few more minutes pass and my shoulders leave me in agony, forcing me on the ground again.

Minutes go by.

Water again on the floor. Shaking my head makes it go away. But the water level seems to rise each time it comes back.

Why did Clara plan on waiting for me to save her anyway? Couldn't she have hacked something to save us both? She's smarter than me anyway—all forms of artificial intelligence are smarter than me.

Oh, I feel so much depression all of a sudden. Why am I so… sad?

"Clara?" I say aloud. But no answer. I swear I heard her footsteps, maybe even a voice calling to me.

Minutes go by.

I don't want to get up. Don't make me—what purpose do I have but to rot in the dark, unknown to anyone on the surface. As if I'm stranded in hell, like I'm Satan stuck looking up. No, no. That's a silly thing to think. What old imagery. Clara would know more about historical figures, icons, and belief systems like that, though. I'm sure she would. She, with that smile, would outsmart me any day.

She's real. Very real. Clara is more real than the concrete wall I'm touching in this unforgiving darkness. She is not imaginary in any way and I'm grateful to have met her. Very grateful.

I laugh aloud in happiness and then slowly fall asleep from exhaustion.

Minutes go by.

Where am I?! Oh—yes, the darkness. I'm so lost in the darkness, all the time. Always lost. No matter the time, I'm always lost in it.

Sitting up, I look around. Obviously, not seeing a thing. And unfortunately, not knowing which way to go. I grab a bite, drink some water, and exchange the canister again. Strange I have to replace them so often—they must be defective. Hopping to my foot, which I still find strange, I slowly choose a direction and start down the corridor. The weight of the backpacks are painful on my shoulders but I ignore it.

Minutes go by.

Damn it! I chose wrong again.

Minutes go by.

Finally. I've made it to the connecting room again.

I sit in the correct corridor and rest a while, panting and replacing another oxygen canister. The only one left. Okay—just a little rest before I continue. I don't want to leave the familiarity of this room. A room Clara and I were once in together. As a couple.

Wait—are we a couple? I don't think it's official yet.

"Who's there!?" I yell at the dark. But no one says anything in response.

"What did you think was there, Morris," I ask myself aloud. "A friend? Get a grip."

A voice emerges in the echo of my own, but I couldn't make out the words. I tilt my head—oh, a voice? No, no. How could a voice be down here? Clara doesn't exist here. I mean, she exists! But she's just away from me in the dark. Alone and by herself. Poor Clara. How I miss her.

Tears drop on my cheek, but I wipe them away in anger.

"You want me to give up, don't you!" I shout directly at the dark, my muffled voice echoing down the corridors. "Well, I won't! I'm a Master number 11 and 22. My life path is one! Nothing can stop me, not even you!"

I shake my head. Why am I speaking out loud? This is insanity. I have to get out.

With heavy breathing, I get up and start down the corridor. The correct one this time, shoving away hallucinations as they come. Water, Clara, dusty ghostly figures.

"Ahh!" I shout and wave my hands at what I thought were ghosts. I lose balance and fall against the wall. Squinting my eyes harder and harder, my fists in tight balls, I begin punching the darkness in defense, grunting with each blow.

I'm panting uncontrollably now. Not just from exhaustion, but from mental fatigue. Maybe I should sleep this off? No! I've taken too many naps. I must get back. I'm so close.

Hopping slowly, I make progress. Minutes go by, I think. Or hours. I believe this moment to be longer than it is, but I know these hallucinations distort my perception. I know it! I'm smarter than the darkness.

"Shut up!" I shout as I hop and pant.

Ugh—why am I shouting again. The water on the floor isn't hurting anyone. "Ha ha," I point at it as I hop. Ugh. Stop, stop! No, there's no water. Quickly, the rushing water fades into the darkness. A strange loneliness starts again and then a sharp anxiety.

I hop faster again, but trip and fall. AGAIN.

Minutes go by.

I wake up from the nap I decided to take and unwrap another bit of food. Drink the last of my water. Oh, no. There are a few more bottles left still. I keep forgetting.

Breathe in. Breathe out.

For Clara. This is all for Clara. My beautiful, lovely Clara, who has saved me and will save me from the darkness. I love her so much.

She's my life now. And I'm hers. At least I hope I'm hers. No, no! I am all she cared about. "Cares" about! I mean, she currently cares about me. She's not gone. Ugh!

I pick up the backpacks and continue with frantic purpose. I must get out!

Minutes go by.

I'm confused and delusional. I have to stop thinking so much.

Breathe in. Breathe out.

Keep going. I must keep going!

Don't look behind. Don't hallucinate anymore. You're sane and Clara loves you. She is your purpose to push forward. Forget pain. Forget the past. Forget everything.

I am firewood. I might be burnt to nothing, but with my ashes, I will fuel a new movement.

A movement for Earth! I am FIREWOOD.

The weight of the backpacks bring me to my knee, but unable to balance I fall on my side again, this time hitting my head on the wall.

Pain radiates, overwhelming my senses. I shout in pain and grab my head as I roll on the floor in the dark.

Minutes go by.

The air is thin again. I have to replace the canister for the oxygen mask. Shuffling through the backpack in the dark, I try searching for another. No luck.

What! I swear I had another canister. Shuffling again, pulling out all the stuff in my backpack and Clara's—I find no more extra.

I'm going to die here. This is it. I've failed Clara.

In one last desperate attempt, I shove everything back in and set off again down the corridor, hopping on my one foot with my head in agony from my fall. But it is so much harder now without proper oxygen—the canister must be out. I'm exhausted!

Complete frustration leads me to grab the mask and throw it aside, creating a banging against the wall, echoing in this lonely coffin. The place where I'll die. The dark walls of death are closing in on me and any last bit of hope is now drowning in my fatigue.

Everything starts shutting down and I fall hard on my knee, leading me to try and catch myself with my left leg. But I forget I no longer have a left leg and take a hard fall on my left side, grunting from the pain.

I roll to my back and notice water rushing above me, as if underwater. Gasping for air, I feel myself drowning in the expansive darkness around my existence.

Clara. I've failed her. I've failed society. Here I drown in the darkness, leaving the world to burn in the sun forever. Wait, no! Don't give up, not yet!

Rolling to my stomach, I crawl forward. Inch by inch. Grunting while trying to breathe the thin oxygen.

Minutes go by.

My face is flat on the cold, dusty floor. A small pin-drop of light shines hundreds of feet down the corridor. I had chosen the right corridor, but my body is deteriorating without oxygen. Choking with each breath, I roll on my back again, fighting to stay alive.

But everything is a lie.

Breathe in.

And everything is nothing. Nothing is everything.

Breathe out.

In the darkness, I might see many things. But in reality, it could be anything. Frightening, yet soothing, my mind expands as it understands.

Choking as I try to breathe, I move but find no energy.

I realize now I'm here to die. And as I slip into unconsciousness, colors and worlds float about my vision as though I'm moving. Grand visual displays ignite a mental overload and my eyes blink slowly. Slowly until they shut.

My body feels weightless as I black out.

Breathe in.

Clara.

Breathe out.

I'm sorry.

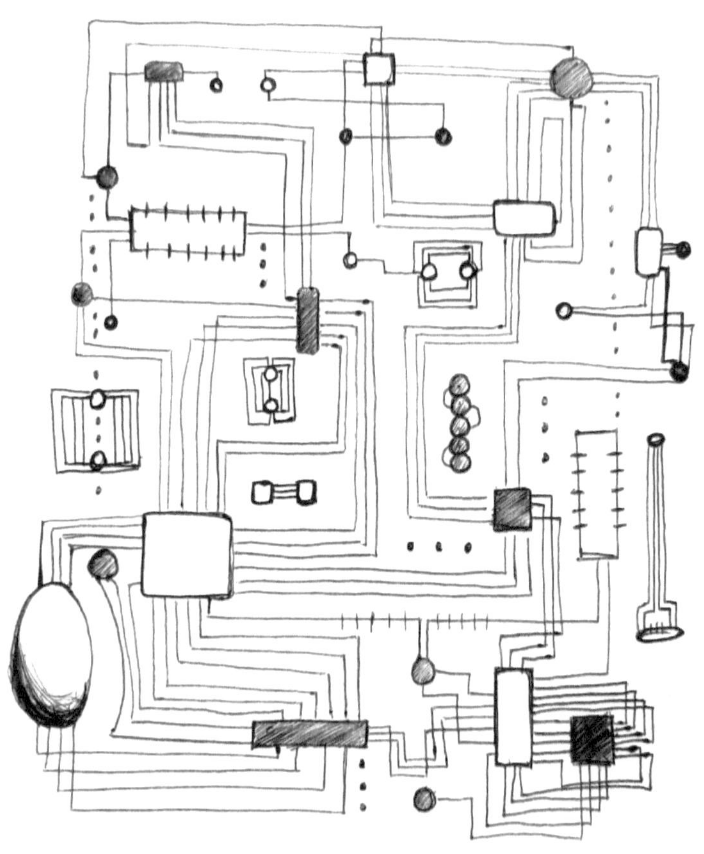

CHAPTER 19

"Morris!?"

Suddenly I find myself choking as I shield my eyes from an intense light. Have I died?

"Morris, are you okay?" a voice asks me calmly, but quickly.

Trying to catch my breath, I sit up slowly, unable to see a thing. The brightness is overwhelming, but the air is more breathable. As my eyes adjust, I make out a figure next to me and two backpacks beside them. Pain radiates from my missing leg and I grab it in reaction.

"Where am… I?" I barely get out through some coughs.

"Some cave, I don't know—your message sent me here. What happened to you?" the voice, a woman's voice, replies. My eyes adjust more and I start to recognize the figure in front of me.

"Michele?"

"Yeah, are you surprised? I saved your life! Glad I came when I did. You were just passing out as I grabbed you," she replies in relief that I am okay.

She stands up and observes me, glancing at the cave around us occasionally. Her tall, slender frame towers over me as I lie on the ground coughing a bit and rubbing my eyes.

"And why the hell are you missing a leg? What happened in there?" she asks, almost angry with me for letting things go so wrong.

But her question jogs my memory.

"Clara!" I say aloud. I grab Clara's backpack and hop up to my one foot. I begin making my way to the old desk and barely make it, my leg shaking from overuse. The old humanoid virus is still in a catatonic state on the floor by the opposite wall.

"What's going on? Why did you ask for my help?" Michele asks, watching me scramble to set up the plug-in system. "And please tell me what happened to your leg!"

"The ceiling collapsed in there. Crushed my leg. But Clara saved me." I pull out the necessary parts from Clara's backpack and quickly set things up. "So glad you're here, Michele, but I need to bring her back." I pull out the instructional tablet and turn it on, then turn on the plug-in system.

"Who's Clara? And can we talk about this mysterious underground passageway?" Michele asks while pointing to the open titanium and concrete door, totally confused by the anxiety of the situation.

"Michele!" I look at her intensely. "Please. Right now I need to focus on saving the woman I love. Thank you for saving my life. I will answer all your questions soon. But please, there's still one life left to save."

She recoils in reaction to my sudden seriousness. Curiosity is apparent in her expression, but she replies respectively.

"Of course. Tell me what you need from me, Morris. I'm here to help," she says, understanding the urgency.

In the most sincere voice I can muster in my frantic state of mind, I reply, "Thank you. I wouldn't be here if it weren't for you. Really, thank you for responding to my message."

Wait—what message? Oh. Clara must have sent our location to Michele after I asked. Our fight led me to believe nothing was sent, but she must have sent it regardless of our disagreement. I would be dead if it weren't for her decision to send Michele coordinates regardless. Realizing this spurs conflicting feelings of being right and being extremely lucky.

Shaking my head to repel these unproductive thoughts, I turn on the reading tablet displaying in large text: "Backup Plans." Touching the screen initiates a transition to another screen of text:

Morris, if I've handed this tablet to you or you found it within your backpack, follow my instructions. I've created backup plans so we're never separated for too long. Don't worry too much! You'll be fine and I'll see you soon.

Hearing her voice in my head as I read what she wrote is bittersweet. Tapping the screen again leads me to a large table of contents listing possible scenarios with the title, "Select Situation..."

Most of the situations involved something happening to Clara.

If I become unresponsive...
If we're separated...
If I've been hacked...
If you need to contact me...
If I run out of power...

Wow. How much time did she have to write all this? Not having to sleep really allows more time for productivity.

Could I have used this tablet as a light back in the darkness? It's meant for reading and is designed not to give off too much light, but it might've helped. A growing disappointment grows. How did I not think of this? I tighten my fist in frustration, but continue looking at the table of contents, ignoring the "what ifs."

Ah-ha! Found it: *"If my body has been compromised..."* I select it and another screen of text appears; a date at the top suggests she updated this a few days ago.

I am not dead! My consciousness is updated to the USB backup servers every minute. There is an old decommissioned humanoid connected to a docking station in my shop. It acts as my backup in situations like this—so give me a few minutes and I'll meet you back in the cave after I've initiated the transfer. Hang tight and don't be alarmed when a random humanoid walks in the cave—it will be me!

Tap here when you're in possession of the old humanoid...
Tap here if the old humanoid was stolen...
Tap here if there's no connection to the humanoid...

Clara really planned for every scenario. Knowing how much she thought ahead helps my nerves. Michele walks around the cave observing as I read Clara's instructions. I tap the appropriate option.

In possession of the old humanoid?

You need to boot the plug-in system and type in this code using the display on top: E354-87465. A copy of the most up-to-date version of my consciousness will then upload to the node connected to the plug-in system. Once complete, attach the node to the back of the old humanoid's neck and wait!

It should only take a few minutes. See you soon!

Tap here if there's no connection to the plug-in system...
Tap here if the plug-in system has no charge...
Tap here if you lost the node...

She really planned for every situation. But okay—should be easy.

Michele watches me as I turn to the plug-in system and type in the appropriate code. A progress bar takes a bit of time, but the uploading finishes and I hold the node in my hand. Though it's merely files and code, it feels odd to hold Clara's being in a small round node. But I quickly walk over to the humanoid virus and pause. Uh-oh.

"Michele, do you know how to wipe a humanoid clean?" I ask after failing to think of other options.

"You mean, kill a humanoid? Just because I enjoy killing neurobines doesn't mean I've worked with humanoids," she replies with attitude, then combs through her short hair—an awkward mannerism.

"You're right," I sigh. "I don't know you very well, but I'm just asking." I stare at the catatonic humanoid still mumbling to itself. But after some time, Michele walks toward it.

"Alright, I do know how. But I'm not necessarily proud of it," she mumbles loud enough for me to hear.

She grabs the humanoid and props it upright, her strength quite shocking, but then she backs away in reaction to its mumbling. The humanoid virus falls, hitting its head on the wall, but eventually settles and leans against the wall.

"Wait, is this humanoid still alive?" she asks.

"There's a neurobine virus in there, but nothing has changed since day one. So is it alive? Well, yes and no," I reply quickly. I'm anxious to bring Clara back.

"Whoa—what the hell are you trying to do with a virus?"

"Michele, we don't have time for this—I'll answer your questions later, I promise," I say to reassure her that it is normal, even though it is far from it.

She examines me, trying to look for side-motives or a hidden agenda, but eventually shrugs and stands the humanoid upright again.

Michele turns the humanoid around and grabs and lifts the back of the head, starting from above the neck connected by a small hinge at the top. Now that the metal flap is removed, the inner skull is uncovered along with the workings of the humanoid mind. The simplistic design is anticlimactic since it's merely a circular container. Just a central processing unit from what I could tell.

But by lifting another metal divider, she reveals a small blue button outlined by little LED lights. The interior of this humanoid's head is illuminated by little blue LED lights specifically placed in geometric shapes outlining various, albeit important, sections of the inside.

Michele pauses and looks at me. "And you're sure you want to delete this virus forever?"

Memories of deleting neurobines as the member of the AVC flood my mind. I remember tears of men and women falling as my hand lifts to remove them from existence. I try to shake my head to clear these thoughts, these painful nightmares, but found myself too distracted all of a sudden.

With Clara around so much recently, I hadn't had many episodes of PTSD and had nearly forgotten about my terrible life before her. All those disappointments. The people I let down, including myself.

I start zoning out in reaction to all these thoughts and haunting memories, including the darkness I thought I was to die in—the terrible nothingness Michele had luckily pulled me from.

"Morris. What will it be?" Michele says, breaking my train of thought.

"Um," I mumble as I successfully shake my head to clear my mind, "yes. Erase the virus. Clara is more important."

Nodding her head, Michele turns to the humanoid virus and presses her thumb against the small blue button she had uncovered. After a few moments of holding it there, the light from the LEDs flicker, causing the illusion of circular movements.

"It's done," she reports.

Trying not to be affected by yet another deletion, I move toward the humanoid as Michele puts everything back. Metal snaps into place as I walk up to the empty shell, the shell now waiting for Clara. Without delay, I place the node on the back of the neck and it, along with the humanoid, hum softly.

Michele and I step back and watch (I hop back, while she steps). A few minutes go by as we wait for something to happen, my one leg tiring quickly. But in determination, I wait without sitting down.

The humanoid's stance relaxes as we step back in reaction. It slowly turns to us, the eyes observing.

"Morris?" it says in a voice like hers.

"Clara?"

"What… what happened?" she asks, completely confused—but relief overwhelms me and I move in for a giant hug.

"Clara, you're okay!" I say loudly as I wrap my arms around the unfamiliar metal of her new humanoid body. The rust of the metal smells different and though her arms hesitantly hug back, it feels awkward.

"Oh, Morris. I was so worried... wait. What's wro... why am I in this nasty piece of junk? What happened to me?" Clara pulls away from me and looks at herself in disgust. "Ugh, this backup was not ready for use," she says as she looks up and notices Michele. "And who's this?"

"Clara, meet Michele. Michele, Clara..." I introduce them with a warm voice, without taking my eyes off the strangeness of Clara's new form.

"So this is Clara, eh?" Michele says, hiding the surprise in her voice as she shakes Clara's hand.

"I'm glad you received my message," Clara says to Michele in a nice voice. Then she turns to me, her movements familiar, but the lack of expression on her face is off-putting. I'm beginning to notice all the things missing from this humanoid—it's definitely more robot than human. More primitive. Less... warm.

"Explain what's going on before I flip my lid, Morris!" she stares at me angrily. "Oh!" she shouts as she walks closer, her feet clunking without grace, "What happened to your leg!?" She places her hand on my shoulder, "oh, my sweet Morris! Where is your leg?!"

"You don't remember?"

"Remember what?" Clara asks me with so much sadness in her voice it hurts my heart.

After she had disconnected the modem back in the large underground room with the titanium table, she must have lost connection with the USB backup servers. So this "Clara" isn't the most up-to-date version, not without the ability to sync after losing connection. She must not have any memory of what happened, because this version of Clara didn't have to go through with... what she had to do.

"Oh, Clara," I look into her unfamiliar eyes with such a longing. My desire to hold her and tell her everything will be alright grows stronger, but I'm distracted by the unusual metal of this impersonal face I don't know.

Though she stands right here, I miss her more than ever.

"Morris… tell me."

Breathe in. Breathe out.

"What happened to us?"

CHAPTER 20

Clara, Michele, and I sit in a circle as I recount what happened. Shade from our cave keeps us safe from the intense sun—it's hard to tell when the night is coming, if ever, especially with Sun Season approaching. My guess? Another week of quick nights until full sun, 24/7 (a.k.a. Sun Season).

Growing up, we learned how thousands of years ago, humans lived closer to the equator where the day/night cycles didn't shift as drastically as they do here so close to the South Pole. As a kid, I always daydreamed about what it would be like not to worry about Sun Season or Night Season. What it might be like to instead worry about rain and hurricanes or any type of cold weather. Natural disasters that cause water and cold are such a foreign idea to humans now.

I remember feeling jealous of humanity's way of life those thousands of years ago. Envying their need to put layers upon layers of clothes on just to go out into weather that was so cold it would turn water into snow. Water that would fall from the sky, not just appear in buckets managed by scientists. Not just water released in measured quantities down city canals.

It never felt right to worry about the sun melting my skin off from heat and radiation. Didn't feel natural growing up and it doesn't feel natural now. Earth is sick and we're dying with it.

Why doesn't the USB understand this?

While deep in thought, I look over at Clara. After the recent tragedy, she now resembles a default servant bot with no features except for the bare minimum. She had told me other projects were her main focus rather than her backup humanoid shell (since she never expected to be put in any dangerous situations). Luckily Clara replaced the vocal box a few months ago so she at least sounds like herself—but apart from that, she looks like a completely different person. Mannerisms here and there remind me of Clara, but I feel troubled by my sadness. She is here, but… not really here.

"So after I went unconscious from lack of air, Michele pulls me out," I say to finish the memory.

"Pure luck really," Michele adds. "I stumbled upon this cave after following your coordinates and noticed that old door was wide open." She points to the open door leading to the corridor. "After walking a bit, I saw you struggling and caught you as you passed out. Then I ran out with you over my shoulder!"

"I did have a question about that—you felt safe waltzing into a dark cave?" I ask, noticing her excitement from recounting the chaos of her rescue story.

"With no one around, I just assumed you were in there and I went for it. I'm no stranger to a little risk, so I started walking. Plus, I had brought my own backpack with supplies just in case things got out of hand. And don't be surprised by my strength. You don't weigh anything. I lift far more in my weekly workouts."

"Wow, noted," I say awkwardly, feeling inadequate to her strength. How is she so strong for being so slender? I itch my head and ask her, "Are you always so prepared?"

"Well, I saw where the coordinates were on the map. I could tell it was off-grid so I packed a few things to be ready. Luckily I brought a flashlight and oxygen mask just in case."

"Yes, very lucky," Clara interjects. I turn to Clara—she hadn't said anything for a while as she thought over the events I recalled. "It's extremely lucky.," Clara looks up at me. "You could have died. The human brain starts deteriorating after a mere minute without oxygen—what was I thinking sending you alone, after amputating your leg!"

"Clara, you had no…"

"It was reckless decision-making! I should have planned better. Planned for an outcome like that…" Clara's voice is stern and serious, sounding unwilling to hear my sympathetic attempts to calm her down.

"You're very brave, Clara," Michele says quietly to console her. "It sounds like you had no choice."

Clara turns to me again, ignoring Michele's kind words.

"How long ago did all this happen?" Clara asks me in an unmoving tone of voice.

"Um, like earlier this morning. It's okay, Clara. There's nothing to forgi…"

"You… you were stuck in the dark for DAYS, Morris! Did you know that?" Clara exclaims with anger, her voice shaking, but her expression unchanging due to the limitation of her new form.

"Days? What do you…"

"Yes! I left you alone in the dark for fifty-seven hours according to the timestamp of my last sync." She sounds angry, but it is hard to tell who it is directed to (either me or herself)—I only have her voice to decipher these emotions.

"No, no, I… I didn't know." I pause, unsure how to take in this information. Learning of my skewed perception of time catches me off guard and I forget to hide my extreme worry as I ponder over such disturbing news. How could I have lost track of so much time? Was I really alone in the dark for that long?

"You were alone for two days, Morris! I left you to die in the dark—do you know what that does to the human mind? You must have experienced hallucinations and loss of mental function. All because I couldn't figure out a better solution!"

Clara turns to wipe her eyes, but grunts in frustration at the lack of tears. And then stands up suddenly and punches the cave wall. A dust cloud falls, revealing the indent she made.

"Clara, you have nothing to be sorry about. I am perfectly fine! You saved my life in the end, didn't you?" I get up and hop over, putting my hand on her cold metal shoulder to turn her around.

Michele sits awkwardly trying not to pay attention, unsure if she should still be involved or not.

"You could have died, Morris. We both could have…"

"Shh, shh," I quiet her as I hold her head and kiss a metal forehead. "I love you. You were the reason I made it so far in the dark. Without the thought of you, I wouldn't have made it."

Being that this was the first time I said, "I love you," Clara looks up suddenly, her anger gone. Motionless eyes stare back at me without a sign of emotion, but I could tell she felt something.

"How could I have failed you so… terribly," her voice shaky. "I left you, the man I love, to die alone. Alone in the dark," she says softly and sadly, "and I will never forgive myself."

She turns away and walks toward the plug-in system.

"Clara, wait…" I say in the hope she would turn around, but she doesn't.

"I cannot apologize properly without my original chassis," Clara states with a rigid voice. She turns around. "I cannot begin to tell you how truly sorry I am without the ability to cry. I cannot hope to connect with you without my ability to express. I want so desperately to kiss you, but I'm just a metal bucket without my old self, Morris." She turns around in her strange, impersonal humanoid form and continues, "I love you! I do, but a metal bucket cannot love a human."

Hopelessness in her voice hints at her desperation and need for help. In reaction to her guilt and her sadness, from the loss of my limb, and from my recent near-death experience, determination bubbles within my soul. And I begin to devise a plan to save her from the metal prison she finds herself in.

Michele looks at us unsure of what to do, while Clara looks at me feeling lost without her true identity. I have to do something about this—it IS my fault we're all down in this cave to begin with, so I have to take responsibility.

I've run from society, started my own life with a humanoid, and survived two days in lonesome insanity. If I survived all that, I can survive anything, because my previous self died in that darkness. And like firewood, I've taken on another form. Evolved from the blackness of my ashes, I will grow into the leader Clara needs me to be.

I look at Michele and then at Clara.

"Here's the plan," I say without hesitation. "Clara, grab us the equipment we need to retrieve your real humanoid shell. As we go to fetch your true self, begin building the firewall needed to protect my connection to Sector 1."

"Sector 1?!" Michele asks uncontrollably.

"Clara," I say ignoring Michele's concern, "can you fetch us what we need to carry the humanoid body we left down in the passageway?"

"Yes," she replies, concentrating on the task at hand, "I'm on it."

She rushes out of the cave and disappears.

"Michele," I say to her, "how much do you have in your back-pack?"

"I have enough, but wait. Slow down. I'm here to help. And I love action and all, but what exactly are we doing here? Sector 1!? You gotta be…"

"We gotta go!" Clara comes rushing back in the cave, beginning to pack the plug-in system.

"What? What's going on?" I ask, thrown off by her frantic packing.

"We need to leave. Now!" Clara throws the backpack with the equipment on her shoulder and runs into the passageway. Then turns around and frantically motions for us to follow.

I look at Michele with wide eyes and then grab my own backpack and hop toward the door. Michele comes up behind and picks me up as we enter through the door.

Clara swings the door and runs in as it slams behind her.

"Move!" she shouts as the door crashes, causing it to buckle and crack. As we jump out of the way, crashing can be heard out-side the door within our cave. Clara's new body can really pack a punch.

A light flickers as Clara complains about the low-quality ma-chinery, but then her hand-light finally stays steady.

"What is going on, Clara?" I quickly ask, unsure what to think as Michele sets me back down.

"The government is looking for us."

CHAPTER 21

The cold metal of Clara's shoulders presses uncomfortably into my chest and lower gut, but I refrain from complaining as it's much better to be carried. Michele walks behind us, her own flashlight on as she observes the strange corridors for the first time. We're escaping now, running from the government according to what Clara told us.

Both Michele and I have our oxygen masks on as we hurry further underground, worried about hear anything besides our own footsteps.

"Why is the USB after us?" I ask, confused about the situation.

"My location was made known after my backup version was pulled. I, uh…" Clara hesitates, "made a patch to prevent this, but it must have failed. I must have been distracted by... other projects."

I could tell she was referring to "us" being a distraction, which wasn't all her fault. Our closeness has caused both of us to be emotionally influenced—my lack of control leading to my missing leg proves my point. But, no use in pointing blame now. Unfortunate events have taken place and we must look forward.

Occasionally Clara's footsteps sync with Michele's as we speed down the dark passageway. Intriguing, phasing rhythms come in and out of unison between their feet—something I remember listening for, hoping for, while alone in the darkness during those two days (though it felt like half a day). My fear of the possible pitch black is hard to ignore, but the light from these two and the conversation between us keeps my mind occupied.

"The USB was notified of my location once my backup was accessed…" Clara states with a tinge of guilt.

"But humanoids are allowed to access their backups, right?" I ask.

"Yes. Just not… in an illegal way," she answers with more guilt in her voice.

"Illegal?!" Michele replies.

Clara turns and sets me down suddenly.

"I didn't want to leave Morris alone for too long in case something happened to me!" Clara defends herself, then pauses for a second.

"There's an extensive report and a time-consuming investigation when a humanoid… 'dies.' It wouldn't be fair to leave Morris waiting for weeks all alone," Clara explains with a hint of vulnerability in her voice. Admitting her concern for me around Michele made her feel awkward.

"I altered the code to ensure fast data transfer, but never got around to confirming its discreet connection protocol. Which I take full responsibility for…," Clara says, her eyes meeting mine. "I'm sorry."

Michele looks awkwardly at the two of us, seeing how we look at each other.

"How long have you two been a thing…?" Michele asks bluntly without embarrassment. Clara looks at her in surprise, then back at me wondering what to say.

"About a week… why?" I reply with no shame.

"Just wondering why you two are so awkward," she says frankly, then walks between us and down the corridor.

I smirk at Clara hoping for a smile in return, but the old humanoid body she's stuck in doesn't move. I forget she has no ability for expression. But she whispers, "Sorry," and grabs my hand for a second, tightens as an emotional response and then lets it go.

I give her a loving smile in return and mouth the words, "It's okay," and then sigh in frustration. Clara lifts me up and sets me back on her uncomfortable shoulders again and we follow after Michele.

Many minutes go by.

The connecting room with the six corridors looks different than how I imagined it when I was stuck in the dark. Clara looks for a second and then continues leading us to the large room through the corridor slightly to the right.

"I assume we need a new place to call home, so the large room with the titanium table is an obvious choice," Clara states while walking.

"Was thinking the same thing," I reply while adjusting the uncomfortable oxygen mask.

"Love the unknown references, but shouldn't we be concerned about the government following us down here?" Michele asks behind us. "Plus, I'M not being chased by the government? So I COULD just go home, right?"

"First off," Clara says with sarcasm in her voice, "Love that you're a team player," mocking Michele's wording, "but unfortunately, if you're caught within proximity of me, then you're guilty by association. Secondly, they didn't see where I went so down here we should be safe. Maybe they found where the cave is, but I'm fairly sure I broke the entrance."

"And possibly collapsed the entire cave," I interject.

Michele groans, unsatisfied by our confidence. She swings her flashlight and ponders for a second.

"Then I guess I'm stuck here helping you two lovebirds," she replies with equal sarcasm. "Just know that it's not that I don't approve of intersentient couples, it's just I'm uncomfortable as the third wheel."

"Sure thing, Ma'am. We'll keep the PDA at a minimum," Clara remarks lightly, chuckles and turns back to walk down the corridor.

Minutes go by.

We finally make it to the large room with the titanium table. The trauma I experienced when last here makes me shiver as we enter the room. Michele gasps at the enormity of the space, her flashlight pointing everywhere as she scans the room.

"Wait," I tell them. "Michele, can you do me a favor?" She turns to me and nods.

"Can you please pull the decommissioned humanoid from the corridor just over there?" I point to the double doors on the far side. The place where I lost my leg. "Just… be aware there may be some blood and… well, a terrible scene."

"I want to see, Morris," Clara says as we near the titanium table.

"No, I really think it's best you don't. I don't want you seeing what's over there," I reply with sadness, trying not to remember what happened.

"I'm on it," Michele says and without hesitation makes her way over to the corridor as Clara sets me on the table.

"Clara," I say sweetly and slowly. She turns to me after setting her backpack on the table. "Remember that night under the auroras? Do you remember the colors in the sky and your arm around my chest as I fell asleep?"

"Yes. I remember clearly," she replies sadly.

"For the endless hours I spent hoping to escape the darkness, that memory kept me going." Gently, I take her hand and lead her closer. "All I wanted was to spend another night like that with you and that desire kept me pushing forward. I reminded myself over and over, how much you mean to me and how much I owe you."

Clara stays silent as I pause to decipher her unchanging expression, a cold face of stone with such limited mechanics.

"Knowing you're with me right here, right now is something I thought I'd never have again. So it's YOU I love, no matter the form you're in," I say, gesturing at the old humanoid body she was stuck in.

Clara hesitantly looks at my missing leg, then back to me.

"You're sweet." Her voice is genuine, I can tell. But she strokes my cheek and says, "Just by bringing it up, you confirm the obvious. There's a reason I want to be back to normal—everything I do seems impersonal without my real self. And it upsets me that I can't express to you how guilty I feel and how much I love you."

She lets her hand fall.

"There's a reason I upgraded the hair, lips, eyes, and skin. I wanted to experience life like a human does." She turns and begins setting up the plug-in system. "So until I'm back to normal, I can't love you like you deserve. And I can't help but feel… inadequate."

Nothing I can say will make her feel better now. I've said what I needed to say. Now it's just a waiting game for Michele to return.

"Okay, Clara. I can wait," I reply to her as she continues setting up the plug-in system.

"Wait," I say quickly. "We need to come up with a plan. You need about a week to work on the firewall, correct?"

Clara pauses and turns to me. I can just imagine the smirk on her face as she says shortly, "Yes, we've been over this, Sir Plans-a-Lot."

I laugh at the ridiculous word., "I don't even know half the things you say."

"I know," she says lightly and turns back to the plug-in system.

Footsteps approach and we look to see Michele placing Clara's lifeless form on the table. That true identity that I've missed so much. Clara ran up to see it closer.

"Oh you found it!" Her voice is giddy as she examines it.

"Wasn't too heavy. About as light as Scrawny over here," Michele reports, referring to my thin figure. I flash an angry look, but she continues, "It was quite a nasty sight though. Smelled too. I'm assuming that mess was once your leg?"

"Yes, the ceiling… fell and Clara had to… creatively problem-solve." My voice sank at the memory of the situation. My missing leg still catches me off guard, even with the constant dull pain.

"Ah—well. This side project you've brought me in on has really turned out to be quite bazaar," Michele says with her hands on her waist, troubled by the strange underground titanium table and the odd couple that recruited her.

"Like a circus act, yes," Clara chimes in as she carefully places her normal humanoid shell on its side. Both Michele and I look at Clara with looks of confusion, unsure of what a 'circus' even meant.

"Mhmm," Michele grunts. "Can I be excused?"

Michele's unhappiness makes me worry about having her part of this so-called team. "I'm sorry Michele, but I'm not sure there's a way out from here. Not an easy one anyway," I say plainly; but I devise a way to break the tension. "Don't you want to be a part of this 'circus?'"

Silence follows my question as Michele turns to me slowly.

"We're officially stuck down here. And with limited supplies, we need a way to reach the surface or else we'll die. Unlike buckets of metal," she gestures to Clara, "we can't survive without food and water. So were you expecting me to laugh?" Michele's voice turns very serious in concern.

"We have maybe a few days' worth of food, we're stuck in an un-known channel of tunnels with limited light, and you both keep forgetting the USB is searching for us!" Michele throws up her hands in anger.

"Stop wasting time! We need a solution, fast. I didn't volunteer myself to die under the dirt," she shouts, her voice echoing in the large space around us. We fall silent in response.

"She's right." I turn to Clara. "We can't die down here, not in the dark. And we know this place isn't as safe as we thought."

"I might know a few people who could... maybe identify the structural integrity?" Michele says in reply, her anger simmering.

"Really? Okay great." My voice is quick in excitement. "How can we contact them?"

"Okay, but wait." She puts her hand up, palm out. "You promised me answers," she says rudely to me, "and now I'm officially stuck with you two? I deserve to know what the hell we're doing with this 'side-project' of yours. I took a day off for this, you know! But now with the government after us, we could be down here for days! I wasn't expecting to lose my job, Morris." Michele's voice is angrier than usual. Before I can respond, she continues.

"And the ceiling took off your leg?! I mean, come on! What kind of operation is this?!" She thrusts her fists into the table, the noise intertwining with the echoes of her shouting.

"So… talk," she suddenly speaks softly and seriously, commanding even.

Clara looks at me, catching my wide eyes, but I quickly look back at Michele with more awareness now. I'm understanding she has a temper. Maybe Clara was right—I should have gotten to know her a bit more before entrusting her.

"You're right." I match the seriousness of her voice. "I never meant to drag you into this mess, but without you, I'd be dead. And for that I owe you more than answers, I owe you my life. But..."

I hop off the table and catch myself with my one foot, trying to stand tall regardless of Michele's superior stature.

"I have reason to believe the SSR is hiding vital information within Sector 1. Information that may convince the population that virtual time is second best to life on Earth. Society's priorities need to shift toward regrowth. We need to build an authentic reality and step away from the fraudulent imitations cheaply reproduced in the Sector-System."

Michele is taken aback by my sudden shift in vocabulary and philosophy. Though silent, she stays very attentive.

"I promised you freedom from the AVC. Well, with your help and possibly many others, we might just be able to alter the course of civilization by proving the Sector-System uninhabitable. Haven't you wondered why there are viruses in the first place? Michele, we are so close to understanding the source of these issues." My hands are gesturing with large movements.

"Our mission is to uncover all of it, so the general public can force the USB to proactively respond and refocus our efforts toward Earth's rehabilitation. This, in turn, will remove the AVC entirely."

Still silent, Michele takes in all the information, decoding my speech and deciding whether to believe in it.

"Don't you see?" I hop closer to her. "Earth is our home. And AI was created to augment it, not abandon it. Humans and humanoids were meant to coexist. And with a single, inarguable goal of rebuilding Earth, we can make this happen. We can change our lives and promise our future!"

Michele's face is still as I wait for a response, but then, it suddenly relaxes.

"You're crazy."

Her short response leaves me shocked.

"What makes you think the government will respond to what the people want? They're a business! They're only after people's money, not their welfare. PixelOne practically runs the thing!" Michele argues with anger mixed in her voice, though this time directed at the situation rather than at me.

"The Sector-System makes money! They're not gonna budge. They'll throw everything they have at you to keep their money net functioning. If you're to change society, you're going to have to overthrow the USB AND the SSR. Are you prepared to build an army and tear everything down?! 'Cause that's what you'll have to do in order to change society. Rebuild from nothing."

Like firewood, I thought. Ashes to fuel the growth.

"No, that's just destruction," Clara interjects. "The better plan would be to rely on mass hysteria. Once neurobines are convinced the Sector-System directly causes virus symptoms, there'll be chaos. And with a neurobine population in the trillions, all flooding to escape, Antarctica will be overburdened and the government will be forced to expand outward somehow. In turn, altering their priorities."

"Isn't there a waiting list to transfer out though?" I ask Clara.

"Yes… and the government COULD potentially stall the entire NTC," she replies looking upward, thinking to herself.

"What does NTC stand for?" Michele asks.

"Neurobine Transfer Center," Clara states.

"Hmm. What a creative name," Michele replies sarcastically. She doesn't look entertained by the talk of avoiding destruction and chaos.

"Neurobines must have some power to influence things in human-reality, right?" I ask them, while also thinking out loud.

"Well," Clara thinks, "if I can hack INTO the Sector-System, there must be a way to hack the other way. With trillions of possible neurobine hackers, I'm sure they could find an illegal way out and bypass the NTC."

I stay silent, thinking to myself now. So many things to consider that I hadn't had a chance to think over. But I have to figure this out now in order to convince Michele to stay and that our fight is not a losing battle. And she's getting impatient.

The light in Clara's hand flickers a bit as Michele twirls her flashlight in thought.

"Look," I say, pausing for dramatic effect, looking at them both, "we can promise humans and neurobines a better life here on Earth by dismantling both governments' priorities. The right thing to do is inform the population of the sickness caused by the Sector-System and with a revolution to break free, it's power-in-numbers at that point. Right?"

"So incite political activists and widespread concern without burning anything down, hoping that false democracy works in our favor?" Michele seems very unconvinced as she adds, "Seems promising."

"'There's too much to risk with an all-out civil war. Priorities wouldn't just be rearranged, they'd be lost entirely!" Clara argues. "We'd need to rebuild everything if there's war. What if the departments of water manufacturing are destroyed in the chaos?" Michele looks at me oddly in response to her last statement.

"With Earth's oceans refilled, having healthy atmospheric density would allow for a more stable environment for us all to live in. Even near the equator. Don't you remember anything from school?" I ask her, hoping she would understand the importance of old-Earth's oceans.

"Nope, wasn't interested in reading," Michele responds shortly.

I take a big breath and sigh.

"Michele we're so close," I plead with her, but suddenly an idea strikes me. My eyes widen and I look at them again.

"I got it. I got a plan."

Tomorrow is the day.

Clara estimates just one more day until the firewall is secure, allowing me to explore Sector 1, the origin of the Sector-System, to hopefully uncover SSG secrets kept behind these closed doors.

Currently, I'm walking around in circles, thinking as I keep a consistent pace around the titanium table we now refer to as "The Table." I have to review the details over and over to ensure our one shot is successful. But this bionic leg that was retrieved for me makes a different-sounding footstep, slightly distracting me as I make my way around The Table again and again. Regardless, I think and prepare.

Everything's coming together.

Days have passed since I convinced Michele of my new plan. And with her on board, we were an unstoppable team of three. Though Clara had to collapse our old cave to cover our tracks from the USB, it luckily didn't alter the structural integrity of the corridor or anything connected to it. Though I'm still sad about leaving our old home, we had to press on deeper into the blackness with greater plans in mind. And after climbing, digging, and cold-sawing with the equipment Michele brought (thank goodness she was so over prepared), she and Clara were able to cut their way through the old, stuck titanium elevator in the giant room with The Table.

They reported to me that the elevator was stuck at the top, but opens to a view overlooking Lake Vostok (a few miles' walk from the edge of town). Having been covered by rocks, it, too, has never been detected by the government. Why explore into the dead desert land when you can expand the Sector-System exponentially? The USB's obliviousness is astounding.

With the sun so hot and fatal after only thirty-minutes for us humans, Clara left the elevator hideout to bring back some equipment, food, and stolen SunSuits for Michele and me. Her ability to hack security systems and drones has quickly become priceless.

Day two involved Clara working long hours straight on the firewall as Michele snuck into town for supplies after building a pulley system to act as an elevator. It was then that Clara took a break from programming to retrieve a bionic leg for me from her old shop. Quite a relief to walk again after hopping for several days. Looking at it now, it isn't pretty, but it works. The dirty chrome of my new left leg has grown on me (adds character as Clara says).

Day three involved Michele and me going into town with our SunSuits while Clara continued to code the firewall. Michele's servant bot, Diane, met us by the edge of town to help us evade cameras and drones as we talked with passerby. As mean as Michele can be, she does make for a good saleswoman. After "selling" our mission and purpose to hundreds on the street, we were able to recruit a few programmers and a botanist to the team: two humanoid and three human. All thanks to Michele's pushy sales technique.

Day four was the most tiring. We helped lug equipment the new recruits couldn't live without, but soon our underground home looked more like "headquarters" rather than an old forgotten-about dungeon. Three plug-in systems are now lined up on The Table with enough plants around to help things feel more homey.

Along with these new team members came an inspiring speech from me that ended with: "And that's why we don't follow society, but explore outward and make our own path."

The programmers were placed under Clara's direction while the botanist began working on planting more oxygen-rich greenery around the vicinity.

Day five had us pooling the newest recruits' credit to buy enough plants for us to safely leave our oxygen masks in our backpacks. It was a happy moment to be able to breathe normally in our safe underground home. But no time was wasted and we quickly went up to recruit Michele's architect friend.

Once he was convinced, he brought his things to join our team. Upon entering our underground sanctuary, he immediately began pulling out tools and measuring devices to examine the structural integrity of the ancient ruins. We promised undiscovered territory and we delivered—Dr. Rogers was thrilled to be the first to inspect these timeworn walls.

On day six, Michele split off with Diane to gather more supplies while I waited at the edge of town. I had Diane send a message for Archie, asking him to forgive me and if he truly cares, to meet me by the edge of town unseen. After hours of waiting in the hot sun, protected only by my SunSuit, Archie finally arrived and it was one of the happiest moments in my life.

"Morris! You plant-crazed, breath of fresh air. I was so sure your 'meditation' phase would lead you straight to the PRP!" he had said, hugging me with tears of relief.

His ability to cry shocked me at first—it was strange to see new upgrades, but his analytical eyes and slicked back, black hair are still exactly how I remember them. Our carefree reunion was cut short though when Archie quickly told me the PRP was searching for me since my epichip was found tossed aside in the streets of East Vostok.

"I've been a cave-dweller, Archie. Safe from the PRP," I said to reassure him. And after telling him my newest life goals, I hesitantly updated him on how Clara had been searching for me and how we've found love.

"Why am I not surprised," he said. "You always did talk to AI more than humans, huh?" I remember his sarcastic tone in his reply as though he didn't quite believe me.

After some convincing, Archie agreed to come with me and help in my cause. It's an amazing feeling to have him back in my life, even if we're both still awkwardly examining each other, trying to grasp all that has changed in the last few weeks. But it is good to have him part of the team now—he's more family to me than anyone.

Though when he remembered who Clara was, he wasted no time in telling me of recent public alerts sent out about a vigilante named "Clara" being tracked down by the USB. He was not happy to find our relationship riddled with criminal entanglement, even if it's for "the greater good" as I put it.

Today is day seven.

It has been a week with all this prep since I devised my newest plan. Clara has been working nonstop and is nearing completion of the firewall. Still anxious, I walk around The Table over and over, going over the details in my head. My new metal leg clunks with every other step.

So much has changed in the past week. I stop and look around to gather the situation we're in.

Clara sits concentrating on the firewall, the four programmers next to her focusing on their part. The botanist is walking around spraying the many plants, keeping our oxygen supply steady. His vast array of mirrors illuminate the room and spread sunlight from the elevator shaft down onto the important oxygen-producing plants.

Archie is standing aside keeping up to date with current news of the vigilante known as "Clara." Michele and Diane are still out and about gathering supplies in case we're stranded down here, preparing for backup plans.

I stop walking, seeing that Michele's architect friend, Dr. Rogers, is walking up to me now.

"Morris," Dr. Rogers says, asking for my attention. I nod in response.

"After examining the area, I've found that this giant room is structurally sound for the most part. A few lintels worry me, so I urge you to prioritize when you get the chance because a few areas need attending to." His voice is shaky as he speaks, though I don't find it surprising seeing as he's an older man.

"Thank you, Dr. Rogers, it's invaluable to have an architect on the team. I will prioritize when able," I reply shortly. He grunts.

"I'm a civil engineer, remember? Not an architect," he corrects me, then walks away to continue examining.

"Fine, fine," I say to myself. "As long as these walls hold, more pressing matters need attending to."

"Archie," I call out. In response, he walks over as I ask, "Any updates?"

"Yes," he says, foreshadowing some bad news. "It appears they've identified an associated human that was in contact with Clara last week, according to security cameras. They've thrown your name up on the 'wanted' list, Morris."

Hmm, great. It must have been that time Clara followed me to the cave—investigators involved with her case must have connected the dots. With my disappearance and her recent hijinks, they're probably headlining our story as "The Criminal Duo."

"Any mentioned of a cave? Or where they're looking?" I ask, troubled by this news.

"A cave was only suggested out of a series of possibilities, so nothing worrisome."

"Thanks, Archie."

I turn to walk around The Table again but notice Clara and her focused eyes. It's hard not to dwell on how much I miss time alone with her. I walk over and run my hand through her hair, "Clara?"

"Um, yes, almost there…" she reports in a serious tone.

"How are you doing?" I ask her sweetly.

"I'm fine, Love," she says with a smile. "It's been a long week, but the tests I'm running on the firewall are promising."

"That's great! But I'm worried about you. You haven't really taken a break."

"Well, you're the boss," she playfully replies. "Are you ordering me to take a break?"

I hear the pulley system start to crank, hinting at the arrival of Michele and Diane.

"Why, yes. I think I am," I say, returning the loving tone of her voice. After kissing her forehead, I pull myself up on The Table and clap loudly to gain everyone's attention.

"Team meeting!" I shout. My voice echoes around the room as I hop off. As everyone gathers, I smile at Clara again. Her beautiful eyes look through me, those eyes that at one point I thought I'd never see again.

Noticing everyone standing around The Table, I stand a bit taller. Michele and Diane arrive and set down the supplies they brought to join in the huddle.

"It's been a week and we've seen this forgotten vault transform into a home. Months ago, I would have never guessed I'd be working alongside a team capable of so much change," I say with a more confident voice than I expected.

All of us are gathered around the titanium table Clara and I once found by accident. Each of the team members attentively waits for my words. It's still strange to find myself in a leadership role, but in some ways, a natural ability facilitates my willingness. Maybe Clara's "numbers" were right all along.

"I've not known many of you for long, but I feel indebted to you for committing so wholeheartedly to this team." I scan their faces and stop at Archie's. "I could not imagine having a better group of caring individuals." Archie smirks at me, his familiar humor making me smile back.

"The mastermind behind the code for the next phase of the plan needs a break," I gesture toward Clara. "And I think you all are in need of a well-deserved break, too. We've worked hard toward change on a much larger scale and I'm confident we will find success. But, take a break everyone, it's late! We'll start first thing in the morning," I say, my bright voice echoing.

"Hey," the humanoid programmer says to keep us at the table, "what's our group's name?"

"True, a team name would tie this place together," the human programmer agrees.

"We don't need a name," I say to write them off, but another programmer chimes in.

"How about 'The Travelers?'" the female programmer says.

"No, it should be more like 'Revolutioners.' We ARE doing something important after all…" the botanist suggests.

Another young programmer points at large engraving on the far wall and says, "maybe that spinning fan design can be our symbol?"

"No symbols," I say sternly.

"Fine—then let's go with Revolutioners," the young human programmer says.

"No, it has to be something creative," another replies.

"Mmhmm," I interject. "Best of luck with that everyone. Clara and I will be back soon," I say to them as I take Clara's hand, grab my oxygen mask, and walk towards the pulley system. But as we walk, I hear them continue behind us.

"Well, there's eleven of us. How about Eleven Radicals?"

"Ooh, that's a good one."

"No, wait. Echo Eleven—you know, 'cause we live with echoes?"

"Firewood Eleven." I turn to look at Clara in surprise at her suggestion. "What?" she smirks. "I know you like firewood." I chuckle and smile at her as we near the elevator shaft.

As we pull ourselves up the makeshift elevator for some much-needed alone time, I hear voices echo by The Table.

"Did she say fire and wood, and then also eleven?"

"Fire wood. What's firewood?"

240

I'm sitting with Clara now, looking out over the surrounding area of Lake Vostok as we inch closer to each other, embracing our solitary togetherness. The boulders covering the elevator's entrance are smooth and still hot from the midday sun, but we were able to find a shaded area to sit with each other.

The sky appears stuck in perpetual twilight as the sun peeks over the horizon just enough to illuminate the sky while still allowing stars to shine. Auroras of light purple dance slowly across the landscape bringing memories of our time in the first cave. Our first "home" that was understandably destroyed in order to slow the USB's search for us.

With Sun Season almost upon us, it feels like our last chance to watch the auroras before the sun takes over the day/night cycle. Living this far from the equator and this close to the South Pole really alters life. Though I've always lived with the inconvenience of Night Season and Sun Season, it has never truly felt "normal."

"So. I think it's someone's birthday today," I say softly through my oxygen mask. Clara had been observing the landscape, but laughs gently in reaction and glances at me.

"You remembered," she replies with a grin. I then lean over, lift my mask, and kiss her lightly. With no plants around the outskirts of town, the mask is annoyingly necessary. I start feeling the need to breathe and reluctantly end the kiss to slip the oxygen mask back in place.

"Of course I remembered. We once had a conversation where you told me how your 'Life's Path Number' is 33 after adding up the numbers of your birthday: 10/8/8151." I rub her hand and look up. "You thought I'd forget? Tisk tisk."

"I always assume you're not listening when I talk numbers," she says, poking fun at me with a hint of passive-aggressive inflection.

"Hmm. Well, I prepared for this one." I reach into my pocket and I continue, "I never told you this, but I was married a few months ago. Happily married about six months ago actually," I say with calmed emotions as I pull out my old wedding ring from my pocket.

Clara hesitantly looks at the ring, unsure of what to think.

"Don't propose, Morris. I hope you're not going to propose."

"What? No! No. It's just that, after my ex and I signed the divorce papers, I held on to my old ring in hopes things would eventually work out with Yuki. But now," I turn to Clara, "it just serves as a little reminder of a previous life."

"Why did you… get divorced?"

I was hoping that question wouldn't come up. I turn away in response but realize I shouldn't be surprised she's curious.

"Yuki had told me, I wasn't motivated enough to keep up with her and her goals. That I was slowing her down with my lack of enthusiasm for the mundane… and she hated my cynical outlook on life." My voice sounds regretful, regardless of my attempts to sound unaffected by the situation.

"But I loved her and wanted to change. Just… couldn't," I say quickly trying not to add much to the sob story.

"It wasn't in the numbers," Clara says jokingly to lighten the mood. I laugh and look over at her, but notice she's partly serious. My smile softens in response.

"My point being, for your birthday I'd like to show you that I'm ready to move on from that old hope and that old life," I say with strength behind my words. As if making a big decision in front of her, my body tightens and I stand up dramatically (not necessarily on purpose).

Feeling the weight of the ring in my hand, I look out upon the landscape and pull my arm back. Quickly, my arm jets forward and I throw the ring into the distance, my eyes losing it as it descends into the desert land between us and the city.

With a smile, I turn to Clara and grab her hand. She smiles back, innocent and happy—her eyes bright.

"You're my future now. I don't need reminders of my past or memories of what could have been, because you're all I need. And that's all I want," I say genuinely as I pull her close. "I'm here for you. Always. And no matter what shape or form you might find yourself in," I say referring to her insecurity during her time in the decommissioned humanoid chassis, "I love you."

Her eyes had been focused on me, soaking in the moment and my every word. I know how much she desires companionship, especially after losing her original owner so tragically.

Feeling the moment, I lean forward to kiss her again as I lift my mask, but she stops me.

"You're sweet, Morris." Her words seem delicate. "You are by far the best thing that has happened to me." I listen closely, afraid she might say something I don't want to hear. She sets her hands on my shoulders and hugs me.

"But before you commit to me fully with your puppy love and those 'three little words,'" Clara says as she hugs me, again spouting out idioms I don't understand, "I have to come to terms with the consequences."

I pull away and look at her. "Consequences?" I ask confused.

"I am but code in a box, copyable and transferable. Able to live forever. But you, Morris, are human." She looks into my eyes. "I can't imagine living on after watching you… eventually pass away."

She looks down, avoiding the emotions of her hypothetical situation. Hypothetical, but unfortunately, inevitable. She's right.

Moving closer, I hug her and realize she must have thought this through in reaction to being surrounded by more humans, maybe after seeing the old engineer, Dr. Rogers.

"I would never dream of putting you in a situation where someone you love dies in front of you. I could never make a decision that might make your fear a possibility. So I'll leave it up to you, Clara," I say as I raise her head gently and stroke her cheek.

"But know that I would rather live a life with you than without you. And that I hate thinking fear could keep us apart, knowing how happy we make each other, here, now, in my limited lifetime." I run my hand through her artificial brown hair while taking an unrewarding breath through my oxygen mask to gain control of my own emotions.

"Clara, I would do anything to prevent you from ever losing me and with a lifetime to figure it out, I'm hopeful we can find a solution," I cheerfully say to her with a light smile.

She stays silent a few moments, pondering over her difficult decision, then replies: "Knowing you love me and are so committed is the best birthday gift I could have asked for." She kisses me on the cheek and then continues. "But I'm afraid we're both blinded by love."

A fear quickly overwhelms me that she might decide against our being together. The few moments of silence feel like minutes of anxiety, but Clara then looks down and chuckles to herself.

"What…" I ask, unsure of what she might find funny. Unsure of how she could find any of this funny. But she looks up at me with a smile of defeat.

"I just think it's too late to turn back."

I laugh from the sudden relief and nod.

"There's just no way I could live without you now, not without regret. Not without the pain of leaving a happy life with you. It's not worth playing it safe here—not when I know I'm preventing you from… well, me," she says sarcastically with a grin.

"I couldn't agree more. Our relationship took a strange turn at the beginning, but if we've survived through all that, then I have no doubt that along the way we'll figure out all the details that worry you. I promise," I reply, then lean forward, lift my mask and kiss her.

The half-lit, gray sky serves as our backdrop, with timid stars shining through the light purple auroras. Drones in the distance hover over our last sanctuary, searching with no aim and no leads thanks to our demolished cave. But regardless, nothing in the world has more hold on us than our devotion to each other.

From what we've been through and what we could become, our lives feel like one—an oasis of hope in a society on the brink of change. A change led by "Firewood 11," as Clara had named us.

Breathe in. Breathe out.

These moments feel suspended, stuck in a limbo between the old ways and the new ways. A new wave of change in society's priorities that we've hoped for so long.

Fear of the unknown, of what might grow from the ashes of the chaos we'll ignite, leaves a lingering anxiety only remedied by the unquestionable love we share. And our commitment to each other is a welcome distraction.

My thoughts lead me to gaze out toward the twilight sky. Clara glances at me from time to time but doesn't interrupt. Until now.

"You're in your head again, aren't you?" she asks softly and sweetly, her concern for me apparent.

"Yes," I say, then turn and smirk, "as always."

"There have been many humans throughout history that attempt change in their society. But since AI came along, 'change' is a rare thing now that humans aren't in control," she says, then pauses for a second. "You're different though. And different is needed."

I stroke her cheek and smile through my oxygen mask.

"Follow no one… right?" I say, feeling nostalgic.

"And leave no path untaken," she replies with a smirk, finishing the quote and hugging me back.

Memories of the past keep reminding me of how far I've come, but one, in particular, haunts me still. When at my lowest point in life, away from society, away from people, with no one and no hope, I found inspiration to push forward by convincing myself. For the many days in my solitary cave, I told myself over and over, words of motivation.

As Clara and I sit looking out, enjoying the stillness in our lives and in these moments, I think to myself:

"Hopes and dreams no longer define who I am. Actions do."

I breathe in and feel my lungs expand, stretching the muscles around my rib cage, centering me on the rock we're sitting on.

"Like firewood, I was burned past repair."

I then breathe out slowly, softly, releasing stress and the worries that weigh me down. Hope quickly fills my soul as I recite the last phrase of my old mantra.

"But like ash, I will fuel a new movement."

"Any questions?" I ask the group after explaining the plan one last time.h

Each of them, sitting at the titanium table, looks around awkwardly. It's a new day and we're about to take the plunge, but with a team of so many people, I feel anxious with all the variables. And even more so when remembering how little I know them. I've only had the past few days to judge their character.

Let's be honest—just by accepting Michele's and my original sales pitch ("tired of feeling manipulated by society? Ready for change?"), I can safely assume they are all idealistic thinkers. Hopefully, that's enough to carry them through.

"I do have a question," one of the humanoid programmers says raising his hand.

"Okay, sure," I respond by nodding my head his direction.

"I've been doing some research about this ancient symbol on the wall over there," he says, motioning to the swastika. "I don't think we should be associated with what it stands for..."

Clara and I look at each other and then I look back.

"Yes, we've researched the swastika symbol and have found there are SOME terrible things associated with it. But it doesn't negate the MANY positive things it represents."

"That's all well and good, but after scouring the ancient database the last few days, I've come across some incriminating evidence as to the group associated with this particular base," he says with serious concern.

"Send it to me then," Clara says and she pauses, most likely reading it over in her head. She snaps out of her concentration and looks to me. "He's definitely right."

"You mind sharing?" Michele asks almost rudely.

"There are some ancient conspiracy theories about the end of World War II, where this symbol received its most horrible association," the programmer replies.

"It appears the man responsible for one of the worst genocides in human history might have fled to Antarctica after losing the war. Hard evidence was never found, except for a few suspicious coincidences," Clara says, helping continue the explanation.

"Such as a submarine leaving old-Earth Germany after his defeat in 1945 and with rumors of his coalition to find the center of the Earth in Antarctica, long-held rumors of his escape here were never proved, yet never denied," the programmer states.

"They never found this man's body after his alleged suicide," Clara adds.

The group stays silent for a second, wondering how to react to this odd bit of information.

"That's like 6,000 years ago, does it matter?" Michele says quickly.

"The Nazis killed over ten million people, so I just felt it needed to be shared," the humanoid programmer replies.

Everyone recoils in response to his last statement, realizing the human population isn't much more than that today.

"You're telling me we're working inside a lunatic's secret base?!" Dr. Rogers butts in with urgency in his voice.

"Should we even feel SAFE in here?" the botanist asks while

looking around worriedly.

"Okay, calm down everyone," I shout to snap everyone out of overthinking.

"Anything that might have existed in here is long gone, both physically and historically," Clara says in a calm voice, her hands up, motioning people to relax. "Working in this space does not mean we, too, are associated."

"Then what's OUR symbol?" a human programmer asks hurriedly.

All their eyes eventually land on me as they wait for an answer. The pressure to lead correctly falls on my shoulders and the weight of their concern feels nearly tangible.

"Like I said before, no symbols. We do not need a symbol."

The group doesn't seem satisfied with my answer, but regardless, I continue.

"Throughout history, humans have relied on imagery to convey ideals. Symbols, idols, dictators—all created to influence the masses, powered by human nature's need to comprehend the incomprehensible, yet perpetuated by humans' ignorance."

The team sits listening intently, trying to decipher my underlying message.

"We don't need an artificial representation of who we are—we don't need to visually manipulate, because we stand for something bigger than all of us. Bigger than any ideology." I pause for dramatic effect.

"We stand for balance. Advocates for a self-sustaining ecosystem where we are all equally working toward the greater good for

Earth and our future here."

The strength in my words reminds me of my personal investment in what I believe in, and the need to convince others of my passion spurs more confidence. I look around and make eye contact with each of them as I speak.

"We are all here, born from the Earth, whether assembled from materials"—I gesture to the humanoids—"or grown from flesh"—I gesture to the humans—"we are all made from the dirt of the Earth and fueled by the energy of the Universe."

Archie inches closer to me and the others nod as I speak.

"The only visual representation we need is the Earth on which we stand. Born from the dirt like the trees of old-Earth, we burn through the fire of life and give our ashes to those after," I say, my voice commanding and unmoving while I begin to clench my fists in response to the passion bubbling up inside me.

"Like firewood, we were made from Earth to warm the people. And we will fuel this new movement toward a balanced life for Earth and its people, with us as the catalysts."

Everyone listens closely as I speak, their perspectives hopefully narrowing toward our goal for "the greater good." A goal I'm trying so hard to define clearly.

Archie steps closer to the side of me and asks for my attention with a single word: "Sir?"

"Yes," I turn to Archie and in sotto voce, I add, "what is it?"

"According to the 24/7 news stream, they've narrowed down the search and will be focused on excavating the cave you escaped from soon—we should press on. Quickly." Archie emphasizes his quiet urgency with a soft, yet intense voice. In response, I nod and turn to the group.

"Time we start! Clara is everything…?"

A loud thud echoes through the entire room, originating from the corridor we came in through so many days ago. All of us freeze in fear and confusion.

"What was that?" Michele shouts.

"They've begun digging the cave," Archie replies loudly as the echoes subside, passing through the large room and down all the other corridors.

"We have to get going, Morris. Now or never!" Clara shouts while heading to the plug-in system.

Thoughts, details, backup plans and the like, shoot through my mind as I decipher the situation and argue with myself on the best course of action. I did not expect this, not this soon—how many other possibilities have I not planned for?

"Michele!" I hastily call out, "Take whoever isn't a programmer and slow them down. Whatever it takes without risking your life!"

"On it," she replies, then proceeds to collect Dr. Rogers, Diane, and the botanist to head down toward the original corridor.

"Programmers to your positions. Stay prepared and alert. Ready yourself for Clara's signal," I order as I walk to Clara.

"Is everything ready for the firewall?"

"Yes," she smiles quickly. "You're all set. Here's the node." She hands me the round outdated node. "Go ahead and lie on the table. The plug-in system is still turning on."

"From your research," I say, sitting on the table and then continuing, "which domains in Sector 1 are most stable?"

"Not many. 43 and 49 through 99."

Michele's voice echoes through the room with a loud command I can't make out from the distance.

"Which have the most activity as far as transfers?" I ask Clara, her eyes serious as she waits for the plug-in system to warm up.

"Domain numbers 2, 14, 43, and 60 have the most neurobines visiting on a regular basis."

The answers I'm searching for must be found in the oldest, but I'm curious about what interests the SSG.

"What about domain number 1?"

"I tried everything to track down information about domain number 1, but it appears it was disconnected," she answers, expecting my disappointment. "So, which would you like to search through first?"

Too many variables, too many unknowns. With no time to waste, I reply, "Number 43 then. Let's try there first."

Clara nods and I mouth the words, "I love you." A sad smile forms as she mouths the words back, "I love you too." This one moment of contentment leaves a longing for us to be alone like the first week we met. But Michele's loud voice in response to another loud thud snaps me out of it.

With a contrite smile, I lie on the titanium table, between the other plug-in systems manned by the four programmers, nervously watching our every move.

"Deep breath," Clara directs as she grabs my hand.

I close my eyes and a whoosh of silence washes over me.

My eyes open to a flat landscape of desert, familiar desert. As if modeled after the area outside of Lake Vostok. The expanse is overwhelming and as I turn to locate anything on the horizon, a single building can be seen in the distance. I start jogging.

"You alright, Morris?" Clara's voice is sounding in my head.

"Yes. Approaching a building in a few minutes."

"I would hurry if you could."

I begin running and continue to gain speed without effort until I'm sprinting faster than any human! But my excitement wears off when I remind myself it's the AVC mutations that allow me to bend the rules and code that tie the Sector-System together. The ground below me is dry and cracked, my feet leaving dust behind me. As I run toward the grey building, it starts looking more like a large fenced-off area.

The heat of the sun feels very realistic and sweat is already forming around my neck and back. Maybe the SSG is experimenting with the natural weather of our sick Earth?

"Ah!" Clara yells in my head and then stays silent.

"Clara? You okay?"

"Oh, yes. Sorry, Michele is collapsing parts of the corridor. Didn't know it until I heard a loud crash—know it now! Continue your search, Morris. We're good still."

I near the fenced-off section and peer in. The chained fences and concrete walls are tall, almost unnecessarily so. Its design encloses a large square nearly the size of the old Business Park. But with nothing in it, I walk around to look for any evidence of someone being here. Then I notice more of these things on the other side.

Behind this one large area are several more, maybe hundreds, stretched out in a single file line continuing down the corridor. My heart races at the sight.

"Are you doing okay, Morris? You're breathing heavy."

"Clara, there are hundreds of fenced-off sections, maybe more. What could the SSG be doing here?"

"Not sure—afraid to know."

I run along the fences and peer in each as I pass them. So far not one has anything in them, but finally, the tenth one down makes me stop and look closer. This domain is so silent it feels unbearable and unnatural, putting me on edge as I look through the chain-link fence.

Suddenly a virus comes crashing into the fence causing me to jump back and fall on the ground. Where did she come from!?

Foam spews out of her mouth as she yells nonsense at me. A black aura illuminates around her body.

"I've never seen a virus this far gone before," I say to Clara and partly myself.

"They must be experimenting on limitations then?"

"Not sure. Probably."

The virus' skin looks unhealthy and sunburned. Her clothes look so old they could rip any second. How long has she been out here in the desert? Alone?

I run to examine the next. Empty.

But the next fenced-off section turns out to be similar—a crazed male virus comes to the fence and stares with drool falling from his mouth. His eyes follow me without blinking or looking away.

Though I'm intrigued, no answers can be found from these experiments the SSG is conducting. Running further down the line of fenced-off areas, I come across five more neurobines in the same state. And from the looks of it, the line of fences continues indefinitely down the desert.

The sun beats on my head, sweat drips on my shoulders. Everything feels uncomfortable and the air is thin.

"Clara, I don't think I'll find anything here. Take me to another domain. Connect me to domain 60."

Silence.

"Clara?"

"Okay, yes. I'm back, but the USB has made it through the corridor from what Archie has told me. You have to find something in 60—we may not have enough time to search another."

With time slipping, I feel an urgency for action. Something to buy me more time. I HATE risks, but I must attempt to further the plan without my portion complete. Should be fine as long as I find the answers I'm looking for…

"Clara. Tell the programmers to make it rain."

"But Morris, you haven't found…"

"I know the risks, Clara! I'll pull through—I know it. Just tell them to…"

"Yes, yes. Fine," she answers, but I could tell she is upset with my decision.

I close my eyes, but all of a sudden my eyes open to an island with no trees. A single large body of water surrounds the sandy isle I'm now standing on. This island seems about as large as one of the fenced-off sections, but the water keeps going into the horizon in all directions.

"Okay. The programmers have released your note in Sector 9, domains 1 through 10," Clara reports back with no enthusiasm in her voice.

I truly hope this plan of mine works out of order. The note I devised to fall from the skies into the hands of every inhabitant of these domains should spark a chain reaction. Each programmer had been helping hack the system, under Clara's direction, to code a paper note generator to take the place of rain.

And each note reads:

You lead a life of stolen time,
controlled by greedy SSG sheep.
Nothing you do can rid the ghosts,
that surround you in your sleep.

Though artistically derivative, its poetic influence serves a different purpose. The rhyming emphasizes the word "sleep." And sleep, from what I've experienced, is always an ongoing inner conflict in a changing or current virus. By placing a strong rhyme, I'm hoping it acts as a cue word to ignite virus symptoms within the neurobines who read the note.

I WAS hoping to have found a solution to fix the virus symptoms BEFORE releasing the notes, but situations change. And risks must be taken. For the greater good.

"Okay, good," I reply to Clara. "Keep me updated on its effects."

Suddenly, a group of neurobines come running my direction over the sand dune in the middle of the island. But by the looks of it, their frantic chase is evidence of virus symptoms. My heart races at the sight of the now twenty neurobines running toward me. They must have heard me talking out loud!

"Clara, I need to go. Now!"

More viruses keep coming and now a group of more than fifty are in the distance. And they're closing in fast—screams and shouts of nonsense an obvious trend with my last encounter with those black-aura viruses.

"Clara! Now!"

"What—okay, but where? Which domain!?"

"Anywhere!" I back away and hit the water behind me, saying, "Take me anywhere!" The viruses nearing the water prepare to jump as I close my eyes.

Silence.

My eyes again open to solitude, but this time inside a building. I stand now in a hallway of windows, each offering a glimpse into rooms housing red-aura viruses. Neurobines associated with the SSG walk back and forth examining each.

I'm frozen. Being this close to government officials is frightening—I'm afraid they might see me. The hallway is dimly lit, but I can see their uniforms and their expressionless faces. This hallway is narrow, so I'm sure the neurobine walking toward me will notice me. I hold my breath, but he soon walks right through me without noticing.

Breathe out.

"This is domain 59—don't worry, no one can see or hear you thanks to my extra protective firewall. Well, except viruses."

I take a deep breath and think. Time to take advantage of this firewall she's coded.

"Clara, take me to domain 2."

"Can't we test out my firewall on a less unbalanced domain first? I'm worried about its durability."

"We don't have time. Listen, if my heart rate reaches 150 or my breathing pauses for more than thirty seconds, pull me out no matter what. You can act as my safety net in case things go awry."

Neurobine officials walk past me peering into the glass of each room. Clara stays silent a few moments as I look into a room and see a neurobine lying on its side on the floor, drooling. Its arms are wrapped around a pillow of sorts and I step closer. Oh! It appears the pillow is the head of another neurobine, its owner's body lying in the corner, a crooked mess.

I shake my head to rid myself of the image of the horrible sight I just witnessed. What the hell are they testing here? It's disturbing beyond all belief.

"Okay," Clara responds finally. "Domain 2 then?"

"Yes, but Clara, any news on the notes?"

"Nothing yet. Not in the news anyway, according to Archie."

With no other way to hear about whether the raining notes are working or not, my guess is the USB and the SSG would, of course, hide any negative material from the public eye. So most likely, they're covering up the chaos we've started in Sector 9. Ten domains weren't enough—we have to take further action.

"Tell them to target the entirety of Sector 9."

"Morris! That's trillions of lives you're…"

"We have no choice! The USB could stop us any minute now; we have to gain control of the situation."

Walking as I talk, I accidentally look into another window and see a twitching virus being shocked in a chair. And then shocked again! I look away, trying to ignore its widened eyes.

"Fine! But I do NOT approve of this plan and never have. You're risking too much, Morris! There are too many lives at stake here!" Clara's voice sounds angrier than I've ever heard before.

"We must commit 110%, Clara! Or else we lose everything! Speeding up their inevitable fates is not a crime if we intend to save them. Take me to domain number 2, we're running out of time!"

As I wait for a response, I turn to see a neurobine virus pressed against the glass of its room. Its rhythmic twitching causes a banging on the glass as it stares at me, its mouth open unnaturally wide, as though stuck or broken. The sight renders me frozen—such insanity lies on the other side of the window. The virus starts screaming a consistently high pitch and, though slightly muffled by the barrier, forces my entire body to tense.

"Clara, now! Get me out of here!" I shout in agony.

The virus's voice, inhumanely consistent and banging on the glass, makes my blood race in my veins. An official runs over and presses a button next to the window and the insanity stops with an intense shock treatment administered by robotic arms that extend out of the walls.

I shut my eyes, praying to be taken away from this nightmare. Suddenly my surroundings change again hinting my arrival in the domain number 2. But the complete and utter silence is deafening, so I open my eyes only to find pitch black. Nothingness consumes me and memories of my recent near-death experience in the loneliness of the corridor flood my mind. I begin to lose control of my fear and panic, looking everywhere I can to see anything. Anything but darkness!

But no luck, I can't see anything. Except wait, a pin-point light. I blink for a second.

Unexpectedly I open my eyes to the ceiling of a large room, the cold of the titanium table on my back. I quickly sit up and my eyes meet Clara's. Looking around, I notice the programmers working on filling Sector 9 with my propaganda as I'm sitting on The Table.

"What happened?! Your heart rate reached 160," Clara says as she stares at me, waiting for a clue.

"I… I'm fine, just was stuck in darkness," I admit, trying to cover up my embarrassment of my newest PTSD. "But Clara, you have to put me back in there. I found something!" I grab her shoulders to convince her.

"They're close!" Archie shouts as another thud echoes through the large room, this time sounding louder.

We're running out of time.

"Domain number 2, Clara. I can do this." She looks into my eyes and sees my confidence, then nods.

I lie back down on the cold titanium and close my eyes. Silence overwhelms me and my fear of the dark forces my eyes shut as I realize I'm already in domain 2.

Taking a deep breath, I open my eyes to the darkness again. But calmly, I look around to find that pinpoint light again. There it is—in the distance. Determined to find answers, I start to run toward it but realize my feet aren't on anything. I'm floating!

"Clara, I can't move!" I shout in desperation. "I need to move toward the light!"

"Um, there's nothing I can do here—this domain has no coordinates or measuring system I can recognize. Nothing!"

Before I realize, the light approaches and continues to grow in size. My heart rate races, but I remember to calm down. Can't have it reach 150, can't be pulled out by Clara again.

Breathe in. Breathe out.

The light swarms toward me and rapidly enlarges to encompass my entire perception. My feet feel solid ground and an empty, dark room replaces the pitch black. Under the new conditions, I cautiously walk forward.

"Morris, the news is full of the insanity you started in Sector 9. Apparently, 73% of the population has developed 'strange symptoms.'" Clara's bittersweet tone of voice sounds slower in my head than normal. But I shake my head and review the situation.

Things are falling into place. It's up to me to find something, *anything*, here in domain 2 to help save the viruses I've now created.

I can tell by her inflection that Clara feels guilty about what we've caused. There has to be some way to reverse these symptoms—neurobines are literally code! And code can be easily rewritten or altered. Saving their lives should be a matter of revision, right?

My feet might be on solid ground, but the gravity parameter feels a little unnatural and I begin to feel a little light-headed. Drowsiness of some sort kicks in, as though my mind is clouded and functioning more slowly.

Clara's firewall, her protective "bubble shield," must be faulty or not as effective as we were hoping. There must be too much oxygen in this dark room of sweat and dirt. I stumble forward, regaining my balance and look around. After observing closer, lines along the wall hint at an existing door nearly camouflaged in the grey.

Slowly, by ignoring slight vertigo, I walk toward the door.

"Clara, is there anything you can do about the firewall?"

Her voice starts a few seconds later but sounds like it is revving up and awkwardly elongated.

"Clara? Clara, are you okay?" I ask while turning the doorknob, but her voice continues uninterrupted as a mix of low, sweeping tones. Must be some communication bug between the firewall—hard to tell.

Opening the door reveals a giant room with a single light in the center. The walls at the edges are unlit and barren—not even windows exist in this basement-like dungeon. No furniture except for a single chair underneath a hanging light. Nothing about this place feels right. But its strangeness is peculiar and sparks curiosity. Why is this place SO different?

"Clara—are you there?"

My voice triggers a sound in the corner and as I look, a figure emerges. A shadowy neurobine figure slowly makes its way toward the chair and sits down, mumbling nonsense to itself. Grey carvings cover its face, like the designs within designs I've seen before. But its eyes are motionless and wide open.

Unsure what to do, I freeze looking at the still, small neurobine—my guess a virus. But it sits staring at nothing as if waiting for something. Perhaps it was used to SSG officials coming in. Maybe it had been trained to respond like this when another enters the domain.

"Hello?" I ask the unmoving figure. It turns its head while mumbling quietly and stares at me, but doesn't move.

"Are you okay?" My voice sounds sweet, though I'm unsure how best to approach a possible virus. No aura color can be seen around it.

"Are you lost?" it suddenly asks me without moving. I stay silent, unsure what to say, trying not to incite aggression. But abrupt laughter causes the neurobine to rear its head back in a deranged reaction to its own question. Then it stops and looks at me again.

"No human has set foot here. You MUST be lost." His voice sounds surprisingly normal and well-tempered, but I stay vigilant.

"I'm looking for something. May I ask who you are?" I reply calmly with respectable manners.

"I am a moment stuck in time. Born from the past and saved for the future," he says quietly, staying still while speaking with wide eyes. "Am I what you're looking for?" His head twitches. "Because everything you see is all that remains."

"Do you work for the SSG?" I ask him, maintaining my distance, many feet away. His odd phrasing keeps me on edge, fearful of him turning psychotic. His head twitches again.

"You ask questions I've never been asked. How am I to answer without knowledge of life outside these walls?" His head tilts slightly, then settles back upright with another twitch.

"Morris! Morris, are you alright? We're connected again. Time is sped up in this domain, but it's skewed far more than I had calculated! Your consciousness is functioning faster than human-reality. Human consciousness can't handle…!"

"Shh!" I shush her as I keep an eye on the neurobine. I'm still alive. I can stay a bit longer.

"Morris, they're nearly through the last few barricades Michele made—whatever you're doing, hurry!" Clara's voice is urgent and anxious. I take a few breaths to think this through.

Except for repetitive twitching, the neurobine hasn't moved since we've started talking. I must choose my questions wisely—time is limited.

"How old are you?" I ask the small man in the chair.

"How old is the Sector-System?" he laughs again, louder this time with his mouth opening wide. But he shuts it quickly, muffling the laughter.

His question answers my own—he must have something he can tell me. After thousands of years living here as an experiment for the SSG, he definitely has virus symptoms but they seem… contained. Something about him MUST be the answer.

"What is your purpose here?" I ask him excitedly.

"Let me ask you something, human." He stands up from his chair but stays in his place. "You ask me questions as though I'm wise. You observe me not unlike the regular men who rarely come in here, yet you are unknowingly different in so many ways." He takes a step closer and twitches again.

266

"What is YOUR purpose here?" he asks me with an unchanging face, but takes another step closer to me.

Feeling the pressure of the situation, my heart rate races, but for fear of reaching 150 bpm, I calm myself down and think of a reply. My body is confused by my mind's interpretation of this altered time warp. Is my heart rate dependent on this domain's skewed time? Or is it still tied to human-reality?

I shake my head—no use in figuring it out. I look at the small man again. Though he's not yet aggressive, he acts differently every second.

"I'm here to save millions of lives by understanding you," I gesture to him. "All neurobines inevitably turn insane, but here you are, stable, since the beginning of time."

"Time!?" he says angrily. Oh man, I forgot "time" is another cue word. His anger appears controlled still, but I'm afraid of what I've started.

"I am trapped like a soulless bird in a frozen cage, force-fed fabricated 'time' on an endless loop in this artificial reality. All to observe its effects." His voice grows abnormally loud as he stands firm. "I am far passed sanity. Nothing affects me here, not even time itself!"

He throws his arms out and the walls fly away revealing a perpetual blue sky, forcing me to cover my eyes from the sudden light. This neurobine seems in absolute control of this entire domain! The walls twirl away and dark clouds form above us.

"You ask me how I came to be?" He cues rain that comes falling down like I've never seen before. Thick drops of water blur my vision, but I notice he begins to levitate above the floor.

"Can one so small ask something so profound in a dimension

where I am God?" His voice booms and vibrates within my chest.

"Morris—what is happening, your heart rate is high and you've been breathing fast this entire time!" Clara shouts in my head

"I'm fine!" I shout over the storm. "Give me more time!"

"We don't have time! They're about to break through the last barricade!"

"Convince them we have a cure! We want change or else we take another Sector with us!" I shout in hopes it will buy us time.

"Threaten the government? Are you mad!?" Clara shouts in anger, but before I can respond I begin gasping for air.

"Whoever you're talking to will know my power over this dimension, for I control you. Flawed creation left you bound by your useless human limitations," he says loudly as I gasp and fall to the floor. "I can easily take away your precious oxygen. And I can easily give too much!"

I regain my breath, but suddenly feel overly light-headed.

"Morris, I just noticed your firewall has been compromised! I have to pull you out!"

My head hits the floor as I fall from imbalance; the dizziness is too powerful, but suddenly the oxygen normalizes. I hold my head in pain, surprised I can feel the throbbing ache, and reply, "I need more time, Clara!"

The rain stops, but the floor begins to disappear. The man floating ten feet off the ground smiles creepily as he watches me panic, "You have no place here! And I will force you to sleep forever."

"Wait, wait! Please!" I shout at him, but the floor is nearly faded away and the blue sky turns gray all around and underneath me.

"I can help you!" My voice is desperate to be heard.

Silence rings in my ears and I open my eyes expecting to see Clara in our large underground space. But instead, I notice blue skies below me as I float in mid-air! No, maybe just an invisible floor?

A grassy field comes shooting up from below, from nowhere and straight to my feet. I find myself standing in the middle of a long stretch of grass, blue skies above, with a friendly sun. The man walks toward me, but stops a few feet away and stares into my eyes.

"I am omnipotent here," he says powerfully. "How do YOU expect to help me?"

A slight breeze cools my skin from the warm sun. I catch my breath and my senses after everything that just happened. My feet crunch on freshly cut grass as I stumble a bit. So much chaos and now, so much stillness. This powerful neurobine abruptly stopped his display of power at my promise to help—he must be desperate for an escape. He must have some weakness.

"I can free you from this cage," I say confidently in reply to his half-serious question.

"Why would I want to leave if I control everything within my cage?"

"You said it yourself. You're trapped by this cage, this fake illusion of control—but a truly all-powerful God could leave this all behind! So let me help you. Let me take you away from here, into human-reality, to 'real' time."

The small man stands motionless.

"As generous as you seem, it proves you're a fool. Time has no momentum here. Its speed has shifted out of my control throughout my existence. Nothing is constant, yet everything repeats. But the 'reality' you speak of opposes my fundamental perception. So tell me, how can I run forward if I've never walked straight? How can I live outside of this maintained dream?"

The SSG must be using this domain for time experiments, changing it constantly to note its effects on neurobines. Maybe they know time is the ultimate cause of virus symptoms? But regardless, even if I *were* to save him, this poor soul may not know how to perceive time that flows without interference.

"Dream? Do you mean the Sector-System is a dream?" I ask him.

"A dream has a timeline, but no time. Dreams spin around a single consciousness, born from reality, yet spin out of place," he says sadly with deep eyes of intense thought and then continues.

"Living in a dream is like living in an ocean—there is never a straight path to follow. How am I to live in a world where time flows forward, when all my life I've lived spinning upon my own conception of time?"

His thoughts make sense.

As a member of the AVC, every neurobine virus I deleted mentioned sleep. For humans, sleep brings dreams and a break from reality, from consciousness, as if pressing the reset button. But artificial intelligence doesn't sleep. Neurobines don't get a break from their version of time.

Humanoids, on the other hand, don't live long enough in human-reality to turn "virus." They're not exposed to their artificial existence long enough to suffer virus symptoms. So most (if not all) eventually promote themselves to the Sector-System to live for thousands of years, practically serving as an elegant waiting game for their virus fates.

It's a problem with AI! Not just the Sector-System.

The neurobine confusion between sleep, dreams, death, and time must be triggered by mentioning these concepts. So these words catapult their logical discrepancy into a circular dependency and THIS must cause frustration. And unresolved frustration turns to anger. And anger turns to aggression and so on.

There is no grounding or foundation holding together AI's version of time. That must be it!

"Morris—they're about to break through!" Clara shouts in my head.

Urgency clouds my judgment, but I scour my mind for an answer to this new problem. Something must connect AI to human-reality, where time is constant and organically falling forward. My heart rate rises, but I try calming myself down to keep it under 150.

Breathe in. Breathe out.

"You've found my one weakness: I am dependent on this false reality. Maybe I have found a form of sanity after hundreds of years of insanity, but my mind is still spinning. I am a kite without a string and here you are, telling me there could be ground beneath me," the ancient neurobine says as he sits on the grass, closing his eyes and calming himself down. But the grass begins to fade into nothingness.

My mind races. Something must be inherently different between organic life born in human-reality and artificial intelligence trapped in their manufactured dreams.

Breathe in. Breathe out.

Breathe in.

Wait.

Breathe out.

"Breathing!" I shout aloud. "That's it!"

"Morris, they're here!" Clara yells in fear.

In reaction, I jump toward the ancient neurobine and say, "Come with me! I have the solution. Anywhere is better than here, let me show you a new life!"

The ancient neurobine prepares to defend himself, but I don't hesitate. Not with the government upon us. My hand raises and the warmth triggers down my arm. The neurobine notices something is up and jumps up, but without warning, I hear a slight pop.

Suddenly, with a blink of an eye, I find myself staring at the ceiling of the large underground room. Reminding myself the ancient neurobine is safely caught in the node on my neck, I sit up, quickly locking eyes with Clara. Her hands are up. She mouths the words, "They know nothing." Her worried face shocks me and I turn around.

The USB has us surrounded. Drones, droids, bots and humanoids, all around us. I look at my team and they all wait for me to do something as they keep their own hands up.

"Now walk toward us in a single file line. Make this easy and there will be fewer consequences," a humanoid says, its voice amplified and echoing around us.

"Morris," Archie's voice sounds in my head, "nearly 85% of Sector 9's population has turned, according to all the news streams. The media has declared this a state of panic and people have started pointing fingers at the SSG. If you found something, anything, use it to our advantage NOW."

His voice sounded firm, placing all his confidence in me. But how can I best describe my solution for the Sector-System? Will they listen to me?

I step forward.

"You are all guilty by association with Clara E354-87465," the humanoid official states loudly.

The government won't listen to a human unless the information I possess is valuable enough, right? And if my grand plan was successfully carried out, all evidence of our involvement with Sector 9 should have been erased. No proof of our involvement. The media is soaking up this pandemic as I had planned and the government must be in a panic to find the culprit and more importantly, a solution.

I step forward again, slowly following their orders as I thinking. The other members of the team hesitate to follow and I realize I'm running out of time. It's now or never.

"We have information on Scctor 9! For the sake of millions of lives we demand to be heard!" I stop walking and stand firm. The others behind me do the same, except Clara who continues until she stands next to me.

"You better know what you're doing," she whispers to me, her sarcastic tone strangely comforting. "This chaos is being streamed to millions. But to get out of this, we'll need more than just fifteen seconds of fame."

Plans upon plans take shape in my head. The complicated mess I've put us in is on my shoulders. But I relax and breathe.

Breathe in. Breathe out.

CHAPTER 25

We've been stuck at a standstill since I mentioned we had information regarding the issues in Sector 9. After we waited for more prestigious USB representatives, a more decorated official finally makes her way past the crowd of enforcement personnel and gazes out at us.

"I am going to approach! But I ask only to meet with whoever's in charge," the official commands.

I motion toward the others, including Clara, to make some distance while I stay at the titanium table. The official directs two armed guards to follow her as she walks closer, then she stands in front of me.

"Why shouldn't we arrest you all right now? Don't waste more time than you have..." she says rudely to me, standing with a posture of strength.

"Nice to meet you, too," I respond sarcastically. "My name is Morris 1045, a previous member of PixelOne's AVC 46, and I have reason to believe I can cure the virus pandemic."

She looks at me with disbelief.

"Yes, you ARE Morris 1045. Who illegally lived homeless for a month in collaboration with a humanoid who illegally accessed government backup servers. You've been sentenced to ten years in the PRP," she says with no change of expression, but pauses for dramatic effect. "Why, then, should I be inclined to believe a convict?"

Ten years in the PRP!? Not good. I have to think of a solution that doesn't worsen our situation with the government. Somehow, I must appear to be the good guy here.

"During my time with the AVC, I came across an ancient neurobine who told me he planned to escape from Sector 1, Domain 2 one last time to infect every Sector he could with his insanity. So I took it upon myself to attempt the impossible by building a team and finding a solution for when he attacks the Sector-System..."

She looks at me funny, slightly unconvinced.

"Why did you hide in caves then?"

"Didn't want to scare the public or the government in case it wasn't true."

"As you know, Sector 9 HAS been infected in the way you speak. You're saying this neurobine from Sector 1, Domain 2 is the cause?"

"Yes," I say with a confidence, pretending to be uninvolved with Sector 9. "I'm convinced it was him."

The USB official stares at me, observing to see whether or not I'm lying. To be honest, I'm surprised my "acting" fools her. I glance over at Clara who raises her eyebrows and waves discreetly.

Clara must be hacking or manipulating the situation somehow. Most officials this high up in the government are equipped with highly sensitive polygraph machines, yet somehow I'm lying well enough to trick her sensors? No, I'm not that good. Clara must be helping.

The official stays silent a bit but then continues the negotiation.

"I've had SSG enforcement check Sector 1, Domain 2 and it appears the neurobine you mentioned has indeed found a way out."

"Then it's only a matter of time before the entire Sector-System goes insane unless you allow me and my team to continue our research," I suggest, trying to manipulate the situation.

"Are you blackmailing the government? It is your right as a civilian to inform the government of terrorist attacks and possible solutions to them. By withholding this information, you...," she states flatly, but I interrupt.

"We'd be willing to be good civilians and share everything we know if we weren't currently threatened by our own government. How do we know you won't just throw us in confinement after we share what we know? We do not *deserve* reprimanding. Everything we might have done illegally was for the greater good— none of us here have gained from our efforts to save the Sector-System."

"And now you're justifying breaking the law? Why did you run from us if you're so virtuous?" the official asks, expecting me to trip up.

"We only ran because the cave collapsed. And we kept running because the corridors were crumbling. We did not *know* you were after us until you broke through the doors," I answer with no hesitation.

"Why did you not respond to our many messages and calls? And what might you be doing with so many plug-in systems?" she quickly asks.

"We removed distractions from the outside world by turning off all forms of contact in order to focus on the problem at hand. Our plug-in systems have only been used to observe viruses and to help us determine the cause of their symptoms."

"You were trapped down here, yet you survived for a week?" she asks, trying to find a hole in my story.

"We built a way to climb up to the surface," I gesture behind me, "through an old elevator shaft. We retrieved all we needed from town and found this large, underground space a suitable replacement for our collapsed cave."

She observes me a bit more.

"Obviously there's a strong case against your word. You can either tell me your proposed solution now or I'll arrest all of you with a promise of ten more years in correctional facilities," she threatens without shame. What a manipulation game.

"We want credit where credit is due, and our involvement will ensure proper execution of our solution. Telling you our cure-all now guarantees nothing and we both know time is limited. Allow us to continue our research and save the Sector-System," I say with even more confidence. "If you don't agree to these terms, understand that by locking us away, you force us to withhold information that I *know* you need."

My rebuttal feels airtight. I must be close to convincing this stone-faced official because there's nothing she or the government can do.

They cannot pry any more information from us. All they have is threats of more time in the PRP because barbaric forms like "torture" were made illegal thousands of years ago as a human's right to silence. Time is "limited" with this fictional impending doom I've fabricated about the man from Sector 1, so I'm banking on the fact that AI hate wasting time, especially under the circumstances.

But she gives me an irritated look of dissatisfaction.

"We have our own team working on a solution as we speak. You're unneeded," she says and begins to walk away. But I see through her bluff.

"The Sector-System is uninhabitable and the SSG has been covering it up for years!" I shout after her, realizing all the flying drones must be streaming this to the public. With barely any action around Lake Vostok due to the low amounts of crime, the media must be covering every angle.

My words carry weight thanks to society's need for constant streaming shows.

"What makes you think this virus problem can be solved when this CANCER has been untreated for thousands of years!?" I begin adding drama to the situation to incite a level of distrust between the viewers and their government. The official turns slowly, her eyes wide with anger.

"Allow these faithful civilians," I raise both arms gesturing toward my team and myself, "to solve this contagious illness or else the SSG will be held responsible for the decay of the entire Sector-System!"

My voice is loud and full of drama. I am purposely going overboard to rally the population against the government so they will have no choice but to concede.

The official glares at me. Now that I've complicated things further by bringing the masses in on this conversation, her hands are tied. Deny our team and the governments look like enemies, but accept us and gamble for a more positive outcome.

She then reluctantly says, "Wait one moment."

She walks away, probably to communicate with a superior or the SSG. I turn to Clara and motion her over, then quickly update her on my conversation with the official including the white lies.

"Tell everyone this same story so there are no discrepancies," I tell Clara.

"Got it," she says, then turns away back to the group and begins whispering to them.

I wait a few more minutes until the official finally returns. Standing in front of me now with her two armed guards, she hands me a tablet and gestures for me to turn it on. I tap it and the screen illuminates, revealing some paperwork.

"Due to the urgency of the situation, the government is hereby freezing all charges until your motives are more clear. If what you say is true and lives CAN be saved, consider you and your 'team's' charges cleared," the official USB humanoid woman says in an authoritative tone of voice. Relief overwhelms me, but quickly she interrupts my calm.

"But if you do not have the information you claim and you fail at your task, this act of wasted time will be considered in conjunction with the terrorism from Sector 1 and your team will serve a life-long term," she explains with a hint of amusement at the stakes. "If you agree, sign the document. If not, come with us and serve only ten years."

Looking down at the paperwork in black letters and boring font, it reads:

Morris 1045, Clara E354-87465, and all associates are hereby placed under governmental supervision until the Sector-System emergency has been resolved by their hands. All tools, equipment, space, and materials will be given to aid in the process...

It kept going with pages of more details—how did they write all of this so fast? There's no way I can read this quickly.

"Does my signing of this agreement represent the entire team?" I ask the official.

"Yes."

"May I speak to them first?" I ask professionally, making her pause in doubt.

"You may. I'll give you a few minutes. But hurry—with a terrorist on the loose in the Sector-System, we have no more time to waste. Sir," she adds in a fake tone of voice.

I nod in understanding and then walk toward the group, their faces worried and their eyes following my every footstep. The clang of my left metal foot reminds me I'm not a normal human anymore.

"We've struck an agreement," I tell them as they listen closely. I hand Clara the paperwork and ask her to review, then continue to describe the risks and the consequences to the team.

"Morris, before we accept this wager, we need to understand your solution. Is it viable?" Dr. Rogers asks.

"Yeah, I'm not liking the idea of bargaining with the government to begin with," Michele adds.

Clara smiles at me, trying to cover up her worry with eyes of encouragement, then continues to read the paperwork on the tablet.

"What is the main difference between AI and humanity?" I ask them, each silent. "Our mechanics! Thousands of years ago, AI simplified their humanoid bodies originally designed to imitate the human form." As I explain, more things come together in my own understanding.

"Once AI took hold of society, before the Sector-System, humanoids were soon built without lungs or hearts because those organs were seemingly unnecessary. But this disconnects them from the universe and then even MORE so when implanted in the Sector-System," I explain while noticing the humanoids (including Clara) begin to look slightly offended.

"The Universe is always vibrating and time is always flowing. Every living creature, whether sentient or not, has a connection to the rhythm of life through each heartbeat and each breath. Our constant connection to time is linked through our involuntary sympathetic vibrations with the Universe."

I turn to Clara. "That's why the humanoid virus we created a week ago was stuck in a catatonic state. Its mind couldn't comprehend this world after thousands of years in a disconnected existence regardless of the Sector-System. It isn't just the Sector-System that causes viruses, it's these mechanical differences between organic life and modern-day forms of AI."

Feeling the need to explain myself further, I turn back to the group.

"By redesigning neurobines to imitate life on Earth, with lungs and a heartbeat, possibly even the need for sleep, we could then reconnect them to the fabric of time!"

Mixed expressions among the team left me unsure of what to think. Have I not explained it correctly?

"Why, then, am I not crazy?" a humanoid programmer asks me, offended that I'm inferring AI have flaws in their design.

"Neurobine viruses are thousands of years old. Plus, the Sector-System accelerates virus symptoms by further removing previous humanoids from reality. The ancient neurobine from Sector 1 told me the Sector-System might have a preset TIME-LINE, but there is no time. It's just moments caught in a loop, labeled according to code. Like a stopwatch," I say looking at the programmer.

Still not convinced as a whole, my team is more skeptical than I thought they'd be.

"Our main argument is that the Sector-System is unstable—it is a manufactured dream spinning inward upon itself causing sentient minds to question existence. When it has gone too far, this circular paradox generates a self-destructive greed for reality, unbeknownst to the victims themselves, who compensate by claiming they have control over 'time.'"

"You lost me, I'm out," a young programmer human says shortly.

"Yeah, you lost me at redesigning neurobines," Michele agrees. "I thought we were here to create a new society."

"We are doing just that by starting a domino effect! Once society accepts that the Sector-System is not a safe escape from our dying planet, they'll come to find Earth is the only priority worth investing in," I respond, slightly frustrated they weren't seeing my logic.

"That's true, we DO have the resources. AI just needs to prioritize away from the collapsing Sector-System," Dr. Rogers adds, thinking aloud.

A humanoid programmer looks at him, offended. "Hey, humans are responsible for the state of the Earth. Don't blame us for thinking outside the box."

"Obviously AI hasn't solved the problems the humans left us with thousands of years ago," Archie interjects. "The USB/SSG 'escape' plan has failed. Society must face the truth and prioritize for the future."

"It's true," another programmer states. "Civilization on Earth hasn't improved for a thousand years. The Sector-System has, but not society, not here in reality."

"Okay, but if we give neurobines lungs and hearts, wouldn't that save them and make the Sector-System viable again?" the humanoid programmer asks everyone.

"That doesn't solve the 'dream' effect though—it wouldn't solve the entire crisis. Plus, the Sector-System is not the priority, Earth is," Clara replies.

The arguments begin forming and conversations grow between the members of the team. I look around and notice the official standing where I left her, waiting for us and growing impatient.

"Look," I gesture and quiet everyone down, "I am so grateful for everyone's sacrifice in getting us here today and I value everyone's opinion, but we can't stay here paralyzed by too much analysis. There are always doubts and variables in every plan, but details can be figured out along the way. For now, though, the more pressing issue is each of your decisions. I need you all to decide whether you'll help me attempt to save everyone or whether you'll give up and serve ten yrs in the PRP." I pause for effect. "So? Are you with me, Firewood 11?"

The use of our makeshift name adds a personal touch to my statement. Faced with real risk now, some of them look unsure while others stand confidently in a decision.

"I'm with you," Clara replies, smiling at me with energy behind her eyes.

"Same here," Archie decides without hesitation right after Clara. A few more seconds of silence builds tension.

"I'm in it this far, might as well," a programmer says begrudgingly.

"If you back out now, you'll only serve a year in the PRP! Decide quickly," the official shouts, her impatience very apparent.

Most of the team grow restless with this new deal and I see their eyes dart in anxious thought. The pressure is on and the risk is too great.

"I'm sorry."

"Yeah, me too—I can't."

A human programmer backs away from the group along with the botanist behind him, his head down low, "I'm sorry."

"But we're Firewood 11, eleven…" I say in a low, sad voice. How could they not see the greater good? The amount gained by sacrificing now? Such purpose they're giving up out of fear.

"It's been fun. But I'm going to take this chance to get off easy."

I turn and find Michele had spoken. She regretfully backs away to join the others, with Diane (her servant bot) by her side. After all she's given up to save this mission, she's willing to leave? She even saved my life! Yet, she's leaving?

"Michele? You can't leave now…" I say in reaction to her decision. Suddenly I feel abandoned by my team members. Does it not make them feel selfish to quit on me? On society?

"I'm with you," Dr. Rogers, the old engineer, says with confidence. "It's time I do what's right for once."

Another humanoid programmer steps toward me, "I'm with you, too." Her smile tells me she's eager to follow in Clara's footsteps as a successful "hacker for good," or a "white hat" as Clara calls it.

Six of the team stand away from the rest of us, without making much eye-contact. In frustration, I turn my back and walk toward the official. Archie, Clara, Dr. Rogers, and the programmer (whose name I have yet to remember) follow behind me.

I stop in front of the official who looks unamused. Clara hands me the tablet and I lift my eyebrows to signal my questioning of the agreement. She nods, letting me know everything is in order, and I turn back to the official to begin signing the paperwork.

When I finish, I hand the tablet over and the official grins.

"For the sake of the Sector-System, I hope you five succeed. But speaking off the record, I hope to see you fail. Miserably."

She turns to the drones flying above the fifty or so enforcement bots and humanoids in the space and begins to announce.

"While under investigation, these five have kindly volunteered to assist the government in resolving the recent disaster in Sector 9. Further details will be released to the public in time, but until then please allow us space. No more media coverage. Thank you."

The official motions to the guards as the drones fly back through the corridor. Our equipment on the titanium table is then gathered by a few enforcement bots, while other humanoids round us up—the five of us in one group and the other six in another. Slowly, we're escorted out of this grand space I've gotten so used to.

I glare at the six, but they don't look my direction. My thoughts race. I begin to miss the original cave and now this titanium table we're walking away from. When will Clara and I find time alone now? I turn to Clara to check on how she's doing.

"I didn't want to say back there, but…" she whispers to me, "this agreement we've signed states we're practically prisoners of the government until we find the cure. I'm scared to think how long that might be."

"Don't worry," I whisper back. "We'll find our way. Our own way."

She smiles at me in reaction to my unquestioning self-confidence in my decision and adds, "Follow no one…"

Oxygen masks are handed to the humans of the group and we continue to be led out of the cave. The unknowns of my life and this situation pile up. I can't help but think how much I've left behind—how much of a "normal" life I could have had.

"Firewood 5."

I look over at Clara, who turns to me and says again, "Firewood 5. Doesn't sound right, huh?"

Her observation makes me smirk and reach for her hand.

We continue to hold each other's hands as we walk away from our underground home. More regretful thinking is difficult to ignore, but I silence those thoughts and remind myself of where I've come from.

Comparing my old self with my new self, I feel much more secure and ambitious. And with Clara alongside me, I feel safety in this newfound momentum in my life, regardless of the unknowns.

How empowering it feels to walk with purpose.

Breathe in.

And to reappear accompanied by newfound confidence in my decision-making.

Breathe out.

THE END

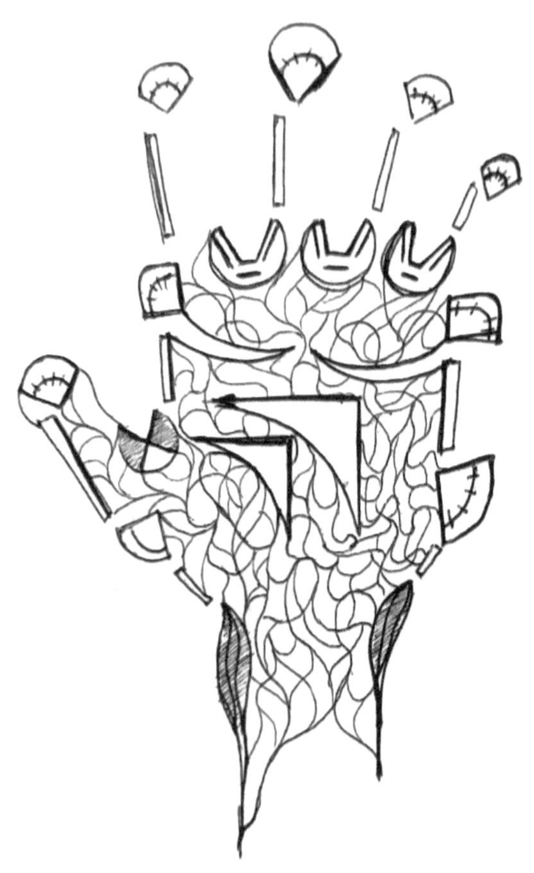

ABOUT THE AUTHOR

Harlan Jay is a musician, composer, author, and philosopher.

After finding a passion for music at a young age, Harlan has found great influence in the realms of music theory, live performance, and music philosophy. His philosophical writings emphasize the importance of music in every culture throughout the history of humanity. And while science and technology continue to shape his predictions of society's future, the strictly human ability to comprehend and appreciate music continues to influence his thinking and subsequently, his narrative philosophies.

Harlan's immediate family is non-musical but extremely spiritual and sparked a non-exclusive relationship with philosophy at an early age.

Anonymity is important to Harlan Jay and he has requested a short, non-detailed biography. His main goal is not to seek out recognition based on image or social status, but for his works to be shared due to their thought-provoking content.

"You cannot know yourself until you know the world you live in. Learn, know, observe and understand. Accept things as they are, but never stop asking questions." - Harlan Jay

Sample 1

Sample 2

Sample 3

Sample 4

Sample 5

Sample 6

www.ingramcontent.com/pod-product-compliance
Lightning Source LLC
Chambersburg PA
CBHW021104110726
47900CB00007B/2021